TWICE B[...]

Leela Soma

Price: £6.99

For my family

To Chris,

Best Wishes and Thanks.

Leela

xxx.

Acknowledgements

I am grateful to my mentor Professor Willy Maley of Glasgow University whose enormous help and faith in my writing was the spark that helped me complete this task. To Frances, Alison, and Ian a special thanks for being my first readers. All my buddies in the writers group and other friends for their help, criticism, and advice that made me work on this novel. Thanks to my nephew Karthik forunquestioning help. Last but not least Som and Nita whose patience I often tested for their understanding and support.

Prologue

The horoscope was written for Sita, the new baby. Date, time, star sign, all significant sources that would rule her life. The horoscope would entwine her with a partner - her future etched in Sanskrit and Tamil. The astrologer drew a neat square, divided it into sections, placed the nine planetary positions at the time of birth and recorded it in the family book. Sun and Moon, followed by the five major planets – Mars, Jupiter, Saturn, Venus, Mercury – and the two nodal points of the Moon - Rahu and Ketu. The black ink traced her traits and her destiny on the virgin paper. The astrologer smiled, pleased with his work, and pocketed his payment.

A breech baby, Sita arrived upside down, feet to the stars. The family doctor announced that the baby was healthy and left.

Her granny remembered the tiniest details and recalled the ignorant comment made by the midwife.

'Oh, not another girl! Coming upside down, that does not bode well! She does have pretty features, but I'm sure an upside down life for this one.'

Sita's mother had stopped her granny reiterating it constantly.

'All these old sayings are traditional. What one achieves in life is important. Remember Sita, happiness and contentment come from within.' Her mum's words of wisdom remained with her.

Sita was curious about everything and posed questions that her dad wished she would not ask, but he had always nurtured her interests, whether in fiction, music or general knowledge. She stood before him now, asking questions that his other children never bothered about.

'Dad, why are we called Brahmins?'

'Well, the caste system places the Brahmins at the top as they were the priests well versed in the scriptures and they could interpret the scriptures, explain the rituals that have to be followed in the temples and were the guardians of the spiritual side of life. It's a bit like the Archbishop of Canterbury being revered as someone above the Monarch, so he can place the crown and bless the ruler when they start their reign.'

'But why do they say twice born? It's strange. More like science fiction.' Sita giggled.

'Twice born are people who have realised God. All the boys have to go through a simple ritual called the upanayanam (the thread ceremony), like the Jews have their bar mitzvah. After the ceremony, they are known as twice born, they have realised God and are willing to continue with propagating Hinduism or at least practising it. That is when they are given the 'Gayatri Mantra,' whispered in their ears.'

'What is that dad? Is it a secret? Why whisper? What does it mean?' Sita insisted.

Her dad shook his head at Sita's constant questioning.

'Go on now and play with your sister.'

She would not give up.

'Dad, when is my upanayanam?' Sita asked expectantly.

'No, the upanayanam is only for young boys.'

'Why?' Sita did not look pleased.

'The girls become twice born only when they marry a Brahmin.'

'That's so bad, I think it's terrible, saying you are born high or low and they treat us girls differently. I don't like it.'

'I can't justify it Sita except to say that Hinduism is one of the oldest surviving religions in the world. They divided society in the way they thought was right at that time. Even slavery was condoned by deeply religious countries. Things happened in olden days that are not necessarily right. The caste system is outlawed anyway in India now. The

6

class system is all over the world now. Your money buys you a place in society.'

'But dad at least you can move up a class if you better yourself.'

'True.' Her dad agreed. 'Now go and play with your sister.'

Sita ran over to Gita who was shouting at Anjali, the maid's daughter.

'I said bring me that ball not the bat you stupid girl,' Gita's voice rose up in a scream.

'I'll get it for you Gita, stop shouting at my friend.'

'Your friend! You are stupid too,' said Gita and slapped her.

Sita cried, but as always, her mum made her apologise to Gita and took them both back into the house. Sita sat with her book, soon was lost in it. Gita cuddled up to her mum and cried a few more tears.

Chapter 1

Glasgow 1999

Today was an anniversary. Twenty years to the day since Sita had arrived in Glasgow, a new bride beginning her life with Ram. She was not to know that today was to turn her world upside down.

It was a glorious Saturday morning, the sun streaking the tarmac gold. Change of seasons still surprised Sita. The autumn colours had changed the green leaves to gold, some maples tinged with a bright red. Nature the artist, had painted the scene with a palette of rich hues. Some trees had shed their leaves; they lay in small brown mounds on the pavement. A large brown leaf swirled onto her windscreen briefly, before the breeze swept it away. It was a day to feel the joy of life, the golden shades a contrast to the normal grey as she drove towards the surgery.

Radio 4 had that quintessentially British programme where eccentrics broadcast strange anecdotes to the nation with a certain pride. She giggled as she heard the man talking about his passion for ferrets. He spoke with such a passionate interest in what she thought of as a vile little creature. Yet she could not but admire such devotion to raising animals. Such a British thing, the love of animals, she concluded, smiling to herself.

There was a new car in the driveway. Perhaps one of the other doctors had bought one, she thought to herself. She walked into the hallway, her mind on the work she needed to finish. This was the best time to work in the quiet. Carrying some of the sheets of paper in her hand, balancing the bag, she opened the door to her room. It swung right into someone's face.

The tall person moved back. 'It's okay. I always knew I needed a nose job...,'he joked.

'Oh, I'm so sorry; I didn't know there was anybody in my room...'

'You must be Dr. Iyer. I'm Neil, the new partner.'

'Call me Sita, please,' she shook his hand. They both looked at each other and said sorry at the same time.

'You go first,' he said with a smile that lit up his face, 'I don't want to cross you again.' He held his arms up in mock surrender.

'I came to catch up on some paperwork.'

'I can see that,' he nodded and glanced at the papers. 'You weren't here when I came down from Aberdeen for a visit, were you?'

'No. I only work part time.'

'So this is the room that I have to share with you. I came to put some of my things in to get an early start on Monday,' Neil said.

Sita straightened the papers. The room seemed to close in on her. The pale blue paint, worn out at the edges of the walls was cold to the eye though she felt warm. She sat at the edge of her chair. The faint smell of disinfectant was barely distinguishable. Her family portrait – Ram, herself and Uma posing stiffly – took pride of place on her desk. She moved it closer and turned it towards her. They worked quietly for sometime.

'How about a coffee? Shall I put the kettle on? Then you can warn me of all the patients that I should watch out for.' Neil moved over to the sink. 'You must have the Internet-Know-It–All, the I–Need-A–Specialist, and of course the Hypochondriac.'

Sita giggled. 'Yes we also have The Meek One, No-nothing-Wrong-With-Me, Wisnae-My-Fault, or It's-The-Pills-You-Gave-Me patients. Every surgery has them I'm sure.'

They laughed. The kettle boiled. The steam rose slowly up in tiny wisps. She got the coffee jar and mugs out.

'Take milk?' Neil opened the fridge and moved closer. Sita changed her mind.

'I need to pick up my daughter, sorry,' she mumbled looking at her watch.

'Surely a quick coffee? Remember you were going to tell me all about those interesting patients.'

'Sorry, I didn't realise the time.' She picked up all her stuff. 'I really need to go.' She rushed out of the room.

'See you Monday,' she heard him say.

She looked back and waved a quick 'bye, bye.' He looked puzzled.

At the traffic lights, she looked at herself in the mirror. The car behind hooted. The lights had changed to green. She drove to her favourite spot at Loch Lomond which was heaving with weekenders. The waters of the loch lapped on the shore in gentle waves, calm, eternally the same. She felt different. This new feeling was sweeping her away. She sat on a bench, picked a pebble and held it tight. Rocky hard to touch, the pebble was smooth as if hundreds of years of water had flown over caressing its edges to silk. The coolness of the pebble was comforting. She played with it, and then threw it into the loch.

An old couple leaned on each other, the man with a walking stick, his skin like a peeling onion, translucent, withered looking and ready to drop off in layers. They looked happy. Sita bought herself a coffee at the shop overlooking the Loch. The spoon made weird designs on the stirred surface. The froth merged with the dark liquid, the tiny bubbles vanished. The hot coffee was soothing. She tapped the sugar packet, turned it up and down, finally ripped it and the brown granules cascaded into a shimmering heap on the saucer. Time slipped by in an irrelevance; dreams and reflections reared up. The deep recesses of her soul stirred afresh, hastily brushed aside by an inner voice. 'It is the ornament of the wise to preserve evenness of mind,' the Tamil Thirukurral couplet came back to her. Sita dipped her finger in the sugar granules on the saucer, thinking, when the unexpected arrives, the peace is disturbed, the mind shatters into brittle pieces of heartache.

The mobile phone rang loudly.

'Mum where are you?' Uma said 'I'm just leaving for the flat, see you tomorrow, maybe.'

'Oh, I'm just on my way. Can't you wait till I come home?'

'No mum, Ewan and I are going out this evening. See ya.'

'Uma, tell dad I'll be there soon.'

'Okay, bye mum.'

Back in the car, her eyes on the road, the reflex action of moving when she had to, braking, slowing down were all done almost in a trance. The speeding cars were racing like bullets forming a silvery arrow glinting in the weak sun. The metal rasped the road. She was clutching at the journey of her life, its highs and lows. Hazy memories flitted across the windows of her mind, spooling distraction, her hands on the gear, on automatic pilot. The young teen with a wispy dog walked slowly on the pavement, ears plugged to music, paused to look at the brash youth racing past, loud music blaring from his car. Sita slowed down. The past spun in the distance, and came back in relief and rose like dust on a muddy road. She drew into her driveway, with no recollection of how she had got home. Sita opened the door gingerly. Ram was reading the paper, reclining on the old red sofa. The Saturday papers with their magazines were neatly stacked on the coffee table beside him.

'Working at weekends again? You really need to be organised, Sita,' he shook his head.

'I know,' she said and ran up the stairs, glad he was engrossed in the paper again.

*

The first time she had met Ram…

Madras 1979

Madras, early morning was cool and dew showered, the blue skies tinged with an orange glow as the golden sun rose. It would slowly change to a scorching white midday. Would this morning's brief encounter affect the rest of her life? Sita was meeting Ram, the suitable boy her parents had arranged for her. After a restless night, Sita woke up to the early morning raga on 'All India Radio.' Her father tuned into it without fail each morning. Her mum had begun the pooja, the reassuring early morning worship that was part of their lives.

The sounds that woke all of them rarely changed. The aroma of fresh coffee beans rose as the cook roasted it in the kadai, the balti shaped pan, followed by the sound of his energetic turning of the handle of the coffee

11

grinder. The clanking as the Ghurkha opened the gate. The servants were busy getting the hot water ready for the morning baths, giving instructions to each other on the next task. The old boiler was at the back of the house, the servants' children had various jobs of polishing and checking that everything was in place. The young boy on the bike delivered The Hindu newspaper, ringing the bell on his way out. Her dad started reading the paper on the veranda. The drama unfolded, the crows and sparrows starting their day, flitted about noisily. The quiet of the morning soon broke up into little chunks of activity and colour. Sita saw Ayah, the maidservant drawing an intricate kolum, patterns drawn on the freshly washed veranda. The dots threaded together like pearls of life's experiences, a cultural tradition handed down to generations, drawn in perfect symmetry. A piece of art, made with rice flour in front of the house. It was an elaborate one this morning, made with colour. Her restless mind noted all the familiar sights. She sighed and wondered what lay ahead. Her mum's voice broke her reverie.

'Start getting ready, Sita. I have a lot to do today. Here, have your coffee first.'

Her mum handed her a steaming hot, sweet cup of coffee.

'I even had to cut short the pooja. Choose a nice sari Sita, and be sure to wear some of your best jewellery.' Her mum bustled away, onto her next chore.

Her desk strained under the weight of her medical books and some of her favourite novels. A sense of freedom after the gruelling finals was wonderful. The bookshelf filled with books of fiction, a motley collection that she had time for now. Some hardbound copies, old-fashioned well-thumbed classics that her father had relished and given to her. Sita had treasured them. Her parents were proud of her achieving her medical degree, now they wanted her to be 'settled'. Her father had broached the subject cautiously.

'It's our responsibility to see that you are happily settled. You know that it will never be a forced marriage. We will introduce you to suitable boys and you can decide.'

'If only I had met my soul mate at the medical school,' thought Sita. She longed for love. She had seen her close friend Jyoti with her little baby. Jyoti and Suresh had a happy life, and the baby added to that perfection. Sita was ready for a new chapter in her life.

The delicate issue of choosing a life partner was fraught with difficulties. Horoscopes had to match first, and then the families needed to make discreet inquiries asking mutual friends before proceeding further. Her parents kept to their side of the bargain. Sita had rejected the first boy they had lined up for her.

'What's wrong with Sekhar? He's from a good Iyer family, your horoscopes match and he is an engineer.' Her dad looked bemused.

'He was a bit aggressive, bragging about California. He went on and on about his life, seemed full of himself. I'm sorry dad. I didn't like him at all.' Tears welled up in her eyes.

'You know we'll never force you to marry anyone.' A great sense of relief flooded over her.

After a decent period, her father came back with the details of Ram the young medic working in Glasgow.

'He seems like an unassuming young man. Our matchmaker was all praise for his family and vouched for the boy. Sita, it is such a good match of horoscopes. A really good family. His father is a civil servant.'

'Dad, it's not the family. I need to like this Ram.'

'I know Sita.' He removed his glasses, wiped his eyes, and then rubbed his forehead.

The 'meeting' with both families present was the custom. There was the excitement of the occasion, like a ripple going through the house. Fragrance from the sandalwood, camphor from the pooja room, and the smell of sweets made with ghee from the kitchen, the gorgeous scent of fresh flowers, roses, jasmine, and marigold filled the air. Sita chose a pale pink silk sari with a small gold border. Gita, her sister came into the room to take her through to the lounge.

'Nervous? Don't be. They seem like really nice people, except...,' she hesitated.

'Except?' Sita's fingers tapped the dressing table top.

'It's just that Aunty Parvati is here with them. I believe she is related to them.'

'Oh, no! Not Aunty Parvati!' a bead of sweat appeared on her brow.

The Unofficial Hindu as they called her was the gossipmonger of the community. The whole of Madras would know the news of this meeting. She would scrutinise every detail and would relay it without compunction.

'Maybe I should just call the whole thing off.' Sita sat at the dressing table and looked crestfallen.

Gita gave her a hug. 'Come on; let's not worry about the old hag. You look stunning. Ram will be bowled over.'

Gita accompanied her to the lounge. The room was full of people. She heard a booming voice as she entered the room, commenting on a local politician. It was Ram's father. He was a striking man, larger than life in every way. A young man sat beside him. Gita guided her towards the ladies who were all sitting in a group.

'Come here, sit beside me, dear,' said Ram's mum and patted the cushion beside her. She had a kind face, a lovely smile.

'Sita, have you learnt Carnatic music?' she asked. Most Brahmin girls trained in classical South Indian music. Brides sang during the meeting of the two families. Sita's grandmother used to joke this was the only way families could make sure that the girl was not deaf, mute or disabled in any way.

Aunty Parvati interrupted.

'She sings really well, I've listened to her before. How about singing a kirtanai, Sita?' Parvati's eyes were busy darting about observing the whole scenario, taking everything in. The silver platters placed as tradition demanded on the table to receive the guests with the auspicious red powder kumkum, sandalwood paste and rosewater, a colourful array in small silver pots. She noted the designs on the platters, checking to see if they were old. Silver heirlooms would indicate whether it was 'old or new money', an important fact for her next round of gossip. She needed to be sure so that she could describe in detail the number of trays, the silverware, the type of flowers, and the sweets that were offered on this occasion.

'I'll not sing now if you don't mind,' Sita replied politely.

'That's all right,' said his mum.

Parvati tutted. 'Young things nowadays do exactly what they like,' she said, smiling, her eyes hard as nails.

'This is Ram,' said her dad. The young man smiled and said a nervous, 'Hello.'

Her kohl eyes veiled by the long lashes looked across at Ram. She smiled and nodded. The conversation turned to general topics, pleasantries were exchanged, and the maid brought the tea and sweetmeats. Ram tasted the sweet and seemed to appreciate the rava laddoo that was on the plate. Sita stole a glance at him. He was wearing a blue shirt and a pair of black trousers. He looked smart. The parents left the young couple.

'Have a good chat with each other. Ask all you want,' said his dad as they moved to the sitting room. Ram walked over to sit beside her. He was tall, carried himself well. Sita blushed as she realised she was staring at him.

After an awkward silence, Sita said softly 'I did my MBBS at Kilpauk Medical, were you at Madras Medical?'

'No, I went to JIPMER,' Ram said, the colour rising in his cheeks. The ice was broken. They were able to talk about the courses. Ram quietened down after the chat on the medical schools.

'What's Glasgow like?' Sita could not resist asking.

'Oh it rains all the time, three hundred days out of the three hundred and sixty five. Glaswegians say that you can have all four seasons in a day,' he said, looking serious. A tiny bead of sweat formed on his forehead. He looked up at the ceiling fan. She laughed thinking he must be joking. The four seasons sounded wonderful. Madras had a hot summer, the monsoon and the rest of the time, it was hot and humid. Seasons were not noticeable.

'So how is work?'

'It's fine, very busy.' He shifted in his chair.

She liked the way a dimple appeared in his cheek when he spoke. He brushed his hand against his broad forehead where an insistent curl fell forward. She liked him. His shyness was endearing in some ways.

'Are there Indians in Glasgow?' Sita asked as Ram adjusted his watch.

'Not many Indians, more Pakistanis I think,' he added, 'I've seen a few Punjabi shopkeepers.'

'Any doctors?'

'Yes, a floating population of Indian doctors, very few from Madras though.' He cleared his throat as if to say something, then stopped.

'Any other interests … Ram?'

'I support the SNP, the Scottish National Party. It's a political party fighting for Independence.' He hesitated as if he wanted to say something more then swallowed hard. SNP was something new. She had not heard of it before. She hoped he would explain a bit more.

The ceiling fan whirred as the blades moved around, while the clock ticked quietly in the background. The marble floors, polished and cool reflected the sunrays that were straying in from the windows. Thoughts drifted in and out, foggy, clear, scattered and fell. Feelings opened up and retreated playing and preying on her mind. The sudden blare of a car horn made her start. She was conscious now of the voices in the sitting room. They smiled at each other. Ram started to say something, but stopped as they heard noise of people coming. The parents were back in the room.

'Did you get to know each other a bit?' Ram's dad asked in his loud voice. Neither of them said anything. She played the demure bride-to-be and looked up as they rose to take their leave. Ram walked behind his dad, turned around and gave her a shy glance, with a hint of a smile.

Gita said to her as soon as they left, 'Well, did you like him, an instant hit like Ashok and me?

'I... he was okay.' Sita shrugged and blushed. The bustle as the maid came to remove all the trays distracted Gita.

'What do you mean okay? Did your heart skip a beat like mine did when I saw Ashok?' Gita followed her back to her room.

'I don't know. There was so much going on.' Sita snapped at her sister.

'Sita, at least you talked to him. I didn't even do that you know.' Gita was busy reliving her first meeting with her husband.

'He was a bit quiet. I did all the talking.' Sita watched as Gita redid her hair.

'Better to start like that, always get your way. Never give them a chance to say anything, just like me.' Gita joked. 'I need to rush off. Call me later if you need to talk.'

'Sure,' said Sita, smiling brightly, perhaps too brightly.

She sat looking at the collection of her books. Madame Bovary, the thick bound book, was on the top of the pile on her desk, the blue bookmark visible. Lying on her bed listening to her tape recorder, the ballad 'Hey Jude' was soothing. Posters of Cliff Richard, Elvis Presley and Mick Jagger stared down from the wall above her desk. The ceiling fan wafted the picture of the Indian god Ganesha gently with its breeze. She sighed as a gecko snatched a fly near the light and swallowed it quick as a flash. The gecko moved around for its next prey. She got off the bed and walked out of the room and heard Ayah and the cook talking.

'Sita'ma is too short tempered. Why, she is not even happy on the day her future husband comes to see her?' Ayah's voice carried over.

Sita stopped and listened.

'These girls study too much. They are different from us,' the cook opined.

'It's the parents I'm thinking of,' said Ayah. 'Must be worrying for them. Anyway we better get on with all the extra work.' Their footsteps receded.

17

As she neared her parents' room, she heard her mum saying to her dad, 'She's rather quiet, I wonder if she likes Ram.'

Sita steeled herself, and walked in. Her voice was low and serious.

'Mum I would like to meet Ram again and have a chat.'

'Sita, I don't know if his family would approve.' The wrinkles on her mum's forehead deepened.

'Mum, I need to, please.' Sita insisted and attempted to smile, the corners of her mouth not quite achieving it.

'I know Sita, its just Parvati's gossip…...'

Her mum phoned Ram's family.

'They've agreed Sita. What a relief!' Her mum smiled.

Aunty Parvati arrived with him, the chaperone. She gushed with enthusiasm.

'Oh this is so nice, such a blessed couple just like the Ramayana. Lord Rama the 'Parama Purusha' the perfect man and Goddess Sita the flawless wife. I'm sure you'll be very happy.' Her beady eyes missed nothing. 'Go on, don't be shy. Just talk to each other. I can already see that you're going to be perfect together.' The more Aunty Parvati spoke, the less they had to say to each other.

Sita sat on the veranda and watched the twilight fading. The tropical darkness would soon enshroud the sky. The tiny stars would light up the navy curtain of the night. Mali brought the freshly plucked jasmine from the garden. The sweet fragrance filled the air. Her mum came over and they sat together to thread the flowers into a garland with a skill almost like knitting. This was a perfect time for her mum to tackle the delicate topic.

'Sita, Ram's family were on the phone. They're happy, want to go ahead with the wedding…'

'Mum I'm not sure. Do you think he really likes me?'

'Of course, why else would he ask for you? I thought you liked him. He is good looking, surely there's nothing wrong with him?'

18

'Mum, I don't know what to say. He is rather quiet, I just don't know…..'

'Sita, it's only natural to feel doubts, but love grows once you marry, he seems a nice enough young man.'

'Mum, I can't make out what he really likes or thinks.'

'Look Sita, this is our way. If you don't like him at all… like the last boy, we can tell them right away though Parvati has already called twice… all my friends have assumed…' her mum's voice trailed away as Sita implored.

'Mum, please let me at least sleep on it.'

The garland turned into a mess. The neat work of her mum was a contrast to Sita's attempt. The threads of her garland had twisted, the delicate flowers crushed, the unfinished piece of work lay crumpled in the basket. She moved back to her room and picked up the book. Emma in Madame Bovary was describing her loveless marriage. Sita spent another sleepless night. After all, they were strangers. How could she expect love? Yet something in her wanted to feel excited. 'Love at first sight,' such a clichéd thing she told herself, maybe only happens in songs or stories. She had to admit she liked Ram and his unassuming manner. The career they shared would bring them closer. The decision that would shape her whole future was confusing. Despite misgivings that she could not quite put her finger on Sita agreed to the wedding, reassured that living in Scotland would kindle the romance that was missing.

Chapter 2

There was more noise, hustle and bustle at New Delhi airport than normal. 'It must be the Prime Minister leaving. They have really upped the security since Gandhi's State of Emergency,' said Jai, as their car swung into the departure's area. 'No wonder it took us so long to get into the airport,' Sita's brother continued. The rest of the family had other things on their mind.

Just three months ago Sita, a bride of two weeks, had waved Ram off at Delhi airport. Now she was on the plane to start her new life with him in Glasgow. She tried to get comfortable in the narrow aisle seat. Never having flown for such a long time in a big jumbo jet, she was nervous. The journey was a nightmare. Her only flight had been from Madras to Hyderabad to attend her friend's wedding, a short journey of just two hours. This seemed to last forever. She looked around, the creamy white interior of the plane was soothing, and the Air India logo of the Maharaja in bright red just above her seat on the overhead lockers gave her a feeling of familiarity and comfort. She turned, smiled weakly at the woman beside her who was battling with a screaming toddler. The toddler's dad, unruffled, did little to help and buried his face in the in-flight magazine.

The glamorous airhostess, with a perfect figure revealed by the beautiful blue silk sari worn tight around her slender frame, walked around each row of seats checking on seat belts and safe disposal of hand luggage in the overhead lockers. A frown spread on her expertly made up face, her nose crinkled, as she had to deal with a horde of people unused to flying at all. Some of the passengers wore no shoes. Some had even brought bedrolls with them.

The strong smell of the food served made Sita feel sick. She ate nothing, just drank some water. She noted to her horror that after the dinner, some spread their bedrolls in the aisle, leaving no place for people to walk to the toilets. The airhostess hurried up the aisle and remonstrated, giving them a spiel about safety rules. The passengers rolled their beds and adjusted their thin bodies back into the narrow seats. The toddler fell asleep. Sita tried to read her book but tears choked her. She missed her family already.

'Do not cut your hair. It's an Indian woman's sign of beauty. Always wear the red bindi. It is a sign that you are married. Do not remove your thali. It's like your wedding ring.' Her mum's words resurfaced. Words, words that floated in her mind, were the only link now with her family.

How would Ram be in Glasgow? Excitement and fear rolled into a strange new feeling that made her palms sweat. How would she cope? A new life in a country that she had imagined from pages of fiction would now be a reality. The smells of the early morning breakfast served on the plane made her almost retch. She was used to only vegetarian food at home. The stale smell of bacon and eggs was overpowering. She was glad when the plane landed in London.

'Non British Passports queue over here.' The board was clear. She dragged her hand luggage and waited patiently. The sunny morning in London, the busy, luxurious and huge airport terminal in Heathrow lifted her spirits. Ram was meeting her and she would at least see his familiar face. The immigration officer took forever. The wait seemed longer and longer. She was people watching, taking in the new experience. There were Indian workers in the airport, mostly cleaners and baggage handlers. There were some signs written in both English and Hindi. She volunteered to help a passenger who could not fill in her disembarkation card. Though she could barely speak Hindi, she helped her get an interpreter by asking the immigration officer if there was such a service. When her turn came, Sita was tired, exhausted from the flight and jetlagged. She heard the question,

'So is your husband here on a work permit?'

'I think so,' she replied.

'Stand aside. You're not sure, are you?' He rolled his eyes heavenwards.

'Well, all my papers are in order. Could you check again, please?' She asked politely.

'Just wait there,' was his curt reply.

21

An attempt after half an hour later brought the same response. He was brusque.

'I'll deal with you when I'm free.' The snort said more than words.

The next time she asked him, he indicated a room for her to wait in.

Confused, she entered it and sat down on the orange plastic chair. The fluorescent light hurt her eyes. There were people of all ages in there. They seemed to be waiting for hours in the immigration detention room, vacant looks, incomprehension etched on their faces. A baby suckled noisily, the mother distracted and worried. Sita looked at an elderly man, his wrinkled hand clutching a wallet with all his papers. His thin shirt was a poor cover in the air-conditioned room. Her head was throbbing with lack of food, and she felt shivery in the cold, clinical room. The lack of noise was such a contrast to the scenes at Delhi airport. She sighed.

Two hours later, Sita noted that a new officer had taken over the shift. She ran over.

'Could you please tell me why I've been kept back?' She explained what had happened. 'I know my papers are in order. Please could you contact my husband? I'm sure he'll be waiting outside.' She was tearful now.

The immigration officer looked over her papers, said that everything was in order, and that she could go. She was relieved yet furious. She collected her baggage, dropped her handbag, her confidence at a low ebb. She picked up her handbag, pushed the luggage trolley and walked out following the green sign that said 'Nothing to declare.' Ram was waiting anxiously for her. She saw the dimple on his left cheek deepen as he moved towards her. Suddenly a bit of shyness came over her not having seen him for ages.

'Are you okay? Why was there such a delay?' He looked worried. He took care of the luggage. She moved close to him. He gave her quick hug then handed her a warm cardigan saying, 'You'll need this, it's a big change from thirty degrees in Madras,' he smiled. He touched her arm, an awkward gesture and moved it quickly back to get hold of the baggage trolley. His face relaxed, the worried frown replaced with the brisk look seeking the way out of the airport.

'The immigration officer was awful,' she said.

'Happens often.' He shrugged. 'I've booked a hotel. We might as well see a bit of London while we get the chance.'

Ram hailed a mini cab to take them to central London. They sat in the back seat. Ram brushed his curl back over his forehead and sighed. Her shoulder brushed his as the minicab swerved. She felt her colour rising. She looked out of the window.

London, the opening chapters of her new world, the beginnings of her new life whizzed past her, as she looked out of the taxi window. Surprisingly sunny, the outskirts of London showed the golden haze against a verdant green, a green so rare in Madras that her eyes widened at how kind nature was to this land. Despite the urban sprawl as the taxi sped out of the airport, she noted the green verges, the neat tiny gardens of the houses along the way. The roses were in bloom, some in colourful bunches. The motorway, the speed of the cars, the clean roads and the traffic was a new experience. None of the ubiquitous cow or auto rickshaws that blocked the traffic in the Indian roads was here. She sank into the comfort of the seat, as the tiredness of the stressful flight vanished and she looked at the sights of this new country. As the taxi weaved its way round inner London, she noted names that were so familiar. To see rather than imagine them was exciting. Pall Mall, Hyde Park, Buckingham Palace. These names had been part of her schooling. The red buses were so similar to the ones she had seen in Bombay. Familiar sights and yet so different.

Back at the hotel, awkwardness returned. After the initial enquiries about the family, Ram said little. The feeling of being with a stranger was overwhelming. They ate, while she chatted away about her flight. Ram kept himself busy, making a list of places to see in London. To sleep beside again him felt odd. That night he turned over to make love to her.

The bright morning sun dazzled her eyes as Ram opened the curtains. He had ordered breakfast in bed. They seemed to walk everywhere. Taking the Tube, working out the routes was fun. She had only travelled by chauffeur-driven cars in India. She liked the freedom of this cosmopolitan capital city. She relished the new experience; the cool weather was a welcome change. Ram was quiet as usual but thorough about taking her around London. There was so much to see and absorb.

'We must see Foyle's, the bookshop. It's a must!' Sita's eyes shone with excitement.

'Why? What's so special about an old bookshop?' said Ram as he busied himself with a list of sights to see. 'We've done most of the famous touristy ones. How about checking out some Indian restaurant?'

'But I'd love to see Stratford-Upon-Avon and ...'

'Southall may even have a South Indian restaurant. I am dying to eat a masala dosa,' Ram continued.

'Ram, we can cook that at home, can we not...' She stopped, saw the disappointment on Ram's face and changed tack, 'Yes, let's go for an Indian meal tonight. I'll need to see if they have anything as good as our Woodlands Restaurant in Madras,' said Sita quickly. Ram smiled.

The autumn evening cast long shadows as they left the hotel. Daylight at eight in the evening was surprising, yet there was a chill in the air. It made Sita cower into her cardigan. The Indian restaurant decor was very different to what she had seen back home. The red flocked wallpaper, the big prints of Indian scenes and the piped loud Bollywood music made the restaurant anything but relaxing. The table had plastic flowers and was laden with strange dishes. Onions coloured a deep red, and popadums on a platter with sauces that glowed in bright shades of orange. Nothing looked freshly made, but left on the table for customers to munch on with their drinks. Ram savoured each of the dishes, commenting on them. The insistent curl fell on his forehead. She was tempted to push it back, in a tender way.

'Could I borrow the menu please?' asked a young English girl.

'Of course,' said Sita and handed it to her. The girl joined the man at her table. He offered her a drink and kept holding her hand as they ordered and giggled at their own pronunciation of the dishes. Later, he fed her forkfuls of food while gazing at her.

'Look,' said Ram, 'this vada is not fried properly, too crispy on the outside and a bit undone inside.'

'Waiter!' He called him over. 'This is not cooked inside properly.' Ram picked one of the vadas and prised it open to show the uncooked batter. The waiter apologised profusely.

'I'll get another plate for you sir.' He took the offending plate and moved away to the kitchen. Ram was pleased. He continued being

24

preoccupied with the meal for the rest of the evening. His understanding of the menu, his vast knowledge of the intricacies of each dish was impressive.

'Ram, we could spend a week here and still have so much to see. It brings some of the history that I learnt at school alive again, the reign of the Tudors and Stuarts. '

'Mm… I suppose. Does your lassi taste okay?' he asked. She nodded.

As they left the restaurant, there was a commotion outside. A group of skinheads had thrown a lit paper on a young Asian boy as he walked alone. They jeered loudly as they raced away. Sita clung onto Ram. 'Just a few ignorant yobs,' Ram reassured her. She shuddered. They took a taxi back to the hotel.

He started to pack his suitcase. Everything was laid out on the bed, and then he set about the whole meticulous order for the task. All the clothes were coordinated and folded neatly. The shoes cleaned with paper, then with a cleaning cloth that he had brought with him, polished and wrapped in tissue paper. The toiletries wiped clean before he packed them in. The military precision made her laugh. He turned around, surprised at her laughter. Sita chastened, opened her case and started packing. She dumped her clothes and cosmetics in willy-nilly; as long as the case shut, she was happy.

'I'll help you pack that case,' said Ram, a frown creasing his forehead.

'I'll have to unpack it tomorrow anyway. I shouldn't have bought these souvenirs I suppose. This is the only way it will fit.' She sat on the case to flatten it a bit more.

'Give me half an hour. I'll pack it neatly.' Ram insisted. He was ready to lever the case from under her and start the work.

'Ram, just leave it. Let's have a walk around the hotel. We don't know when we'll get back to London.'

'Let's get this packed properly,' his brows knitted together, 'I don't want the case falling open.'

'I hope you're not going to keep cleaning up after me or you'll have a big job on your hands.' She giggled, got off the case, cuddled him and gave him a peck on his cheek. Ram kissed her back and then made love to her passionately.

She rested, heard Ram turning the shower on, humming a tune. She sat up on the bed, twisted her long hair into little clumps.

Dressed and ready he went back to the suitcase. He emptied it and started the packing, folded her garments neatly. The suitcase closed perfectly.

Next day they flew into Glasgow, to her new life, her new home. 'What was in store?' she wondered.

Chapter 3

Ram's favourite quote on the souvenir pagoda from Malaysia stood proud on his desk. He picked it up. The inscription on the pedestal read: 'Do not look for a sanctuary in anyone except your self.' The Buddha. He turned it round in his hand, the brown wooden pagoda with its green shiny paint glimmered in the lamplight. Green on brown, his mind raced back to his childhood.

The bright green leaf floating on the muddy water hit the rock and twisted away to the far side. He stood watching. The water was not clear, brown, muddy, not translucent, and dirty to touch or wade in. His backside was still sore. He wanted to dive in and cool off. The sun had burned it, the punishment still coursed through his young body. That morning's row with his uncle resurfaced.

'It was not me, I swear on God. Bharat took it.' The fear in Ram's eyes showed.

'You liar, blame my son, how dare you and don't bring God into it. Your dad can gallivant all over India, but who has to deal with you everyday?' His uncle's eyes blazed with anger.

'But I did not take the ladoo,' Ram cried.

'You're always in the kitchen. It must be you. Stand there in the sun till you realise your mistake and apologise.' His uncle's voice went up a few decibels, as he took the cane away inside. The punishments meted out were unfair and arbitrary. His cousin Bharat never got reprimanded. Bharat was into cricket, sporty, never came home until late, often with his dad. An only child, he was pampered and adored by his parents.

'Your schooling in Madras is the best,' his dad used to announce, giving his uncle a fat wad of notes. 'I can't take you around India on all these projects.' The school that Ram attended was one of the best in Madras, a haven.

27

'You need to talk and laugh loudly, son. You're too quiet.' Dad guffawed as he tousled his hair, teased him, and gave him costly, useless presents. The louder his dad's words and action were the quieter Ram became.

His aunt loved cooking. Ram found a great comfort in the kitchen. He watched her every move, ran errands for her to the shops. The time straight after school when his uncle was not around and aunty would make the tiffin was magical. Tasty savoury snacks of bhonda and bhajis followed by syrupy sweets like Jangari and a South Indian coffee that smelled delicious and tasted divine, hot, milky and sweet. He was the taster, making out the tiniest change in the oil, the spices and herbs that she had used. Ram was happy to be her assistant, chopping, peeling vegetables, when she tried out the new dishes and listened to her local gossip of the day. Her perfection in each of the dishes she made, the care she took creating the everyday meal fascinated him. Cooking was her passion. Trawling the bazaar to get the freshest greens, she chose each vegetable with care. She clarified the butter to make the ghee that enhanced, gave a delicious flavour and taste to the sweets. Occasionally when his aunt fell sick, Ram took over the kitchen. He enjoyed trying out all that he had learned. The closeness and the warmth of his aunt gave him much needed comfort. Perhaps she needed him to be succour for living with a frustrated man whose personality was so different, but as a child, he did not realise this. Looking back, he could see why she had leaned on him.

'Not taking an engineering course? I'm disappointed, Ram,' said his dad. 'A chief engineer whose son becomes a doctor? Now how can I help you in that career?'

Ram stood his ground.

'Why JIPMER? We have two excellent medical colleges here in Madras.' His dad was surprised.

'That's the only place I applied for.' Ram's voice was firm.

'But why? With your marks you can get to the best college here, uncle can look after you in Madras.'

'It's too late now. I've already enrolled at Jipmer.' Ram walked away.

'Strange boy,' said his dad to his mum, shaking his head in disbelief. 'Never says much, don't know what goes on in his mind. Choosing medicine! I assumed he would follow in my footsteps. Can't understand children at all nowadays!' He rubbed his hands on his unbearded chin as he settled down to his paper work. His mum nodded in an understanding way, accepting her husband's words.

*

Pondicheri was different. The beach, the Aurobindo Ashram, the French colonial buildings were all different from the bustle and noise of Madras. The calm of the sea, so accessible in this little town suited Ram to perfection. The town had a village feel to it. On his first day as a fresher, he walked into the hostel looking for his room.

'Oi, you get my room cleaned before I tell you where your room is,' said a senior boy as he wrenched the bag from his hands. Ram had been warned of the 'Ragging' that he would face at his college hostel.

'Yes, sir,' he replied quietly. The guy offered him a broom and watched as he swept his room clean.

'Here's your bag then, second floor, your room,' he grinned and gestured to the stairs. Ram ran up the stairs, and confronted a group of seniors hanging around on the top blocking his way. He put his bags down, sweat drops collecting on his forehead.

'What does sir want then?' The thin guy with a rasping voice and a menacing look blew his cigarette smoke right into Ram's face.

'Just let me get to my room,' his voice pleaded.

'No problem, are we stopping you?' said the guy. The boys parted, a tiny path opened up and he moved on. A few walked beside him and shoved their elbows into him. Ram heard others singing a ribald song, following him to room number 236. His hands trembled as he put the key in, but the door opened. A young man with a bright shirt and a dark moustache ushered him in. The group beside Ram suddenly quietened and walked away.

'Hi, I'm Mani, your roommate. Don't worry, man. That was just a bit of fun for them. The medics follow the old colonial tradition of giving all

29

freshmen a bit of a welcome but they never resort to the crazy things that you hear in other colleges.'

Ram sighed with relief. Glad that it was just a few words and jostling. There were dreadful excesses in other colleges. Ragging was a scary initiation in Indian colleges in the seventies. Having as a roommate, a son of a Congress party member of the State assembly (MLA) made a huge difference. He settled in quickly.

*

The telegram arrived at the end of the first semester of the rigorous final year. A frantic call to his uncle gave him the dreadful news. Ram could not attend her funeral as he was in the middle of the diet of exams. The grief was unbearable. The Aurobindo ashram was the perfect place. Not many students came to the ashram. In the meditation hall, the quiet stillness and walks along the beach helped in grieving for his aunt.

'He is never born, and never dies.

He is in Eternity…

He does not die when the body dies'

The Bhagavad-Gita Gita (c.500 BC)

He took refuge in the great book, comfort in his darkest days. The impression of life, a sari, a thumbed book, a recipe that brought the pain of the loss was not easily compensated by mere memories. The pain was real. The thought of the flesh, bones cremated, and dust-to-dust maybe to reincarnate gave little relief to the agony of not being able to see his aunt again. In the inroads of his being, he sobbed for a soul who had given him a love that was unquestioning.

Exams were over. The nine days of mourning rituals were done. When he arrived on the tenth day, the ceremony was a celebration of her life. The small group of the aunt's family members received him warmly. His parents, uncle and Bharat were busy looking after the guests. Treading on eggshells again, the foreboding returned when he looked around the house where he had spent a good part of his childhood. The kitchen evoked happy memories of time spent with his aunt. He broke down. He left the house clutching a photograph of all of them at the beach in Madras, a rare occasion when they had gone out together. The black and

30

white photograph was the tenuous, tiny treasure of his happy times with his aunt.

*

She was in the seat next to him, a smile of recognition and a nod to acknowledge him spread hesitantly on her face. Ram looked at the young girl who was travelling to Jipmer. He had seen her on the campus at the classes. The quiet one compared to some of the other women students was the reason he had noticed her. After an awkward silence he said,

'Hi, I'm Ram, in my final year. I've seen you around the campus.'

'Vidya, final year too.' She smiled, her high cheekbones sculpting her face and eyes crinkling a little. The gems on her earring flashed as the sunlight fell on it. He felt comforted that he was sitting beside her and not beside a loud-mouthed youth and relaxed into the seat.

'The exams were tough,' he said. She nodded. Silence again. The ticket master came over. Ram took his return ticket out of the bag that was stowed overhead. The label on his bag showed the aunt's address clearly.

'Do your parents live in Madras?' she asked very softly, indicating the label.

He found himself not only talking about his uncle but the whole raw emotion of his aunt's death came surging up. He needed someone to hear his grief. She listened intently. The long journey was the start of a friendship he hoped would never end.

The final semester ended. His friendship with Vidya had grown closer but he could never open up his feelings for her. Indian propriety and his shyness kept that in bay. He had hoped that once they both graduated he would somehow get the courage to broach the subject.

He never did.

*

The greyness of Glasgow suited Ram's mindset. Work was a solace. His training, the kind understanding ways of the consultants and tutors

31

were so different from his Indian experience. There was no 'them and us,' 'sir' and standing to attention to the seniors. However, the loneliness in Glasgow was shocking. In India, family or friends had always surrounded him. Now he had to make an effort to find some. Needing a change from his work and study, he chose the nearest bar for a pint. He was nursing the beer when Jim, the registrar at his department walked in.

'Hi Ram, good to see you here. Thought you weren't the drinking type. Get you another?'

'No I'm fine Jim, just needed a change.'

'Yeah, we all need a change, so what do you do with your evenings then?'

'Not much really, work and study that's me.'

'Oh, we can't have that! I'm just going to a Nationalist meeting. Interested?'

'Don't know much about it.' Ram pushed his curl back from his forehead.

'Just come along and see how we can retrieve the last colony from the clutches of the empire.' Jim laughed loudly, 'Joking man, don't look so serious.' He patted him on his back.

Ram drifted into the world of politics. It reminded him of his good days with Mani at Jipmer. Jim was very focussed about his cause. Ram read up on the history of Scotland, the 1707 Union, the Declaration of Arbroath, and the more he delved into the history the more he was fascinated. They settled into an easy friendship.

In the Clydesdale Cricket Club changing room, Jim couldn't stop teasing Ram.

'Call yourself an Indian. That was pure drivel. Out for duck, and can't bowl either. Now why did I put you in our team?'

'Well, you assumed I could play. Why didn't you ask me?'

'It was good fun anyway, only a friendly to raise money for the SNP.'

'Nice day. It's so much more pleasant playing in the cool here than in roasting hot Madras.' They had changed from the whites to casual wear, sat in the warmth of a late summer's day drinking cold beer and tucking into sandwiches. The rhododendrons swayed their purple blooms in the light breeze.

'This is the life,' said Ram, quite taken with the sound of leather on willow and the lush green against the blue skies. Somehow, he had not pictured it in Glasgow; it was a scene more akin to an English village.

'So why are the Nationalists not able to keep up the momentum of the 1974 election gains?' Ram started on Jim's favourite topic.

'Disenchanted! Too used to the Labour party.' With Jim, one never knew if he was joking or serious. He smiled, 'Perhaps not, maybe I'm exaggerating. I think our party shows its inexperience at government level. The elected councillors and our MPs just don't have the long entrenched following and experience at every level of government like Labour or the Tories in Scotland. But don't worry, we'll get there.'

'The Devolution Bill is a mess, don't you think?' Ram had been following the political debate in the papers.

'You're right. Making the Bill for both Wales and Scotland was too long drawn out. Everything is a compromise. The Assembly has too few powers. The Labour Party is so half-hearted about it.' Jim's voice showed his frustration.

They sipped the cold lager, the political shenanigans of the Referendum on their mind.

They were both thinking aloud.

'Labour has more problems with its own failing government. Don't think they'll win at the next election. The opinion polls show Labour losing.' Ram sipped his beer.

'The SNP will just have to fight back. Use this opportunity. Can't undo three hundred years of the status quo in a few years can we? The 'Yes' Campaign needs to get its act together,' said Jim.

They mulled over the topic, with a few more beers, relaxing after the game.

His close friend Mani's wedding brought him to Madras after two years in the UK. His mum pleaded with him to get married. Ram acceded to her request and decided to marry the first girl his parents chose for him.

He was embarrassed with the ease with which his dad took over at any social event. The ritual of meeting a girl who would be his future bride was awkward enough but his dad's presence made it worse.

Sitting facing Sita who was firing questions at him, his shyness became more acute. He was smitten at the very first glance. The way she walked in, head held high, confident, her vivacious personality, the ease with which she asked him questions attracted him. Her pretty eyes searched for a response from him. He wished he could say something interesting and witty to her. What came out of his mouth were bland answers to her questions. Expecting to find a submissive, shy girl, as terrified as he was her sparkling personality took him by surprise. Ram was more tongue-tied than normal. He had comforted himself with the food on the table.

Aunty Parvati's presence did not help. The words formed in his mind 'I like you, I like you a lot Sita,' but he found it hard to say them in front of the old Aunty. Sita was able to articulate, speak her mind and take the lead. He withdrew just as he did when his father was around. Something in him made him afraid to show his love.

His shyness, his reticence would become a pattern in his relationship with Sita.

Overriding all that was a deep scary sense that he might lose her.

Chapter 4

Grey, a life overcast with doubt shadowed and coloured her life with Ram from the start. The flight from London to Glasgow was mercifully short. The taxi made its way to Law Hospital a good hour away from Glasgow airport. The hospital was in a village. The contrast to London was sharp, the poverty evident. The place reeked of old coalmines, a grey area, with grey roughcast houses with grey people. The houses seemed to have dampness locked into them, fissures dark stained on some of the houses. Slums in Madras were awful but this was unexpected. Council estates, as she was to learn later, abounded. The grey sky, the chill seemed to envelop the dilapidated hospital buildings. The slight warmth that was in London dissipated north of the border. She could feel the moisture-laden air. Bleakness exuded in the barren scenery of Scotland. The doctor's residence where the taxi pulled up looked like a prefabricated hut. Sita was shocked, but said nothing as they walked in to the warmth of the little flat. Later, after she had showered and rested she commented to Ram.

'This is not what I expected of the first world. The doctor's flats are so bare and poorly done up.'

'You're right, but this was an old army barracks, now been used as a hospital. It's okay; we're here only for a couple of months.'

'What do you mean, only for two months?'

'As soon as my rotations are finished we can look for our own flat. The next rotation I have is in the Western Infirmary. You'll love the West End; it's close to Botanic Gardens and the University. The main thing about this flat is it is warm and close to my work.'

Sita looked around the tiny flat. She opened a window to get some fresh air, but it was so chilly she shut it quickly. Everything felt different, almost alien. She unpacked, and then looked out of the window. Grey clouds and the matching grey buildings of the hospital seemed to merge with each other. The morgue-like silence was eerie. The clouds were threatening to burst into a heavy squall. A deep sense of oppression swept over her and she put on another cardigan over her jumper. There was no need for it. The flat was very warm. It was more the lack of a friendly face. Coldness that she had never experienced of being alone in a strange place with a person she hardly knew. Madras was always noisy, bright, sweaty, and awash with family and friends. In Madras the sounds of the street hawkers, the traffic noise as they hooted their horns, even the birds chirping or cawing loudly. This was totally new. She curled up on the bed. Dreams of home and family played strange stories in her head. She woke up to smell of onions frying. She found Ram at the little kitchenette cooking the evening meal.

'Let me help you,' she said and chopped some of the cauliflower that he had left on the countertop.

'When did you learn to cook so well, Ram?' she asked.

'When I was quite young,' Ram's attention was on the radio, on drive-time news.

The smell of basmati rice cooking wafted over. She watched in amazement as Ram worked methodically. Each dish looked and smelled delicious. She chopped some tomatoes and cucumber for the raita. When the drive-time news was over, Ram switched the radio off. Her mind went racing back to the scene at home in Madras and her pathetic attempts at learning to cook.

*

The cook stood looking down on Sita. She was in charge of her kitchen and loved the power it gave her over the maids who did all the fetching and carrying, the preparing of vegetables and cleaning of the rice and other cereals. Now the young mistress of the house was in her domain looking for lessons. She swelled with the importance of her task.

'Oh I don't know. Tuvar dhal? Is it the small and white one or the bigger yellow one?' Sita was ashamed at her own ignorance. The cook's face suffused with pride.

'Come to the storeroom. I can teach you everything you need to know.' She took her into the room with the bottles and boxes neatly stacked on the shelves that lined the wall. Sita looked confused at the large array of bottles with various dhal in different colours and sizes. Her mum and cook laughed at her ignorance.

'I didn't realise there are so many varieties. Oh! How will I learn all these?' Sita looked worried.

'It's easy compared to your medical course. All you need is a few hours of practice each day,' cook said as she started teaching her to cook a simple dish of rice and dhal. The smells of the cooking soon filled the kitchen.

'This is hard work.' Sita was sweaty and uncomfortable. Her heart was not in it. The family meals were filled with laughter as Sita's attempts were tasted, enjoyed or ridiculed.

'I'm glad Ram can cook,' laughed her dad, as he tried her sambhar. Sita ran out of the room sobbing. Her mum followed her and comforted her.

'Look, don't get discouraged. You'll get the hang of it once you do it everyday.'

'Mum, I don't know how I'll manage,' Sita sniffled. 'I'll miss you all.' Sita's lips quivered.

'You'll be all right. It's never easy for anyone to learn new things or to start a new life. Cooking is not difficult at all. I'm sure you'll be fine.' Her mum gave her a hug.

Her mum gave her an English version of Minakshi Ammal's 'Cook and See' the Tamil cookery book that was hailed as the definitive work. Sita found it harder than her medical books as some of the weights and measures were from her grandmother's time.

'You need to try your hand at the recipes. Can't learn just by reading it,' scolded the cook. She tried to get her into the kitchen more often. Sita's mind was on the wedding and lacked concentration. Her attempts at cooking were unsuccessful. The family's teasing about her cooking went on relentlessly. That did little to assuage her feelings of incompetence.

'Thank god, I live in Madras. I'd rather have the cook and maid and the comforts of home. Living abroad looks like suffering to me.' Gita made a crisp remark.

'Oh shut up Gita! Not everyone lives with maids.' Sita slammed the door on her sister.

'What's up with her?' Gita asked her mum.

The reality of going away from all she knew and loved was taking over. Sita's confidence in her ability to start her new life abroad slowly started to ebb.

*

The noise of a plate breaking brought her back. It had slipped from Ram's hand as he had busied himself setting the table. As she helped clear the broken pieces from the floor, she told Ram about her attempts at cooking. She waited for a comment. He went over and switched the TV on.

'Ram, I'm worried about my cooking.'

'Yes, yes...' He was checking the TV programmes in the Radio Times.

'Ram, did you hear what I was saying just now?' Sita asked, putting her arm round him.

'Yes, of course. Shall we eat now?' He sat down.

'Do I chatter away too much?' Sita said laughing.

He muttered, 'No.'

She tried to involve him again.

'This is so delicious Ram. You need to teach me.'

'Maybe...' Ram's eyes were on the TV.

They ate their dinner with the news on. James Callaghan's minority government and the woes of the Labour Party were discussed at length on the television. There followed an item on race riots in the South. Sita cleared the dinner things. Ram checked that all the things were put away at the right place in the cupboard and slid onto the sofa. She plumped a cushion and sat beside Ram. Conversation, a few words was what she wanted most. Ram was quiet. She flicked through a magazine, and then wandered around the flat looking for a book to read. Ram had a good selection of medical books and a few political biographies and some history books. She noted that there were books on Orthopaedic surgery.

'Ram, are you going for an Ortho job?'

'Yes, I want to specialise in Ortho, I've just passed the MRC exams for it. '

'Great, I didn't realise that.' This was another chink in his armour, an ambition to strive for a difficult surgeon's job. Sita was getting to know him very slowly. Sita wanted to share everything with him. She sat beside him again, opened a photo album that she had picked up. She felt the pages heavy with memories of her youth. She recounted all that she could to him as the light paper, almost like a tracing paper, crinkled and rustled. She pointed to each of the black and white photos stuck with four little tabs on the black vellum page. Now she turned up a whole section that she wanted to relish sharing with Ram.

'My school days,' she said and with a flourish began recounting them. The school day always began with the assembly…

'Good Morning girls. We start with a reading from Luke chapter…' said Mother Jean her Principal. They would mouth the words, 'Our Father, thou art in Heaven …' the rituals of a Convent missionary school that they were used to from infant school. At the end of the assembly, the teachers would bark out the order, 'Get ready for the inspection of the uniform and nails.' The class teacher walked up and down the row of girls holding out their hands for inspection.

'Chandra, those white canvas shoes are filthy. Stay back and Blanco them before you enter the classroom' ordered the teacher. Nails were not the only things pupils were pulled up for. Uniform had to be perfect. White, crisp, starched white cotton dress, white canvas shoes, and red tie with the silver badge with the school motto. White, a colour so hard to keep pristine, as they all played in the hot dusty playground- a fact often forgotten by the teachers. Rules were laid out and they had to be followed.

'Did you listen to Binanca's top ten last night? Oh isn't Elvis the best. Wish I could buy his LP's and listen to him everyday,' Jyoti, her friend, whispered to her as they filed into their classroom. They settled down to the lessons and worked hard to do their best, the fear of staying back for detention ensured that. Sita remembered the happy days, hard work and some fun, playing in the subtropical heat. She absorbed the refrains in the house that her mother constantly muttered.

'You need to get a good education to be something in life.'

'Money can come and go but an education is something that nobody can take away from you'

'Three main values of a Brahmin are education, classical music, religion, and never forget that you are twice born but you have responsibilities that go with it.'

These phrases were part of her growing up, as natural as the sun scorched earth in the garden, soothed by the vicious torrent of the monsoon in August of every year.

The start of the school year was always pandemonium in her house. All the kids had to get uniforms, books had to be bought and fees paid. They made trips to 'Higginbotham's' on Mount Road to get their schoolbooks. The smell of new books even now was almost palpable to Sita. She remembered the happy hours covering each book and jotter with brown paper, arguing about the labels. 'I want the label with a sweet puppy,' Gita would shout and the tears and tantrums would start. Pencil cases and bags were fought over with ferocity. Only her mum managed to calm them all down. Soon Sixth Form loomed large and the pressure of achieving the right grades from university was relentless.

'Oh, no Sita, not double Maths again! Why don't they let us choose subjects at least in the sixth form, I hate it , can't do it,' Jyoti would moan- the reason why they got to be close friends- top students in Language, but Maths was a no-go area.

The Convent of the Good Shepherd's School under the headship of Mother Jean, the Mother Superior shaped her to be a liberal, well-educated young girl steeped in an English education that was primed and prepared for the Cambridge, O and A level of the period. She absorbed the grounding of grammar with Wren and Martin and was enthralled with J.B Bury's Ancient History of Greece and Rome. The hours spent wallowing in Milton's Paradise Lost was wonderful.

She never questioned the innate differences of her life at home and a world that was opening up without. As a traditional girl at home with poojas, rituals of all kinds of things important to an orthodox Hindu Brahmin, the festivals, the family get-togethers, were part of the life of growing up, yet the schisms of the dual life slowly emerged. Her parents gave her not only a great education but opened up a world that made Sita in particular able to adapt to life in UK with no great difficulty, a coming home in some ways to the land of the Bard, Swift, and Milton et al.

The swinging sixties even influenced their teen years in India. They could not demonstrate and claim 'make love not war,' no chance of drugs or free sex but the music was in the airwaves. The teenage years saw them being influenced by the Beatles, Rolling Stones, the Elvis King, the lyrics tugging at the heart of young teens, hormones ablaze, looking for love. The Mills and Boon romances, the Bronte sister's seminal works, all filled their mind with a life that was not the norm for Hindu Brahmin girls growing up in Madras. Romance, love filled her heart. Sita talked, and dreamed in English, yet her mother tongue was Tamil, the language that she dropped at senior secondary and did a crash course in French. With this eclectic mix of influences, she was a product of the post Independent India, an Indian in every outward way but with the thoughts and aspirations of a liberally-educated middle class westerner. Her mother tongue remained with her but slowly became more difficult to write, though she could always read the language and speak it with ease. Tamil gave her another dimension that enriched her world but she was more comfortable in English, both in her thoughts, speech and dreams. The carefree schooldays ended all too soon.

'Time to choose your major for University' said her Dad.

'I'll do whatever Jyoti is doing,' Sita joked in her frivolous way.

'Sita, be serious for the first time in your life. This is not something you choose to be with your friends. Medicine is a good career and you have always shown an aptitude for science subjects. How about it'? Dad droned on and she reflected on her Dad's advice and accepted it. Important personal decisions were always made in this way in India of the 1970's and deference to parents was the norm. She was grateful that her parents put her education above the rush to get her 'married and settled' as others did. She had secretly dreamed of becoming a doctor and serving the people.

'Jyoti, I am taking medicine. What about you?'

'Seven years of learning hell,' was Jyoti's reaction. 'I'm going to take Domestic Science and get married at the end of the three years. Not busting my gut to get married and look after the family. I'd rather have a relaxed college life. We'll be married off anyway, so what's the point?' Sita had no doubts in her mind at all. Medicine was the career that she had set her heart on and not even her best friend's rejection of it put her off the hard years of study.

*

Sita closed the album, feeling its weight on her knee.

'Well now you know everything, about me. Now it's your turn.' she said to Ram. 'I'm waiting to hear all about your childhood. Were you a naughty boy or the teachers pet?'

'Nothing much to tell. My school was Don Bosco...I lived with my uncle.' He got up.

Sita waited for more.

'Maybe another day,' said Ram, stretching his arms above his head, taking the album to return it in to its rightful place in the cupboard.

Chapter 5

Sita was pleased to see the young couple on their doorstep. Their first visitors since she had arrived at Law hospital.

'Just wanted to say hello. Tasneem was getting lonely. Not many women she can talk to here,' said the young man as he walked in.

'This is Faraz and Tasneem his wife.' Ram introduced them.

Sita said 'nice to meet you,' and the girl whispered a faint 'salaam alikum'. They both smiled at each other's gaffe.

'I'm sorry, I don't know Urdu or Punjabi,' confessed Sita.

Faraz glowered at Tasneem, 'Say at least hello,' he said, 'that's not hard is it?' Tasneem squirmed and looked down. Sita felt awkward at his harsh outburst.

'We'll manage fine,' Sita said, 'It's so good to see another friendly face. It is lonely here.' She patted the girl's hand.

The bright green salwar- kameez with the gold work on it seemed heavy on the slender frame of the young girl. She had covered her head with the long scarf, the dupatta and looked down when the men spoke to her, almost in deference. Tasneem was just seventeen, hardly out of school and her command of English was rather poor. They smiled at each other, made the tea together and sat with the men who were talking about their patients. Sita joined in then felt guilty leaving Tasneem out so she let the two men talk. Faraz seemed the complete opposite of Ram. He cracked jokes and imitated his consultant with whom he was working. Sita laughed aloud a couple of times, and then checked herself.

'She has no confidence at all. Why don't you both go out, shopping in Glasgow together?' suggested Faraz.

'Don't know if Sita knows her way around yet, she's just arrived her,' said Ram.

'I'm sure if you give me the train timings I could get to Glasgow okay,' Sita said. 'I'm sure I could manage with a map in Glasgow. It would be nice to have some girlie shopping.'

'No, I go with him,' whispered Tasneem.

'Look at her, she's scared of everything. Just like her mother, my aunt.' Faraz's harsh tone was noticeable. He frowned and seemed irritated.

'Oh, are you related?' Sita's eyebrows raised and knitted.

'I'm cousin.' Tasneem whispered again. Faraz explained that it was his duty to marry his cousin, that they had been engaged since a very young age. There was an awkward pause as Faraz tapped his fingers on the table, then changed, with a dazzling smile and said:

'By the way, Ram, I'm off to the Southern General, as a Registrar starting next month. I'm buying a flat on the Southside of Glasgow. There are mosques and more Muslims there. 'What about you, Ram?' Faraz asked.

'Congrats, well done,' said Ram. 'I have one more stint at the Western Infirmary. We'll probably settle down once I get a permanent job. A wee dram, Faraz?' Ram asked.

'Aye, why not?' he said looking defiantly at Tasneem.

Faraz turned to Sita, 'Has he bored you with his SNP passion yet?' he asked, looking away from Tasneem, as if she didn't matter at all.

'He's told me a little bit. I've still not got to grips with British politics. There's a lot of material on the Party in the flat. I've been too lazy to look at it.'

'The SNP have gained a few seats in the local elections back in May this year.' Ram interjected.

'Local elections and that's where they'll stay. They'll never be able to take on the two big parties in Scotland,' laughed Faraz. They continued with the banter on the political party and had a few more drams.

Sita turned to Tasneem, admired the gold work on her dress. She tried to draw the girl into the conversation, but found it hard. Faraz made little effort to translate or help her predicament. Their wedding album was lying on the coffee table. Tasneem picked it up and opened it. Sita explained each of the ceremonies. The South Indian Brahmin wedding was so different from the Muslim wedding. Even Faraz was interested.

'We've a cine film of the wedding. Would you like to watch it?' asked Ram.

They settled down to watch, Sita's eyes were on the film but her mind went back to their wedding day.

*

Their wedding had been one of the grandest in Madras, a three-day affair. On the morning of the wedding as Ram tied the Thali around her neck at the Muhuratham ceremony, Sita had a mild panic attack. The gold chain, the Thali just like the wedding ring was the symbol of their being joined in matrimony. It was done. There was no turning back.

She took the seven steps around the holy fire holding Ram's hand. The first time their hands touched, she hoped he would glance at her, give her a smile of reassurance. Ram was busy concentrating on what the priest was saying and making sure he followed all the rites correctly. Then they both stood on the piece of rock promising their fidelity, respect, care for each other and the children they would bring to the world.

The huge crowd of nearly two thousand people wished them well, threw saffron scented rice and flower petals on them, like confetti. They gave them gifts and murmured their approval. Some were more concerned about the food that they had eaten or the latest gossip than the ceremony. Others were eyeing up prospective brides for their sons and vice versa. The reception finished with a huge firework display. As the crowd departed, the couple were asked to observe the last rite by the priest. He took them aside and pointed to the Arundathi Nakshataram, a star in the sky that was a symbol of fidelity. As they touched his feet, he blessed them with the words 'Beget all the sixteen riches of the world and have a long peaceful life.'

Now came the awkward bit, their first night. A tumble of emotions, fear more than excitement swept over Sita as she changed to a beautiful silk sari, pale lilac with a gold border. The raucous group singing romantic songs and teasing her brought her to the bedroom that had been decorated especially for the Shanti Muhurtham, the first night. The bed was strewn with rose petals. A variety of sweets, milk, water and other soft drinks were kept on the big table by the door. They left her at the door. She pushed open the door, stood quietly and she could see that Ram was sitting on the bed. He smiled and came over beside her and guided her into the room. She tried to remove the garland and found it was entangled in all the chains and her Thali round her neck. She tried to tug it out. Ram noticed and helped her. She hung the garland on a hook on the door and as she turned around, Ram tried to kiss her on the mouth. She turned her face quickly and it landed on her cheek. She pushed him away gently as he tried to embrace her and said,

'Ram, we need to know each other. Why don't we talk and get to know each other before ….' She stammered and blushed.

'What's there to talk about? We're married now. I …like you, I like you a lot …you know that surely?'

'I know, but let's talk. Why don't you tell me about your schooldays? Anything at all. I know nothing about you really.' The tremble in her voice was audible.

'We have a lifetime together to find out about each other. Tonight is the auspicious time. We must consummate our marriage. You know I won't hurt you.'

'Consummate!' even the word sounded crass, a plausible excuse that she found hard to accept. She was confused and upset. She had hoped it would be different. Somewhere in all her wild ramblings of fiction reading, she had romanticised this moment of her life in her own head. As she tried to still her pounding heart, Ram continued,

'I've got a month's supply of the birth control pill. I'll use the condom tonight but you can start the course from tomorrow.'

'Ram, I am not ready for any of this. I need time…..' He smiled at her. 'Look its getting late. We must do as the elders say, it's all for a reason.'

'No sorry Ram, I just can't, not tonight.' He took her hand, squeezed it. She jerked it free; her tears fell on his hand.

46

'Sorry, I didn't mean to frighten you. I was following our age old custom. I didn't know either what you were expecting.' Ram's voice was gentle. With a huge sigh of relief Sita turned to him and said,

'Ram this is what I mean. We don't even know what the other one is feeling.' She sighed.

'You're right. I'll wait till you're ready. It's been a long day.' They smiled at each other. 'Go on, get changed, and let's get some sleep.' Ram's concern touched her heart.

The bathroom mirror reflected the tears of relief streaming down her face. Tired and overwrought, she went back in and sat at the edge of the huge double bed. Ram tapped her shoulder and said, 'A goodnight kiss okay?' It seemed almost comical. The tension she felt before was away, and she nodded. He took her in his arms, kissed her gently. She resisted first then gave in to their first kiss. She felt nothing. He switched off the lights and the darkness spread all over. She moved to the furthest end of the bed, away from Ram. Exhausted, they both fell asleep.

Five thirty next morning, all the bustle of the day had already begun. She soon realised that not just the first day of her life with him but Ram's entire short stay in India would be taken over by his family duties.

'It's our tradition, all newly weds must visit the Thirupathi Temple.' His mother said in the morning. 'It is our family deity; you must offer an Archana to Lord Venkateswara and get his blessings.' Ram's mother's wish had to be respected. The whole contingent of the extended family went over the four hundred miles in a convoy of three cars. The trip was wonderful; the deity on the top of the seven hills was special. Sita had been there before. The cottages that they had booked were small but comfortable, set close to the temple. Though they were together, they had no time at all on their own, always surrounded by the family. She felt closer to Ram, sharing at least the nights with him, learning of his childhood. They were like friends on a holiday together, learning about each other.

'Well, what was wrong with the breakfast then?' asked Ram.

Sita blinked 'I thought the upma was tasty' she said hesitatingly 'Was there not enough salt for you?' She was making a poor guess. She was embarrassed as all the in-laws' eyes were on her. 'I don't know much about cooking,' she confessed.

Ram laughed saying, 'It was the mustard seeds. They had not been properly split.'

'Oh, don't be such a tease! Who can make out such a trivial thing, Ram?' said his mum taking Sita's side to her immense relief. 'He loves cooking. You're a lucky girl. He can teach you all you need to know,' his mum patted her arm gently.

Back in Madras living with Ram's family was a new experience. She had to get used to their rhythm of life. She missed her home but was able to chat to her mum or Gita every day on the phone. The days were filled with a round of temple visits or visiting elderly relatives who could not make it to the wedding. There was also a flurry of activity, getting all the papers ready to get Sita's visa for the UK. Sita realised with a sinking heart that there was no possibility of a honeymoon of any kind.

Their platonic relationship was easy at the daytime, but it was still strange to sleep beside Ram, share his bed. Each night when he tried to hold her, kiss her, she froze. She noticed him taking a tablet at night. 'Ram, why are you taking medicine? Are you ill?'

'No...' he did not answer. Tonight, that bottle of tablets was on the bedside table. He had left it as he went to get the water to take one. She picked it up. It was a bottle of sleeping tablets.

'Why are you taking sleeping tablets?' Her voice quivered, she knew the answer already and guilt spread a rosy tint on her cheeks.

He sat beside her and said nothing. She felt the room closing in on her. She whispered

'I wish we could get to know each other...'

'We've been married almost a week now.' He cut in. Of course, we know each other. I find it hard to sleep beside you...... how much time do you need? Do you hate me so much?' Ram looked angry and sad at the same time.

Sita twisted her plait and bit her lip. The sweat on her brow shimmered in the night light.

Slowly she moved over to him and let him caress her. She returned his kiss. They fumbled together. Their life as a couple began in a way she had not imagined. The quiet Ram was certainly passionate. The tension between them reduced. He was satisfied. Sita's heart was still left yearning.

*

The cine film ended. Ram switched the lights back on. Sita blinked. She quickly covered up her embarrassment by coughing and spluttering a bit.

'Excuse me; I'll just get a glass of water.' She brought a jug of water and glasses for the others.

'We've not seen the film properly ourselves until today,' said Ram and left the projector to cool.

'That was fascinating. Yours is so different from our Muslim wedding. Thank God, we don't have a film of ours. Not recorded for posterity like yours. I can get away from her!' Faraz joked pointing to Tasneem.

'What a selfish guy! Seemed to torment his sweet wife,' commented Sita after they had left.

'Did he?' said as Ram preoccupied with getting the projector packed away.

'Ram, relax, can we not do it later?' Sita felt a trickle of a headache coming on. She rubbed her forehead. He continued as though he had not heard her. She joined Ram in putting things away. The room was restored to its pristine and tidy state as they retired to the bedroom.

Sita made it a point to visit Tasneem, to get to know her better. The girl seemed almost frightened of Faraz and gave little away. They communicated by short words and phrase that Tasneem came up with in English when Faraz was not around. Sita persuaded her to go to Glasgow once with her but the trip was fraught with Tasneem's reluctance to relax. She had little confidence and Sita felt sympathetic towards this slip of a girl, battling with little knowledge of the language and trying to understand her new life. It also gave her a boost of confidence that she could manage so much better in Glasgow, her own new life not a struggle with the outside world at all. Tasneem seemed at ease with buying groceries at the Indian shop. Sita accepted her help. Her knowledge of the spices and dhal and greens showed up Sita's inadequacies with the cooking side of running a home. However, when Sita took her to Argyle Street, to the department stores, Tasneem cowered behind her. Sita's attempts to help the girl come out of her shell were not successful at all.

Sita noticed that her sari in Glasgow was not very practical wear. The edges got damp and even with a cardigan she felt the cold around the midriff which was bare. It was not warm enough. She also felt people staring at her on the bus. Her sari did not seem to matter in London, where every national dress seemed to be worn by tourists in all the places that she had been to. She bought herself some skirts, trousers and warm jumpers. Tasneem did not enjoy clothes shopping at all and kept asking when they would get back home.

Ram was in the kitchen when she arrived back, so she reeled off all that happened, excited about her new wardrobe and her trip to Glasgow.

'Why are the breakfast things not in the cupboard?' Ram asked as put them away.

'I rushed out for the train this morning, remember?' she said dumping the shopping, and chattered away about her day. She unpacked excitedly showing her new clothes to Ram. He took all the wrappers and shopping bags and put them in the bin, then started arranging the spices on the rack.

Sita went upstairs, changed and came running down to show her new clothes to him. She had on a grey woollen dress and twirled around asking, 'Ram do you think this suits me?'

'Yes, fine,' he said 'as long as it's comfortable for you.'

'Ram do you think I suit western clothes?'

The last time she'd worn dresses was when she had her school uniform on - at least a good seven years ago. Since university, she had worn either a sari or a salwar kameez.

'Well, what do you think, Ram?' she asked again.

'Alright, practical I suppose in this weather,' said Ram.

'But do I look okay in it?'

'Yes, yes of course' he said looking at her, and then fidgeted with the pen in his shirt pocket.

Trying on a pair of tights was tricky. She managed to rip the first pair, never having had to use such sheer nylons on her long legs. The trousers and jeans were comfortable. She got into the habit of wearing skirts and trousers all the time and wore saris only for visiting Indian friends or for special Indian functions.

Ram's methodical tidiness began to grate on her. His weekend habit of washing his shirts by hand, spraying starch on the white cotton ones, ironing them and putting them away with a military precision annoyed her. He seemed to lead a life where each hour of the day was filled with tasks or sleeping when he was exhausted. The months dragged on. Ram took her around Glasgow when he could, but hours that junior doctors had to do were punishing. She felt sorry for him. He was doing his best to combine his long hours at work with giving her some company when he was home. He was okay discussing work problems with her. She was happy that she could discuss some of the cases with him. When it came to anything personal, he seemed uneasy. His silence at times she felt was like a carapace that she could not break through. She turned to books again, her first love, managed to transport herself to another world. John Smiths in the city centre was her favourite shop. She bought quite a few books to read. Archie Hind's 'Dear Green Place' was highly praised in all the book reviews. She started reading contemporary Scottish authors, learning more about the city, not just relying on her own experience of it but also those reflected in the books. Before their stay at Law hospital was over she had made up her mind.

'Ram, I'm going to take the Professional and Linguistic exams. I need to pass that to work here, don't I?'

'Of course, I just thought you'd like some time to get used to the place.' Ram voice was gentle.

'I need to use my grey cells or I'll go out of my mind.'

'Okay, I've the books here. You can start straight away.' He pointed to the bookshelf heaving with his medical books.

The work for the exams kept her busy. They moved to the west end of Glasgow. Living in the hospital accommodation in the heart of the city made a huge difference to the quality of their life.

Chapter 6

The books that she had read in India had painted a picture of a first world that had enthralled her. She had wanted to experience it in person. Her expectations were perhaps romanticised beyond reality. Reality hit her sooner than she expected. Fed up with hospital accommodation they had tried to set up their first home. Their first flat hunting expedition was a revelation.

The Victorian building glowed in the evening twilight. The blonde sandstone lightened by the last rays of the sun. The huge bay windows looked out on to the wonderful Botanic Gardens. 'The bed-sit would suit a professional couple,' the advert had said in the Glasgow Herald.

Ram rang the bell. A tall well-dressed lady opened the door.

'We've come about the bed-sit. Dr. Iyer,' said Ram holding out his hand.

A crimson hue rose up the lady's cheeks as she edged closer to the door and said,

'The bed-sit? Oh, it's taken. I'm sorry. It's away.' The lady shut the door behind her quickly as if they might have forced their way in.

After a few such attempts, Ram asked Pat, a friend who worked beside him to go and view the same flats. No surprise! The flats were still available.

'Years of education, democracy, freedom and affluence haven't freed people from their deepest fears,' thought Sita. The liberal west of her dreams and the reality did not add up.

The flat hunting continued.

'Ten pounds a week. The bed-sit is perfect for a young couple like you. The gas fire has a meter, so you'll need plenty of two bob pieces and this is the bathroom.' Mrs. Kerr showed them the flat.

'Two bob?' Sita looked puzzled as Mrs. Kerr explained.

Mrs. Kerr had a kind face. Her white hair tied up in a neat bun, she wore a brown tweed skirt, a cream jumper and sensible brown brogues. She was very friendly and welcoming. Number ninety two Kelvin Drive was just a step away from the Botanic Gardens. Ram signed the lease on the basement flat where Mrs. Kerr lived. Sita looked in awe at the huge bookshelf on the wall. Books filled the room. There were some in piles near the huge bay window. Others were neatly stacked near the hearth of a huge fireplace. Sita liked the warmth of the roaring coal fire. The flames made patterns on the wall, the crackling sounds and the aroma of coals burning was comforting.

'Mrs. Kerr, may I have a look at your books?'

'Of course dear! Books are there to be used and enjoyed,' she said, going back to her paper work. Sita fingered the books on the shelf. It was an eclectic collection. She reached for the Scottish authors whom she had not seen or heard of in India.

'Are there any libraries or bookshops nearby?' Sita asked.

Mrs. Kerr's face lit up with a smile of affection.

'Why you're a girl after my own heart. Just borrow any book that you've not read from me. Hillhead Library is just on Byres road. I'll walk you over there and of course John Smiths and Collins, the bookshops, are in the town centre.' The rapport between them was instant.

'Yes, I do know the shops in town,' said Sita.

Mrs. Kerr became her mentor, a surrogate mother figure. She helped Sita in so many little ways. Sita's first steps at domesticity were made so much easier. She showed her the laundrette, how to work the cooker, the shops, the bus routes into town. To Sita, a complete novice, this was a godsend. The warmth that she got from people like Mrs. Kerr made her life so much easier to deal with. She loved the way complete strangers said 'Good morning, terrible weather eh?' The polite thanks, or sorry, at all the shops that she heard often. Such a delight compared to Madras where rudeness seemed endemic.

At Mrs. Kerr's, their spotless bed-sit had a three-piece suite, a bed at one end and a tiny cooker and wash hand basin at the other. A huge bay

54

window with thick lined curtains dominated the room. There was a dinner set for only four people, cutlery for four, four glasses and basic pots and pans. This was Sita's new life. After the rambling old house in Madras, overflowing with family, friends and servants, this was a radical change.

Just once a month she could afford to call home, an expensive trunk call, costing a pound a minute. Phone calls from home were a painful link often leaving Sita with feelings of being unable to reach out over the thousands of miles. Words that one could say face to face could never be said over the phone, as the calls were short and full of emotion. Hearing her mum's voice made Sita weepy.

'Mum, I miss you all so much.' A silent sob caught at her throat.

'We miss you too. Anjali has had a son. We're all rejoicing. Do you need anything from here? Did you write to Jyoti? Are you warm in the new house? How are you managing to run the house and work?' Her mum's concern always translated to a string of questions posed at such speed she had no time to answer them.

'Mum I find it so difficult ... with Ram.'

Her mum cut in. 'Oh, it's just initial adjustment. You'll be fine. Soon you'll say, mum, I love him so much that I can't be without him.' Her mum spoke about the rest of the family, skimming over what Sita had just said. The three minutes flew by. It was too costly to talk for longer.

Sita put the phone down as droplets of tears fell silently on her cheeks. Memories of home played on her mind's screen. She went over all her mum's news of people in India. Anjali was her childhood playmate. She remembered the child bride's anguish. Anjali had struggled with her marriage. Her life reflected the lack of choice and the hardship of the poor in India. Sita shuddered as she recalled how Anjali's marriage had been racked with problems from the outset. That special day when Ayah announced Anjali's wedding came flooding back.

*

The marble floor in her room was still cool from the air-conditioning previous night. Sita looked out at the garden. *Mali* was busy tidying up the paths, with its luxuriant growth of weeds, the red earth making his

55

job hard. The bougainvillea branch bright with magenta flowers swayed gently in the breeze. The early morning smells of a freshly-dewed earth wafted over, and brushed her skin. Sita reached for her books. She needed to complete the assignment soon. The deadline for submission was scarily near. Ayah handed her the coffee and waited, smiling.

'Sita'ma, I've got some good news this morning. I want to tell you first.'

Sita placed the saucer on the table beside her, and then she sipped the coffee. She looked at Ayah: 'Yes, what is it?'

'Anjali is getting married.' Ayah almost whispered it. The excitement in her eyes was just visible.

'What! Anjali? Isn't she is too young?' Sita was stunned.

'She is already sixteen years old, nearly four years since she matured. My relatives would be unhappy if I let her remain unmarried.' A worried wrinkle creased Ayah's forehead.

'Have you stopped her going to school then?' Sita asked surprised. Ayah had not mentioned this to the family at all. Both Sita's mum and dad had wanted Ayah's child to do well and get out of the service culture.

'Oh yes, last year. It was not a good thing to let her out. Too many boys were eyeing her up, Sita'ma.'

'When did you arrange the marriage then?' Sita's eyebrows arched up, still taking it all in. She gulped her coffee quickly.

'Just last week. The wedding date has been finalised. She has been home, learning to cook and clean.

'Ayah, why didn't you mention this before?'

'You were all so busy with your sister, Gita'ma's wedding I couldn't bother you with my business.' True, the wedding had them overwhelmed with work. Like the other maids she was totally at their beck and call. It had lasted three days, and took six months to organise. Nothing else mattered at home. It absorbed their waking days. The silk saris, jewels to match, ordering the fireworks, the best caterers, the list was endless. Flowers were flown in from the south. The grand wedding was a wonderful affair, colourful, bright, enjoyed by over a thousand guests. Gita and Ashok had made a strikingly handsome pair.

Sita ran over to the veranda. 'Mum, Mum!' she shouted excitedly, 'Did you hear, Anjali is getting married?' Her mum was chatting quietly to dad as he tried to read the paper.

'What? That is great news, Ayah, so soon after our Gita's wedding. Tell me all about it.' Her mum turned her face towards them. It was wreathed in a big smile.

'Amman …' Ayah hesitated, her head bowed down. She never spoke in front of the master. Mum noticed her discomfiture and left her chair. Mum, Ayah and Sita moved back to the room. Mum sat on the bed and asked.

'Who is the boy then, ayah?'

'Amman, he is from our village. My brothers have arranged it.' A happy grin slowly spread on Ayah's face.

'Your brothers! They were no good at all when you had problems Ayah.' Mum was annoyed and it showed.

'I've to listen to them Amman, as I'm a widow. They're the males in the family who make all the important decisions.' Ayah explained, her toes making little patterns on the floor, her face tense.

'So where is this boy working?' Mum wanted all the details. Ayah shuffled a bit. 'He is in the village. He works on the land.'

'Not a landless labourer I hope, Ayah. Anjali has lived all her life in the city. How could you arrange such a marriage?' Both mum and Sita were amazed.

'Amma, he is her 'murai pillai' chosen from birth. I can't go against the family tradition.' Ayah's shuffling increased. She twisted the end of her sari between her fingers.

'How will she adjust to a life in the village? Are the family good?' Sita's Mum continued.

57

'I know very little about them. My brothers arranged it all.' Ayah's unease increased. She bit her lip and sighed.

'Ayah, why didn't you tell me? We have boys in our company who are smart, working and earning well. We could have arranged a good match for Anjali.'

'Amma, my brothers would not agree to any one but Muthu. It's a family tradition to marry as arranged at our birth.' Ayah smiled faintly and then asked. 'Amma, about the wedding expenses...nearly 10,000 rupees...'

'Of course, I'll get it sorted for you, though I can't give you the whole lot. I'll talk to the master. Some will be a loan that you'll have to repay.' Sita noticed that her mum's practical side never let her down.

'Thank you Amma. You've been like God to me.' Ayah was about to fall at her feet. Sita's mum stopped her from doing that.

'Ayah, bring Anjali over. We must give our blessings to the young bride.' She added gently.

'Yes Amma, I'll bring her tomorrow.' A smile of relief spread on Ayah's face.

The door flung wide open, Gita barged in and threw herself at mum.

'Oh I hate that house. I wish I was back home.' Her voice was shrill. Gita was always melodramatic. She was perfectly made up, only the best for her. Her designer jeans, diamond solitaire earrings glinting in the morning sun, the lovely leather Italian sandals, reeked of style. No one could refuse her anything. Her beauty enslaved people.

'Now what's the matter?' Sita's mum's attention turned totally to Gita.

'Mum, they expect me to do some house work. You know I can't stand it, not used to it. I'm not going back. How can they expect me to wash the dishes and cut the vegetables? I didn't marry Ashok to be a maid, did I? '

'Gita, servants do need time off. Surely you can help out.' Only then did Gita notice Ayah hovering around.

'Ayah, get me some lemon sherbet. I'm parched, turn the AC on. It's so hot.' Gita's memsahib voice was crisp and loud. She fanned herself with a paper from Sita's desk.

'Yes Gita'ma,' nodded Ayah. She took the coffee cup, closed the windows, switched on the AC and hurried away to do what she was told. Gita waited impatiently, flicked her long hair, and looked at her manicured hands.

'Mum you always take their side,' Gita now composed a bit, was checking her elegant watch.

'Gita, are you happy with Ashok?' Her mum asked softly.

'Of course. I love him. I just hate living with his family. Why can't they get more maids? Mum, why don't I take Anjali? She'd be perfect help for me?'

'Gita you're *unbelievable*. Anjali is getting married and moving away.' Sita could not resist her sharp voice cutting in. Gita hardly glanced at her.

'What! Oh, Anjali, the poor thing. Why do these maids get married so young and suffer for the rest of their lives?' Gita turned back to mum. Her beautiful face enhanced, Sita noticed, with a new shade of lipstick that matched her hand embroidered silk top.

'Anyway, mum, just find me a new maid, I can't stand it. I won't have anytime for socialising if my mother in law has her way.' She tossed her glossy black hair and smoothed it back.

'Well I'll ask around, but it's not easy to find young maids who are reliable. I also need to talk to your mother in law. She may not like it.' As usual mother did whatever Gita wanted and she was pleased with having achieved her goal. Mum admired Gita's new handbag, which she had flung on the sofa bed. The soft leather in a pale colour had some initials in gold on it. She held the straps that had gold and the leather plaited together.

'This is lovely. Where did you buy it, Gita?' her mum asked.

'Spencer's had a special Italian promotion. I had to get it.'

She turned to Sita who was conscious of her old pyjamas and tee shirt, comfort clothes to work in.

'How's my little sister then, still got your head stuck in books? Sita, by the way, I've seen a beautiful jewellery set. Jade with silver. It'll be great with my new green sari. Will you come with me? I must get it today.'

'No, I need to work on my assignment.' Sita said. She was her sister. She could not ignore her but she hated her perfection, her superficial life.

'You're such a bore, I'll call Sushma. She loves jewellery shopping.' Gita went off to call up her friend. Spending money was her way out of anything.

Sita tried to work on her dissertation, but she could only think of Anjali. Sita had grown up with Anjali. Her mind delved quickly into the scenes of their special relationship when they were children. They had been playmates. She would join her when they were little as they chased the sparrows, plucked jasmine flowers from the garden, ate mangoes and grimaced at the sour taste. The mali would let them have a go at the hand pump and they would water the garden. Anjali was a tomboy like Sita, taking part in the cricket games that Sita's brothers played. The boys would always use them as fielders, giving them very little chance to bat or bowl. Sita remembered how she stood up to the boys and demanded that they were allowed to bat. Anjali stood by her. Being a maid and younger she had very little say, but that bond of playing together was special.

Meanwhile, Gita, her sister, did not like to get her clothes dirty. She preferred to watch TV or play with dolls. Anjali was part of Sita's childhood, a happy time. Those innocent days flashed past so quickly. Sita was whisked off in the chauffeur driven car to the exclusive private convent school. Anjali attended the municipal school. They still played together occasionally on a Sunday, but their lives soon moved in completely different circles. As they grew up their relationship changed in subtle ways. Anjali helped in the house when she finished at school, put the fan or AC on, took care of Sita's clothes, ran short errands for the sisters. Now she was getting married, still a child herself in many ways.

Anjali's wedding was a simple affair in the small hall that they had hired. Special chairs were hired for Sita's family to be seated. Anjali looked tiny, the groom a good few years older and very rough at the edges. He did not have the city slickness that some of the boys in Madras had. His sun-hardened skin, the calloused hands and his old-fashioned shirt showed his village naiveté in many ways. Sita's heart went out to her childhood friend who had few options in her life. She said a silent prayer that her life would be peaceful and happy. The village was not too far from Madras. A good bus link was on hand. Her parents made sure that Ayah got long weekends to visit her daughter.

Within a few months, Ayah gave them the news. 'Amma, Anjali is expecting her first baby. By the grace of god it will be a boy.' Ayah stood with a small plate of sweets. The family wished the young girl all the good luck in the world as they continued with their own lives.

Gita had more tantrums, not getting a proper maid, not getting Ashok to take her abroad for a holiday, his meanness when he put a brake on her never ending shopping sprees. He could not stop it entirely though he did try a few times by stopping the accounts in the big stores. Her sulking and tears made him relent. She managed to get Ashok to buy her dream house away from her mother in law. She installed all the maids and help she needed to run her life smoothly. Gita's life of luxury carried on unabated.

The monsoons wreaked havoc in the city. Floods in different parts of the state were reported in the news. Anjali had come to Madras for her delivery. The mother had to bear all the expenses of the 'confinement' as it was called in India. The torrential rain heralded the birth of a baby daughter for Anjali. The family rejoiced that the baby was healthy. Ayah wiped tears of fear. History was repeating itself.

Sita spoke to Anjali. It was the first time since her marriage. She was happy with Muthu, but afraid of her mother in law who sounded like a dreadful woman. She found life in the village hard. Shyly she made a request.

'Sita'ma, if you can find a job for Muthu, we'd love to come to Madras. There is not much work in the village.'

'I'll ask around Anjali, I have a friend who runs a nursery in the city. Maybe he could give him a job.' Sita hoped she could do this little favour for her childhood friend.

'He is a hard worker, I'm sure he'll not let you down. Please don't tell anyone. My mother in law will not allow Muthu to leave her or the

61

village.' Anjali had genuine fear in her eyes. Sita never forgot that look. It was the first and only time Anjali had ever asked Sita for help. She had to help her out, but do it in secret? Now, that was a challenge.

The week after the baby was born the first ritual for the baby's birth began.

'Amma, will you come to the naming ceremony tomorrow. Muthu and his parents will be there?' Ayah asked Sita's mum hesitantly.

'Mum can't come, as Gita is coming back from her European trip, and she'll need to be home to hear all about it. I'll come.' Sita offered, and relished the idea of not being around while Gita held court over her holiday experience and give out all her expensive gifts.

Ayah had decorated the little one room outhouse. The kolum pattern in all colours outside looked lovely. She had tied some mango leaves on the side of the doorstep. The smell of fresh jasmine was pleasant. The floor of the room had a few new mats where the guests sat. Ayah was so worried that there was no chair for Sita, who sat down on the floor at the back and watched as young Anjali came over with the baby wrapped in new clothes. Soon Muthu arrived with his family to see the baby. The young couple looked genuinely happy. They sat beside the priest. However, his mother started the wailing and moaning as soon as the baby was brought over to her.

'What cruel fate, a girl, no one to carry our family name. My only son. Anjali did not give a first –born son. This is a bad omen. She must take after her mother.'

She moaned at everything. 'Why spend money on a girl, who is going to cost money all her life?' Muthu tried to calm her down. He gave her a cup of juice, carried the baby over to her.

'I'll name her after you Ma,' said Muthu proudly.

'No, I don't want her to carry my name. Call her anything else.'

Muthu listened to his mum's every whim. She would not hold the child or even look at the baby. Sita was shocked at her attitude but kept quiet, letting the family carry on with the rituals. They served some sweets, gave flowers to all the women there. The priest conducted a short service. They traced the name of the child- Padmini - on the rice grains that was spread on the floor. Unfortunately, the ceremony was so short that when Sita got home she still had to listen to Gita's excited talk laced with photos.

'It was the best holiday of our lives,' Gita gushed on. 'Taj tours started in London, then took in five capitals in Europe. Sita, you must see Paris, Rome was great …'

Sita looked out of the window. The soggy garden was slowly drying up as the sun beat down strong and hot.

'Three nights in Scotland was super.' Gita was still going on. 'Edinburgh is fantastic. Ashok even managed to play on the Old course at St. Andrews…Mum, here's some Edinburgh crystal for you. Ritu go to the car and bring Sita'ma's gifts.' The little maid ran to the car.

'*Ritu*? Have you changed her name?' Sita asked incredulously.

'I couldn't be bothered with her long village name. She's okay, a bit lazy, but if I don't shout she slackens. *Ritu*, not that green parcel, *you silly girl*, go and get all of them, ask the driver to help you.' Her voice rose a few decibels. The little girl looked chastened as she ran back to the car again.

'See what I mean?' Gita rolled her eyes.

The presents were soon distributed. 'Coco Chanel for you, Sita. Hope you like it. Sorry I had no time for bookshops; we can order the book you want at Higginbotham's.' Sita took the perfume from her.

'Great, thanks. Did you know Anjali has had a little girl?'

'I heard… mum said that you were with them earlier today. These maids all they do is marry and keep producing kids whether they can afford to raise them or not.' Gita dismissed the event and moved on to showing the family the video of her trip.

A few weeks later Ayah took Anjali and the baby to her village. On her return Ayah looked unhappy as she carried on her work around the house. Sita could sense her worry. She tried to reassure her.

'Look Ayah, it was different in your time. Your husband and mother in law were unhappy that you only had a girl. But those days are over now.'

63

'Amma you've heard how I suffered. Only my husband's death released me from my mother in law's clutches. She cursed me everyday, abused me for years. She threw me out as soon as my husband died. Destitute, with little Anjali, I arrived at your house. Without your family, I would not have survived. I don't want Anjali to go through the same.' Her silent tears now turned into sobs.

'Anjali is young. At least Muthu loves her and the baby. He'll take care of them.' Sita comforted her.

'Amma I'm not sure. Her mother in law already blames Anjali, saying it is her fault.'

Sita remembered Anjali's request. She contacted her friend who owned a nursery. He was willing to take Muthu on a trial basis. If he shaped up, he would give him the job. Sita sent for Muthu from the village, saying that she needed some work done in the garden. He arrived, happy to earn extra money and to buy little toys that he could get in Madras for the baby.

'Muthu, would you like to work in Madras? I can get a job for you.' Sita asked him when he turned up for the work.

'You mean leave the village forever?' Muthu looked perplexed. 'I thought it was for a few weeks for the garden here.'

'Well, I could get permanent work for you in a nursery if you want to. Anjali can move near her mother.' Sita explained.

'You mean here in Madras?' Muthu still looked unsure.

'If you want to. Don't you and Anjali want to come to Madras?' Sita asked him.

'I…. I don't know what to say…'

'Muthu, you have to **decide**. I thought you wanted the city life?'

'I like the cinema and shops here, but my village is my life.'

'Did Anjali not speak to you about this?'

'Yes but …,' he hesitated. 'My ma'll not like to leave the family home. She'll not like to live in the city. It's so expensive here.' Muthu looked worried, scratched his head.

'No Muthu, not all of you. I meant just you, Anjali and the baby.' He looked confused.

'My ma... she'll not agree. How can I leave her?'

'Your dad can look after her Muthu, surely. It's not as if she's on her own.'

Sita left Muthu in a quandary to answer a phone call. It was Gita, excited about her latest acquisition. 'You must see and hear it, it's the latest. Ashok, my sweetie, has bought me a cassette player and one for the car. I'm busy getting my favourite tapes to stack them in the car. I'll come over this evening. Don't know if the *idiot* of a driver will have a clue how to work it. See ya. Ciao.' She rang off.

Muthu did not have the courage to leave the village or his mother. Sita often wondered about Anjali. The second baby was again a girl. Sita's father gave the children enough money for their education. Ayah was part of the family and cared for always.

Soon the pressures of Sita's medical degree exams took precedence. Now that she had the news of the baby boy, Sita felt a rush of joy in her heart for Anjali. At last a longed for son. Her life would be more peaceful now.

*

She shook herself out of the reverie as the clock struck the hour. The huge grandfather clock was almost a piece of art. The rich mahogany wood with grains lending an original design from nature, with its polished brass hands and a pendulum that swung the seconds away. The clock graced the hallway and she could hear the chimes announcing the majestic tones of the hour clearly. Mrs. Kerr's immaculate house had beautiful period pieces that she lovingly maintained. She watched one night as Mrs. Kerr reset the clock, with a big key, a ritual before going to her bed, as timeless as the clock that watched the hours whittle away. Time never stood still. It moved on relentlessly. If only Sita could stop it moving and recapture her carefree childhood days. Time, she thought

65

that man has set to the movement of night and day, that never fails and never stops. Maudlin thoughts never achieve anything, she told herself. It was time to get her head back in the books for her Professional and Linguistic Abilities exams. It was a world away from the problems of her childhood friend in India.

Sita spoke to Ram about Anjali. She was touched by his concern and his immediate suggestion that they send a small percentage of their earnings to India every month for her childhood friend, a little act from Ram that made her heart melt at his kindness. She gave him a hug that expressed more than mere words. He pressed her close to his heart, then moved away to see to the practicalities of setting up the way to pay the amount to Anjali. They were not sure there would be a bank in the village.

'Maybe pay Ayah every month and make sure that she'll help Anjali access it?' he asked.

'Ayah would make sure Anjali uses it wisely,' said Sita, ruffling Ram's hair, and kissed him on his ear gently. He blushed and brushed her hand away, 'It's too tickly, stop it!' he giggled.

'Ram, that's the sweetest thing you've done for me,' she said.

'Maybe I'm the champion of the underdog,' a worried expression flitted across his face. His kindness was the quality that endeared her to him. She remembered the old Tamil couplets of Thirukurral that they had learned as children: 'The wealth of kindness is the wealth of wealth.'

Ram was perhaps too good for her she thought. Nevertheless, the negative feelings that she could not have that sexual chemistry, that feeling of being in each other's head, thinking as one, still rankled.

Chapter 7

Walks were soothing. Nature provided an unquestioning companion and offered solace, though sometimes, even the weather seemed alien. Fat plops of rain fell like small missiles, the cold dampness chilling her subtropical bones. She observed that most of the people wrapped up against the damp. A 'permanently coated' crowd, she thought compared to the white heat of Madras where even the thinnest cotton clung to one's skin. Humid with sweat, cooled only in the evening with the sea breeze. The insipid sun here was such a contrast to the searing heat of Madras. The clouds of gold replaced by shades of grey gripped her soul, steeped her in unhappiness.

The cold wind chilled her to the core, the gusts shaking the trees to shed leaves. The skeletal barks of some trees cast strange shapes in the evening light, and orangey glow interspersed with dark figures of the branches casting shadows on the tarmac. She huddled into her winter coat, reaching out for some warmth. She looked around the bus stop. People were in their own thoughts not sharing a word, some stamping their feet, to keep warm in the chill autumn air. Grey, black, and moist. Her new life exuded these. Not the tropical blue of Madras beach, the gold of summer, or the sheets of monsoon rains. The Botanic Gardens was a haven. The green, the bright green of the foliage in some plants, the moss green of the lawn, the colours of so many roses and other bedding plants, such luscious sights. She loved the Kibble Palace best. The warmth inside when she needed to escape from the bitterly cold wind was comforting. Just seeing the familiar palms or an ornamental banana plant in the tropical house transported her back home.

Her first winter in Glasgow would be etched in her memory. She looked around the vast bed-sit. The ceilings were high, the heating from a gas fire that consumed two shilling coins voraciously. The hearth beside it was cold marble. She could not get close enough to warm her whole being. Her back often felt frozen. She had never felt cold like it. Icicles hung smudged grey, or soot covered and dotted black on the windowsills. The Botanic gardens were no longer a verdant green, the leaves long gone, and the bare branches swinging wildly in the winter gales.

How romantic it had been to read this in the books in India! Books about barren Scotland with gales ripping through the countryside had sounded exciting. Living in it was different. Even the air smelt different, the clothes when she brought them in had a musty smell, not the heated sunny fresh smell that she was used to. The air inside the house was stale. Cooking curry with all the windows shut left a strong lingering smell on clothes, on the curtains, the fabrics of the house.

The language, the 'glesca patter' was a challenge. The glottally-stopped words often seared the heart with unfamiliarity. That uncertain anguish of the ear of an educated immigrant became more heightened when she treated her patients. On the bus she heard the words and phrases that were unfamiliar-'windae,' 'going for my messages' I'm flitting today' 'wisnae'- though she was amused with 'are ye awright, hen?'

She felt the confusion of the familiar and the new swirling together. The Queens English, the received pronunciation of the BBC World service that she was attuned to was replaced by a broad Glasgow accent that was difficult to comprehend. Even the TV programmes such as Coronation Street were strange to her ears. She made an effort to watch them and learn the different accents of the language that was used in Britain.

Slowly she gained confidence, almost like the Clyde merging with the Adyar River of her Madras. The cold grey of Glasgow cooled the humid heat of Madras. Nothing was familiar yet this was all hers to form the next part of her history, a new thread to weave. This would be a tapestry of life that she would weave with her loneliness, alienation, fear, perhaps also with the friendships, the beauty and ruggedness of her new life.

Her success at the PLAB exam gave her the chance of work immediately. She felt her confidence grow. The first job and getting into the way of life took time but there were both humour and hardship in her new life as she struggled on.

Sita had experienced the four seasons. The changes were so dramatic compared to subtropical Madras. The constant rain was harder to get

68

used to, but the greenery and the flowers that were so rare in Madras were a wonderful luxury, compensation that she had not imagined ever having. Her outlook had been very negative those first few months in Glasgow, but living and working in the city gave her an insight into the culture. It was a jumble of contradictions. Warmth and a wry humour railed against a class system that was challenged by a deep undercurrent of socialism. Socialism still had a strong grip on the Scots. After all, she concluded, this was the land that had given birth to Keir Hardie. She compared it to Madras where the poor accepted their circumstances as their fate, resigned to their lot in life. Sometimes she longed for the heat of Madras, the simple buildings that let the fresh breeze in. Glasgow's soot encrusted sandstone Victorian buildings were beautiful but black, hidden under layers of century old soot. The dark buildings of Glasgow, smudged and blackened did little to raise her spirits. The red or blonde sandstone sometimes cleaned in one part, radiated a beauty that was unsurpassed but some others were left screened behind black soot. Yet she felt a rare sense of history. The care that had preserved some of them was so uplifting. In Madras, some of the ancient buildings had been left to crumble away.

This was a tough city harsh with drug-ridden gangs in some areas. The pub culture was so strong that people drank heavily. The city was also divided by sectarianism, a football mad youth riven by religious bile. The Clyde River dark was the lifeblood of the city once. Now the shipyards were closing down, the last heavy industry dying a slow death. The conditions of life in the peripheral estates that she had read about, some newspapers referred to them, as 'Jeelie Piece' estates (there was a new word for her!) were shocking. Her colleagues described at length the deprived areas of Castlemilk, Easterhouse, and Drumchapel when she queried them.

In total contrast, she now lived in the leafy suburb of Bearsden just at the edge of the city where some of her friends lived. Her feeling of affection for Glasgow and its people ranged from highs to lows. On the one hand, when she was homesick and needed her family nothing was right with the city. On the other, the joy of working, having her freedom, sharing a drink with friends made her happy. Living in Bearsden was a change from the hospital accommodation and her experience of the bed-sit land of the west end of Glasgow. However, the suburb had its own unique way of life. To be an incomer accepted as part of the close community was not easy. Both Ram and Sita being doctors helped. She

69

had witnessed the treatment of one of the newcomers, her new neighbours not long after she had been there. The wife was from Faifley and the husband a doctor. The wife was treated with less respect than her doctor husband. The class divide in Glasgow was greater than she had reckoned with.

A blue aerogramme letter was in her mailbox. She recognised the handwriting straightaway.

'Dear Sita,

I got your address from your mum. How are you and Ram doing in Glasgow? Its ages since you left Madras. Apart from your postcards from London and Glasgow, you've hardly kept in touch. Not like you at all. I'm dying to hear all about Scotland. So how are you both doing? Do you still wear the sari? Is it as cold and wet as Ram described? How do you spend your time? Have you met any Indians out there? How are you coping with housework? Tell me all about it.

I'm busy with the family. My daughter is now going to a nursery school. I am expecting a little brother or sister for her. Her ayah is so good, so I'll have help always. My mother-in-law helps too, so life is fine. I had to give you the good news of my pregnancy. We've always shared everything in our lives. I do miss that closeness. Are you that busy that you've not found time to write a few lines to your old friend?

By the way, do you remember our visit to St. Andrews Church? Well, you have kindled an interest in me. I have become a *Scotophil* (Is there such a word?) anyway, I have so found out so many connections between Madras and Scotland that I'm compiling a little scrap book on the topic. You must do the same at your end. There is even a Scottish Highland dancing club in Madras. Can you imagine people twirling in their saris doing the 'Gay Gordon'? I'm really enjoying this new found interest. I may even convince Suresh to take me on a trip to the U.K. It won't be possible now, of course, with the baby on the way. Why haven't you written? Have you forgotten all of us in Madras? I still miss you. I'll be waiting for a long detailed letter that you owe me.

Yours affectionately,

Jyoti.

Sita turned on the radio. Tom Jones was belting out the 'Green Green Grass of home.' It brought tears to her eyes. She switched off the radio.

She took out the Basildon Bond writing pad. The pale blue crinkly paper rustled. The watermark on it was faint in the background. She stared at it, made a stab at the writing, stopped then took the envelope and copied Jyoti's address on it. She was procrastinating again. She had one more go at replying to her dearest friend. Why was it so difficult to write? She put the pad back.

The meeting with Jyoti was not something she would forget. As soon as she saw the letter her heart to heart chat with her replayed in her mind. That was the day she had met Ram for the first time.

*

The phone rang. 'It's for you, Sita,' mum called her.

'Congratulations! I heard the great news. What's he like? Tell me all about him?' asked Jyoti breathlessly. 'Is he tall, does he talk posh, with an English accent, did he set your heart racing?' The questions poured out.

'Jyoti, look why don't we meet up and I'll give you all the details? Are you free this afternoon?'

'Ok I'll make time. I'll get mother-in-law to look after the little one. See you soon.' They met at Egmore 'Kwality Restaurant'.

'Why did you ask me to meet here? I've heard that the *masala dosa* is great in this restaurant but this is not our usual place.' Jyoti was curious.

'Well, I read that St. Andrews Church here in Egmore has a Scottish connection so I thought I'd have a look after we finish our snack here.'

'Oh, so you're already thinking of Scotland. We've paled into the background,' Jyoti teased. 'Tell me all about him. Come on. It's me you're talking to.'

'He is okay to look at, five foot ten, curly thick hair. He is very quiet, deep, doesn't say much.'

'Well, was it love at first sight? It must be. I hit it off with my Suresh straight away; the chemistry was there in an instant.'

71

'Lucky you, I just feel he is …, he seems a decent person, as a medic we have a lot in common…'

'You sound like he'd make a good friend. Where's the sparkle?'

Sita sighed. Jyoti could always read her like a book.

'Jyoti, surely being a good friend is important. It'll be there I'm sure when we start our life in Glasgow together.'

'Can't imagine you with someone so quiet. He sounds a bit …introverted. Hope he loves books like you do?'

'I've not had time to get to know him yet. Don't know if he reads.'

'Are you sure he's the one for you? It's a lifetime commitment and you're going away from home to live with him.'

'Jyoti, he's gentle, sweet even. I'm sure things will be okay. I'm sure it'll work out, Scotland sounds so different and exciting.' Sita's voice was shaking a bit.

'Let's go see the church.' She dragged her friend along.

St. Andrews Kirk as it was known was fascinating. Sita had read the detailed history of how it had been built. It was the finest example of Georgian church architecture and modelled on the plans of St. Martins Lane, London. It was built to serve the members of the Scottish Church serving in the East India Company in 1821. Sita and Jyoti gazed at the lapis lazuli blue coloured ceiling, replicating a star studded blue sky looking down on mere mortals. The black and white marble floors, the rich mahogany woodwork made the interior rich in texture. The lovely stucco work of Madras Chunnambu or lime stucco, the pillars and walls were decorated with a relief of grapes nestled in leaves. Fifteen enormous olive green and gold pipes made up the astounding organ. Sita noticed that the stained glass window was by 'W &J Kier, artists in Stained Glass, Glasgow Scotland'. She felt a shiver of excitement at this tenuous connection between Madras and Glasgow, the place where her new life was to begin.

'This church is beautiful. We never bother to look at our own city, do we?' gasped Jyoti, looking at the beautiful interior.

'I'm glad I've seen it now.' Sita was smiling.

'Hey, you're still in Madras, not in Glasgow yet,' Jyoti was teasing her again.

They walked around the church.

'Remember what I said, talk to him, and be sure before you commit yourself. I know all your crazy romantic ideas.' Jyoti reminded her.

'The wedding is only a fortnight away. I'm sure everything will be fine.' A worried wrinkle appeared on Sita's forehead as she forced a smile. Jyoti gave her a quick hug. Sita held on to her for a mite longer.

'I'll look forward to a gorgeous bride then. I need to rush. Can't let ma-in-law and the ayah get an excuse to moan about me abandoning my daughter!' Jyoti joked and left. Sita went round the church again deep in thought.

*

She put the letter away in a box.

Sita wandered into the kitchen and took out the recipe book her mum had given her. Maybe try her hand at making a new dish tonight for their dinner. A packet of sweets lay on the table. She popped a sweet into her mouth and spat it out quickly. It was a sour chew. Life is like Indian sweetmeats her grandma used to say. Sweet, tangy or cloying. You take what you get and make the best of it. Some of the flavours in the packet of sour chews set her teeth on edge. The colours of the wrappers to attract children were bright lime green, blackcurrant, orange and strawberry. It seemed to describe her life. Grandma was right. Hers was a sweet but tangy life. Later, at dinner Ram commented:

'Sita, the rice and sambhar is super. Your first attempts at cooking, remember? Disasters most of them,' he said his face lighting up. 'Rasam and sambhar, I could not tell them apart, both with the same consistency. Thank God, you've improved a bit.'

'I'm learning slowly,' she said with a smile as she cleared the table.

'I've made halva today.' She brought out the dish, and the sweet aroma of saffron and cardamom rose up as she removed the lid. The heart shaped halva with her name and Ram's entwined that she had traced on the top looked delicious. Ram took one spoonful and laughed aloud.

'This halva is not sweet enough, nor does it have enough ghee to make it scrumptious.'

'I didn't want to make it too rich or cloyingly sweet…'

'Not as good as my aunt's. You really need to improve. I'll make it on Sunday. You can watch and learn.'

Sita moved on to wash the dishes. Her hand shook as she tipped the rest of the halva into the bin.

'How was your day?' she tried to change the topic.

'Okay.' He picked up the paper and folded it neatly.

She cleared up the table with him. He made sure all the dinner things were put away. She seethed inwardly. The TV came alive with the nine o'clock news. They settled down to watch it. 'The Nationalist claim it is Scotland's oil…' the newscaster droned on, Ram was engrossed. She waited for the end of the news. She spread out The Glasgow Herald at the classified page and circled a few adverts. She put the pen down and asked him.

'Ram, do you love me?'

'Of course! What kind of a question is that?'

'You hardly talk to me, or say….'

'Oh. Not that again! Saying I love you all the time is a western concept. We don't need it.'

'Ram, we need to plan our future. We never talk about things that are important to us…'

His attention was back on the TV. She went and stood in front of the TV screen.

'Sita, move, please I can't see the news. What childish behaviour!'

'No, not until you talk to me properly.' Sita's indignant tone made him more look at her.

'What do you want to talk about?'

Ram was annoyed. His usual calm voice showed an edge.

'Anything at all, about us, about our life here. Ask me if I'm happy here, anything at all,' Sita dared him.

'See, there you go again. I'm not sure what you want. Talk about what? I do discuss your work.'

'Ram, my work! That's not something personal.'

'I'm sorry. I just don't know what you mean.' He looked perplexed, strained to see the TV behind her. She moved away abruptly, thumped her feet loudly and felt childish as she saw his eyes back on the TV again. The book, 'No mean City' drew her. After a struggle when the words on the page seemed not much more than black blurbs almost calligraphic designs, it made no sense. Slowly as she calmed down, the words came into focus. The struggles of the family in the novel moved her. Sita was transported to Glasgow's Gorbals in the rough east end of the 1930's. The book shocked her in its portrayal of violence and the slum conditions of the city then. The television sound in the background faded. Her eyes followed Ram. She tensed up as she saw him get up from the sofa, stretched his arms above his head and looked around to see that the place was tidy. He folded the newspaper and put it in the bin.

'I think Mrs. Thatcher is going to win, Labour is finished.' Ram commented. She just nodded, seemed engrossed in the book.

'Are you coming to bed?' asked Ram as he switched the TV off.

'No, this book is amazing. Glasgow in the 1930's.' Sita showed him the cover.

'Oh not fiction again! All fiction books are someone else's imagination running riot. What a waste of time. Now, I can understand if you read something worthwhile like history, biographies or even our Hindu epics. Those great works make you think a bit. These are just stories.'

'Ram I know your preference, but don't mock what I really enjoy. One can learn a lot from fiction too. I just want to read up on Glasgow.' He shook his head in disbelief, left her to get ready for bed. She read late into the night.

Outside the winter night looked like a heavy navy shade lit up by the silvery stars. The moon rays tried to peep out of the chinks in the heavy velvet curtains as Sita drew them together. She got to bed glad of the warmth. Ram moved over, his hands straying between her legs. A few minutes of a wordless union, satisfied him. She wiped away her tears.

Chapter 8

The mandir was part of a tiny house on Gibson Street in the west end. The hall with the altar of gods and goddesses upstairs was already full of women in bright saris and salwar kameez, a few men and children. Ram and Sita stood at the entrance hesitantly, unsure about this mandir's rituals. A large lady in a bright yellow sari ambled over. She spoke rapidly and loudly in Punjabi. Sita shook her head.

'Sorry, neither of us knows any Punjabi,' Sita said in English.

'Hindi?' The lady looked her up and down at her as though she was an alien being.

'I am Ram and this is my wife Sita,' Ram replied in broken Hindi.

'Oh, we've the perfect pair from the Ramayana,' she said 'I'm Balvinder. Where you from?' she asked Sita in broken English.

'We're from Madras.'

'Madras? No one talks Madrassi here.' She shook her head for emphasis.

'No, not Madrassi. It's Tamil, the language that we speak.' Sita laughed inwardly at the woman's ignorance.

'No, no Tamil. You come with me,' she said. She dragged Sita and sat her down beside her in the front of the deities. Sita took in the beautiful marble statues of Radha, Krishna and other smaller deities of Ganesha and Shiva. The altar was small but had been decorated with care. Fresh flowers stood filled in vases around the deities. The older women were singing some devotional hymns, the bhajans. She wanted to prostrate –

do a namaskaram – as was the norm, but Balvinder started her inquisition straight away.

'So when you come to Glasgow? What job husband does? Doctor? Good. We need some here. South Indians all brains but no business sense, no? Where you live? Bought house? No? Look,' she continued without pause for breath. 'I came twenty years ago. Now I own three flats all paid with ten pound instalments here. You want one, we get you one. We have sewing class for women. You join?'

'No,' said Sita 'I'm also a doctor.'

'Aree, aree why you not say you are doctor? We need Indian women doctors. I'll be your patient.'

'I am working in a hospital. I don't think that's possible. I'm not a G.P, you see.'

'No matter, beti. Now put address and phone number here,' she said. She pulled out a small book from her bag. Sita thought that the flood of questions would never stop. She was embarrassed, not just because they were talking when the hymns were being sung but because she really wanted to escape from this larger than life Balvinder who was just the type she could do without, another aunty Parvati, she thought wryly. Having got her information, Balvinder moved on to her next task. 'I go to kitchen see everything is all right. You come every Sunday. I'll look after you.' She gave Sita a pat on her head as though she was an infant and moved away to the kitchen.

Sita closed her eyes and prayed. The songs ended and the priest started the sermon. He quoted the Sanskrit words from the 'Bhagavad-Gita', words that she recognised. The priest talked after about the quotation as was the practice at all temples. Sita sat quietly, not understanding all the words but feeling the rhythm of the familiar language skim over her.

After the aarti they queued up for a simple meal of chapattis, dhal, a vegetable curry and sweet rice pudding.

'I knew at once you must be from the South of India.' Sita looked at the lady resplendent in a Conjeevaram silk sari, similar to the one she was wearing.

78

'We all have the same style, silk sari, thali and the seven stone diamond earrings that's recognisable the world over don't we? She smiled and held out her hand. 'I am Lata. Are you from Madras by any chance?'

'I am! It's lovely to meet some one from Madras.' Sita said excitement evident in her voice.

'We have moved from Edinburgh. We were there for the last ten years. Prasad has managed to get a single-handed practice here.'

'A G.P then? That's why I've not seen you. I am still in training at the Western,' said Ram joining in. Speaking in Tamil was wonderful. Their life long friendship started that evening, a feeling of closeness came that perhaps only happens to expatriate families the world over.

'Don't worry about BB.' Lata giggled. 'I saw she had cornered you as soon as you came in.'

'BB? Oh you mean Balvinder?' Sita smiled.

'Yes, Balvinder Bhal, Butterball Balvinder, BB, not Brigitte Bardot.' Lata laughed again. 'That's what we all call her. Fits her perfectly don't you think? Forty, Forty, Forty, the same all over, like a ball and the butter she consumes helps her maintain it always.' She giggled more.

Lata was a thin woman. Small, meek-looking, her thin sparse hair and glasses gave her the look of a sparrow. She spoke in a whisper in good English. 'No one would probably dare to say anything to her face. BB is a frightful woman in every sense of the word. Her huge bulk, her mouth working overtime, both eating and gossiping is famous. You can't miss her in any Indian gathering. She makes it even more difficult to ignore her as she always wears the loudest and brightest saris or salwar kameeez. It hurts me to look at them in the grey Scottish light.' Lata whispered even more urgently. 'Don't miss her enormous handbag.' She shook her head and hid her mouth with a tissue, laughter lines crinkling her face.

Sita listened fascinated. She looked at BB in a new light.

'BB gets all the information about everyone but don't worry too much. We all had to go through the same. She is a leech. She knows everyone in the Indian community. She's our Glasgow Herald. She does have her uses, though. She knows all the festivities and helped set up this mandir. Rules it with an iron rod, mind. Keep out of her way if you can. She

79

comes over as very helpful but she is a gossipmonger. She keeps tabs on all of us,' Lata added.

Prasad's practice was in the Springburn area of Glasgow. Prasad was the exact opposite of Lata. A rotund man, with his shirt buttons straining, with a keen sense of humour. He told them of the Overseas Doctor's organisation and invited them to the annual general meeting that was to be held in a few months' time. As they were leaving, Sita nodded her good bye to Balvinder. BB was standing pointing out a young girl to the lady beside her. Lata translated her Punjabi gossip. She had heard her 'not so quiet' whisper.

'See, see the way she has cut her hair and dressed that young girl? Give up all things of our culture. Bad, bad, acting like gori. Parents no control their children.' BB looked disgusted.

Meeting Lata and Prasad was a great change for the better for Sita. After spending a long time with little or no social interaction, Sita felt her life improving. The change from life in Madras as a daughter at home now had transformed into one of responsibilities as a wife. The feeling of isolation was slowly ebbing away. Later on in the week they met the couple again. Sita blushed with embarrassment when Ram relayed the fact that she had paid a whole week's grocery budget for a pair of Dents gloves as she was feeling the cold. Lata laughed saying she had wasted a whole month's salary on a string of pearls that she had coveted in a jeweller's window.

'Converting Indian rupees to Sterling pounds seems so difficult for our wives when it comes to shopping, right Ram?' Prasad teased them both. He turned to them. 'You know ladies a pound sterling is not equivalent to an Indian rupee,' said Prasad, but the look he gave Lata was so tender that she could only smile back.

Two days later, at six in the evening the phone rang. It was BB.

'Hello, Sita. It's Balvinder. You okay?'

'Yes, thanks. How are you Balvinder?

'Not too well, beti. I need advice. Ache all over. I come now, you see me?'

This was a pattern that was to follow. BB became part of their lives, often arriving uninvited for free medical advice. If it was not her chronic rhinitis, it was her arthritis, her colds, coughs or any excuse at all. Sita and Ram found it hard to be rude to the older woman.

BB's bag was interesting. Sita saw that it contained everything that one needed to fight against the cold Glasgow weather, Vicks vaporub, packets of Beechams hot lemon, tiny boxes of kumkum, the red powder that she insisted all married women should have on their forehead. She even carried flyers, notes on all the bits of information on the next Indian community meetings, little books with dates of potluck suppers and wedding engagements. Balvinder collected them all. She had a voracious appetite for all that happened within their tight community. Her interest and nosiness perhaps encouraged her to overcome her health problems. She made a career of her role. BB was never bored, never got depressed, unlike some others. She was there to remind the younger ones of the dates of all the religious festivals as she always had an almanac flown in from India without fail every year. She knew the traditions to follow at the various festivals, the dress codes for them and the special sweets to be made for each occasion. The younger ones tried to avoid her like the plague, but were often ensnared. Her sharp eyes prowled around for anything untoward that she could discern.

Sita often wondered why BB chose to befriend them. There were so many Punjabis in Glasgow. The broken English conversations were not easy, so what was the reason for BB's reaching out to them?

It did not make any sense at all.

Chapter 9

The frost lay thick on the ground. The trees were covered in a white cloak that glistened in the pallid sun. The white frost dusting looked like silvery sprays on the skeletal trees, even the grass stood upright with white spikes. The road felt treacherous, the thin black ice not visible to the eye. Ram drove slowly. The two girls on the road were holding on to each other to stop sliding on the glazed pavement. Ram stopped the car.

'Want a lift, girls?'

'Oh, it's Dr. Iyer. Thanks.' They clambered into the car.

'Meet Sita, my wife. She starts as SHO at our hospital today.'

'Hi, nice to meet to you. I'm Eileen and this is Claire,' the blonde girl with the grey green eyes, said with a smile that lit up her face. The quieter one with the mousey brown hair and dark eyes, smiled shyly at Sita. Eileen chatted away. Her ponytail swayed from side to side as she laughed and talked.

'Hope you're no gonny get ol Mc Pherson, the cantankerous old goat,' she said giggling. Claire chuckled quietly beside her. Eileen's frank, endearing personality appealed to Sita. Her gossip of the wards and the staff was to be most useful. Sita became friendly with her during the daily car rides. Soon they started meeting up away from the work environment.

Shopping in Argyle Street with Eileen was fun. They tried on clothes. Eileen always went for the younger brasher styles. Sita also enjoyed buying things for her new home. Lewis's with their basement heaving with chinaware and household goods was tempting. She started her collection of Wedgwood ornaments and some Edinburgh crystal.

'Let's stop for a coffee, shall we?' Sita pleaded, bags straining on each of their arms.

'How about a wee drink instead, eh?' Eileen had a wicked smile. Sita giggled, happy at such abandon. She found her friendship with Eileen liberating, someone she could rely on, talk to about anything and not worry about the Indian community. John, Eileen's partner was a pleasant young man but had no focus in life. He seemed happy to strum his guitar, and hoped to break into the world of pop music. Their friendship strode along on easy lines. Ram and John were often happy in silences, John humming a wee tune, or both would remain quiet staring at their beer mugs. They made a habit of going out for a curry night or an evening at a pub, a foursome that seemed to work.

'So tell us about the Taj Mahal. That's the only thing we've heard about India. Don't know much else,' said John sipping his beer.

'It's fantastic. It's one of the wonders of the world. Not many Indians get to see it you know?' Sita said.

'How?' both Eileen and John looked puzzled.

'It's up in the North. India is a huge country. The distance between Madras and Delhi is almost as much as Glasgow and Turkey.'

'That's amazing,' remarked Eileen. 'We know so little, eh?' she said to John.

'So what's it really like this wonder of the world, as good as it looks in the pictures or a disappointment when you actually get there?'

Ram was happy to talk about it much to Sita's surprise. She left it to Ram to describe the wonders of the Taj. Her mind recalled their trip to Agra just after their wedding.

*

They had to visit Ram's ninety-year great grandmother who could not attend the wedding and lived in Delhi with her oldest son. She was a grand old lady, frail but feisty. Her independent streak still shone through. She was very affectionate to Sita, asking her to stay by her side, and hold her arm. She asked her to sit beside her for the morning Pooja.

Sita was overcome when she handed her a beautiful solitaire diamond as her wedding present to her.

'This was my mother's and I wore it as a nose ring for many years. Wear it as a ring if you wish. It is a blue Jaeger diamond, very special. Look after it and pass it down to your child.'

'Patti, grandma, thank you so much. It is beautiful. I'll treasure it. It's your blessings that I need.' Sita meant it. The grand old lady had words of wisdom for her that helped her calm her mind of all the worries that kept resurging in her mind. The prismatic colours of the diamond distracted Sita's eyes.

'I am sure, child, that your life with Ram will be as strong, and beautiful as the diamond.'

As she was leaving the room to put the jewel away, the grandma called her over. 'Here is a bit of advice from an old one,' she said softly, looking deep into Sita's eyes. 'I was married at the age of nine. I was a child, and I learnt the hard way. Always try to compromise. Adjusting to a man is not easy. A happy marriage is one of great mutual generosity. Having a child also brings a bond that holds the marriage together.' Sita nodded.

Ram's uncle persuaded them to extend their stay by an extra couple of days. 'You can't come to Delhi and not see the Taj.' His uncle was similar to his dad, a powerful man, jovial. He plied them with drinks after the granny was in bed. Sita had never taken alcohol in her life. This was a new experience.

The trip to Agra was the first time that she was alone with Ram. 'Thanks Ram. The hotel is great. Look at the view! We can actually see the Taj in the distance from here. It's perfect.' Sita was looking out of the French windows. The greenery was so calming after the dust of the city traffic, the bustle of the capital.

'Not guilty I'm afraid. It must have been my uncle. Booking the best room, I mean.' Ram had already unpacked his overnight case.

'Ram, come here. Just share this with me.'

'You are a right romantic. Yes it's a nice view.' He turned away. 'I'll go down to the reception and check the timing of the tours to the Taj.'

84

'Ram…' Sita wanted to linger at the window, relax with him. She heard the door shut behind him. She was still at the window when he came back up.

'Just as well I checked. The tour leaves in an hour.' Ram gave her the brochure.

He picked up the phone 'Room service? Yes I'd like some salad sandwiches and some tea please?'

Sita suppressed a giggle, so thoughtful of Ram. She freshened up, but left her case unpacked and in a mess. Ram clenched his fists, was about to straighten the clothes but there was no time and they hurried down.

The air-conditioned minibus that took them to the Taj had a few tourists from America, some Indian families and another young Indian couple. Sita noted that the young woman had a shiny new Thali, obviously newly married. More importantly, she saw that they had eyes only for each other. Furtively holding his hand, the young girl giggled and whispered something in his ear. They spent the rest of the short journey talking and drinking each other with their eyes. Sita looked at Ram, who was busy watching the traffic, not saying anything at all. She put her hand on Ram's shoulder.

'Are you always this quiet?' He gave a faint smile. The drive to the Taj was the usual crazy crawl through traffic. The cacophony of vendors, the cows on the middle of the road, the dust of the streets were visible from the cool interior of the minibus. When they did see the building, all were stunned. The group went quiet for a moment.

The beauty of the monument to love was breathtaking. Sita was enthralled. Even Ram was moved. He marvelled at the engineering feat of the marble edifice. They had their photo taken on the seat in front of the Taj. The photographer gave them a copy as they were leaving. The photo showed Sita looking a bit jaded and tired. Both wanted to see it by moonlight, and they decided to come again.

After lunch and an afternoon nap, they were ready for the spectacle of the Taj by night. Sita was speechless at the sight. The tourist guide had told them that the colours changed at different hours of the day and during different seasons. Like a jewel, the Taj sparkled in moonlight when the semi-precious stones inlaid into the white marble on the main mausoleum caught the glow of the moon. The Taj was pinkish in the morning, milky white in the evening and golden when the moon shone on it. These changes, the smooth talking guide had said, depicted the different moods of woman.

Sita was quiet on their return. Such a stunning tribute, one man's love imprinted in marble, semi precious jewels, a wonder of the world. She wanted that. She wanted to love and be loved with an ache, a pain, a feeling of utter surrender.

*

Fingers waved in front of her face made Sita snap out of her thoughts.

'Hey, where were you?' Eileen was rattling an empty glass and John was grinning, waving his hand to get her attention.

'Oh, sorry, I was miles away,' apologised Sita.

'An Irn-Bru, the other national drink or a glass of white wine again?' asked John.

'Yes, please.' Sita was still distracted.

'Make your mind up, Sita.' Eileen's face creased with a smile. 'It must be the wine,' she added.

'Same again please,' said Sita.

'I wouldn't mind seeing the Taj. Ram spoke more than his usual three words. He was quite eloquent describing it to us.' Eileen giggled sipping her glass of wine.

Sita's friendship with Eileen became closer. Sita was glad that Eileen also loved reading. They joined a book group and met weekly sharing an interest that they both enjoyed. When Eileen ranted on about John's lack of ambition, strumming his guitar and wanting it to make it in the music business, Sita listened patiently. She was hesitant about telling her that Ram too quiet, too set in his ways and about his obsessive tidiness. Sita was not sure if would be a kind of betrayal to criticise Ram, her husband. However, Eileen's cheery demeanour, her fun loving attitude to everything in life made her easy to confide in. The chance came when they had come back from shopping to witness Ram making a catalogue of her videos and tapes.

'Doc, that's good enough to be a library. I'm impressed,' said Eileen looking at the array of videos, tapes in alphabetical order. On a shelf stacked neatly. The English ones, the Tamil and other Asian music all colour coded differently.

In the kitchen, Sita said to her 'See what I mean?'

'I wish John and I were like him. Our house is a tip,' said Eileen

'No Eileen. It's not just that. He hardly talks to me.' Sita sighed

'Och aye, how many hubbies talk to wives eh? That's the constant complaint. Now take my John, he'd rather strum his guitar than have a blether with me.'

'It's.... oh, you'd never understand!' Sita looked despondent.

Sita did not raise the topic again.

Eileen complained vociferously about John.

'He has no idea about a future. Gets on my nerves, so he does. You're mad about Ram being quiet. If only you knew what I've had to put up with.'

'I thought you loved John.'

'Aye, mair's the pity, but sometimes I just want to get away from him.'

True to her word Eileen did find a way out. The solution when it did come took Sita by surprise.

*

Sita opened the Basildon Bond letter pad. The blank pale watermark on the blue page was visble. She poured herself a glass of cold lemonade, twirled the pen in her hand. The sweet smell of fresh roses from the garden came through the open window. The gardener had turned on the lawn mower outside. The whirr of the blades now made an insistent noise in the background. The sounds of summer, long days of brightness that she could enjoy. The reply that was long overdue to Jyoti. She made a start, and then looked out of the window, thinking about the words to her friend.

Dear Jyoti,

Congratulations, a mum again! Suresh must be thrilled.

I am so sorry for not replying to you. There is so much to learn here everyday. Everything is a new experience. I have moved again. This will be our permanent address. We have bought a house in Bearsden, a suburb of Glasgow. It's a nice residential area, very quiet, close to the countryside, green, and very beautiful. I do miss the west end. Shopping was so easy. I wish you had been with me at Curleys on Byres Road, where the lady on the counter said to me that they used to have butter on the counter in a big block! They would cut a quarter pound of solid butter with two wooden spatulas, weigh and pack them in brown paper. Can you imagine butter out of the fridge in Madras? There would be a puddle of ghee everywhere!

I have started to work. The hours of a junior doctor are very long. I am happy that Ram is now off that treadmill. He is studying hard for his fellowship. I hope to go into general practice. We have made some good friends. Judge Krishnaswamy's daughter Lata and her husband Prasad are here. They are very helpful; give us a lot of good advice on our jobs. They helped with our house-hunting and advised us on the areas to buy. They live nearby. I also have my neighbour Angela who I can turn to anytime. Eileen another dear friend makes me laugh as you did when we were at school together.

Scotland is a wonderful country. Only wish the weather was better. It does rain often and the cold is unbearable at times. However, the seasons when they change are wonderful. The reawakening in nature after the dull winter is breath taking. To see the shoots emerging then the little buds in spring, it's like a carpet of jewels, amethyst narcissi, purple, and diamond bright amongst the emerald green grass.

I am intrigued by your interest in Scotland and Madras. Working and managing the house I am unable to do much else. We have been to see some bits of the tourist areas. Robert Burns's cottage in Ayr brought all the poetry to life. The beach in Ayr was not as sandy as our Madras

Marina beach but the landscape here is very beautiful. Three of us doctors, one with his young son, went on a National Trust tour. Dr Singh's son wrote in his diary for school that he had spent his holidays going from one broken building to another! You must do one of these tours when you come over here. Life is hectic, work and running a home. I miss my family and close friends like you. Ram and I are fine.

Yours etc,

Sita.

She walked over to the post office to get the letter weighed and posted. Glossing over the facts was easier on paper than in person.

*

It was a quiet Saturday afternoon. Sita was doing her paperwork. Ram answered the door. Lata and Prasad walked in, laden with carrier bags.

'Hi, we've been to a new Indian shop. We thought you'd like some of the things there, so we bought you some and wanted to share it with you.' Prasad handed a bag to Sita.

'He has a lot of spices and ready-made snacks.' Lata said.

'Thanks, that's kind of you. I'm looking forward to the tasting session already,' said Ram, pleased that he might get some yummy new things to try out. He shut and locked the door carefully as they walked in.

Lata lugged three blue bags of shopping that were weighing her down and followed Sita to the kitchen. They put the bags down on the kitchen table. Lata saw her tear stained face.

'What's wrong?'

Sita's shoulders heaved.

'I know. You're still missing home.' Lata gave her a hug.

'I, I'm so lonely...' Sita whispered, 'I can't explain. How can I feel so lonely in a marriage?'

They heard the men coming through, Sita dabbed at her eyes quickly.

'Come on then, let's taste the snacks.' Ram unpacked the bags.

'Let me get the plates and make some tea,' said Sita and busied herself.

'So this is the new red sofa. Very good, solid, well made, will last for years,' said Prasad as he sank into its comfort. Ram brought the snacks on the plates and served them all.

'I see that you've got Ambala Sweets, from London,' Ram popped a Rassogolla into his mouth. 'Mm… This tastes really good.'

'This new shop has quite a variety of food from London,' said Lata.

They sat eating the snacks. Lata admired the newly done décor. The autumn colours against the pale magnolia had made such a difference to the room. She remembered the dark heavily patterned wallpaper, the old settee, the huge dark old sideboard that had filled the room. The walls were crammed with prints of stormy seas and dull landscapes.

Sita had taken a lot of pride in setting up their first home. She had deliberated a long time over the contrasting things that they had collected already. Scottish and Indian prints, ornaments, souvenirs, gifts and books all made up an eclectic mixture. The lounge with the pale walls and autumn colours was a natural place for the Scottish paintings and prints that she had bought. The dining room with its rich red and gold curtains and pale walls was perfect for Indian prints. In the dark mahogany display cabinet, she had put some of her wedding silverware and the crystal collection. They blended well. In the little spare room, she had made a small Hindu altar with the pictures of Hindu gods and goddesses. Her pooja things were kept on a small shelf.

'You really have a flair for home décor, Sita. This room is transformed. It looks so fresh.' Prasad agreed with Lata. 'Maybe you should take that up as your new career. Very few of us Indians are familiar with home decorating.' Prasad nodded.

'It's Ram who keeps the house tidy,' said Sita, looking over at Ram tenderly.

'I must get Mrs. Chalmers over to you. She is my cleaner and she's fantastic. I'll ask her if she has time to do your house too,' suggested Lata. These little acts of kindness had made life so much easier to cope with in this new world for Sita.

90

'By the way, BB keeps phoning and comes over very often. Do you know why?' Sita queried.

'She must like you. She usually prefers her Punjabi friends.' Lata giggled.

'I'm flattered but I keep thinking maybe she wants something from me.' Sita wondered out loud.

'Well, she's only a few doors away. Maybe she's just being neighbourly.'

'Yeah, I suppose.' She sipped her tea puzzling over it.

'So what's up at the SNP now?' Prasad looked over at Ram.

'Are you really interested or just teasing me as usual?' Ram frowned. Prasad had more interest in Indian politics. Ram found few people sharing his passion for the SNP. He ignored Prasad's titter and noticed a small piece of polythene wrapper sticking out of the sofa. He tugged at it. It would not budge. He got a pair of scissors and cut the little wrapper off the sofa.

'Oh, I nearly forgot, Ram, I came to ask you about the reunion of the class of 1975 at Jipmer. Did you get the letter from the Alumni association? Thought that was your year. Am I right?' Prasad asked Ram.

'It was my year. Maybe they don't have my new address yet. When is it?' Ram was interested.

'I didn't notice the date. We can't go to India just for the reunion can we?' Prasad continued, 'You must have the class photo. Maybe I could check and see if any of my old professors are still there.'

'I'll get the box.' Sita was up the stairs to the study before Ram could protest. She had watched Ram setting out all his things in the study, so she knew where his boxes of Jipmer files were.

The photograph of the class of 1975 at Jipmer nestled carefully amidst all his other personal belongings. Ram's meticulous arrangements of his things meant that they had been filed in order of date, even months at his medical school. Sita brought the box down and Ram rifled through it taking out the picture carefully, making sure that the crackly transparent paper on top of the mount was not crushed or torn if pulled out in haste as Sita was wont to do. She listened, her ears pricking up as he described his roommate Mani and his family's political background. Some of the other photographs that Lata and Sita looked at showed the beauty of Pondicheri town, the beach, the ashram and the French quarter which looked exotic.

'MMC is a dump compared to this, a drab, big, concrete block in the centre of Madras, in the most congested part of the city. This looks so special.' Sita crinkled her nose as she remembered the hot days of her student life. Those days when the lone ceiling fan, high above in the enormous lecture rooms did little to alleviate the heat that seeped through their thin cotton clothes. The wooden seats were hard, the lack of comfort that she was conscious of more now after witnessing the plush facilities at Glasgow University.

Jipmer looked so much better. It was a campus university with a heart of its own. Prasad screwed his eyes looking for old professors that he could recognise. 'God, I must be ancient if all who taught me had left by 1975. Don't see a single one that I know. So, how about a girlfriend then, Ram. Don't tell me you went through five years without eyeing anyone?' joked Prasad.

Ram shrugged, looked down at the box, 'I... I.... don't remember any.' He stammered.

'See, being shy and tongue-tied gets you nowhere.' Prasad gave him a pat on his back.

'No, still waters run deep,' teased Lata as she winked at Sita.

Ram brushed his curl away from his forehead, a gesture Sita realised he did only when he was a bit nervous.

Lata peered at the photo again 'Who is this pretty girl standing so close to you, Ram?' She looked at him directly, still challenging him. 'I'm sure we've all had a crush at least during our college days,' she said and sighed.

Ram stuttered 'No I'm not standing close to anyone, just a classmate.' He grabbed the photo from her hand quite brusquely. 'Prasad, I told you, there aren't any of your professors. I didn't recognise any of the names you quoted.' He put the photos in the box and quickly walked away with it to the study. Sita wondered if he had had any girl friends, something

92

A debut novel by a local writer

Have you read a book about Glasgow seen through the eyes of first generation Indians? **'Twice Born'** by **Leela Soma** does just that. The overarching themes of the novel are the universal aspects of love, identity and betrayal.

Available online at Amazon, Waterstone's and WHSmith.
Price £6.99
ISBN : 978-1849231510
Email: leelasoma@hotmail.com
Website: www.leelasoma.t35.com
www.leelasoma.blogspot.com

I enjoyed your story very much - and also enjoyed learning about the Scotland - India connections. Hope you're working on the next one now. I'm looking forward to reading more.

Dr. Ann McLaren (Vice President, Scottish Association of Writers) she'd never thought of asking as he was such a quiet person. Was that the reason for his detached manner she wondered? Later as soon as Lata and Prasad had left, she broached the subject again. Ram rebuffed her.

'No I told you, I did not have any girlfriend. Are you accusing me of being a liar?' His face flushed and he turned away saying he needed to take a shower.

Sita sat there for a while in silence, her nails biting into the palms of her hands.

Chapter 10

Saturday morning, there was no stress of work to worry about. They had a lie-in, a luxury that they could not have in India. The day began at the crack of dawn in Madras. The family, servants and the noise would wake them up. Here in the peace and quiet, they rested after a hard week at work. As usual Ram was keen on making a special South Indian breakfast of Idlis and Vadas. The elaborate preparations for this simple meal of rice cakes, coconut chutney and sambar took days of planning. The rice and dhal mixture had to be soaked overnight, ground to a fine paste then left to ferment for a day. Ram's care in the preparation ensured that the idlis came out perfectly soft and delicious. Sita showered, reminded Ram about the dress that she had seen and wanted to buy later that morning. He was happy to accompany her as there were no SNP tasks for him that might have made him reluctant to spend time trailing around town. The sun shone as they made their way to Argyle Street. They walked towards Fraser's to the little boutique near the big department store. She talked animatedly about the green dress that she wanted to buy for Eileen's birthday that evening. Ram's mind was perhaps on the by-elections that had taken place in the local wards she thought, as he gave monosyllabic answers to anything she said.

The two guys stood waving their football scarves, high spirited as they came close to them. Another group of supporters followed them singing loudly. As they two men neared them, the tall ginger haired guy leered and said, 'Here comes chapatti and curry'. His dark haired pal thought this was hilarious and grinned madly. Sita's mouth went dry. She froze on the spot, tried to look away, anything to help her ignore the jibe. Then she moved close to the tall guy, dug her elbows into Ram, and with a stunning smile, looked straight at the ginger haired lout and said, 'Here comes mince and tatties.' A look of sheer surprise spread across his big face, followed by a nervous laugh from his pal. 'Big Jimmy' came up closer and said, 'That was brilliant. Not bad! Learnt the patter have you, hen?' The pale blue eyes with a glint of hatred and the sour beer breath made her draw back.

The shards of the sun's rays pierced her back, it's warmth, toasting her subtropical frame, a chilling flame snaking up her spine. Sita felt hot, beads of sweat gathered on her forehead, that sick feeling, the bile rising, almost ready to retch. Her heart raced. Leaning against the concrete of a building, a mocking solidity, Sita took a deep breath. The yellow light of a rare sunny morning dappled against the windowed dummies.

She watched the pair in their football colours as they carried on laughing, enjoying their morning outing and swaggered their way onwards, their 'carryoot' safely tucked in the Saltire splashed yellow plastic bag. The chain of the rest of supporters, a rag- bag group moved on. The other shoppers either watched appreciatively or nodded their disapproval and ducked into the shops quickly. A few words had changed a lovely morning outing. Ram guided her to the shop, as the excited children skipped along, keeping up with their parent's strides, their smiles and chatter coloured the sunny morning rending the air with joy.

'Let's go and see if the dress is still there,' Ram said gently taking her arm.

Sita nodded, blinking against the sun. Clutching Ram's arm tightly, she entered the little boutique opposite Fraser's. The beautiful pale green dress she had saved up for, just what she needed for the party tonight, was still there, hanging on the rail. Pale green, pistachio, mint, was her favourite colour. Cool to look at, cool to touch, and cool to douse her burning mind. She tried the dress in the fitting room while the young shop assistant hovered around and offered help.

'It's perfect on you. Going somewhere special tonight?' the young girl chatted away, giving a chewing gum smile.

The mirrors in the fitting room were cold and unforgiving, the florescent shade stripping and showing flaws that she had not noticed before. The blue white glow cast a greying effect on her skin.

'We have some accessories,' the young girl continued, 'like this lovely bag to go with it,'

'No, thanks. I'll take just the dress.' Sita paid for the dress and they walked out of the shop.

'The Times!' cried the guy selling the paper, an early edition of the Evening Times plastered with the headlines of the SNP gaining seats in local government elections. The pressure on Callaghan's government was getting more evident. Ram bought a copy. Sita noted his interest. What little free time he had he spent helping the Party. Jim, his SNP friend as she called him, was always calling him and discussing plans for their next piece of work. Sita resented this. The Devolution Referendum was now the event that Ram was working for. He talked about it to Sita at home. Try as she might she could not get any enthusiasm for a political party that was on the periphery of mainstream politics. She was not a political animal and she was bored with his keenness for it. Sita saw the paper also mentioned the Queen's Silver Jubilee tour starting in Glasgow. The Royal Family, fashion or the arts, interested her more. They sat in their blue Vauxhall Viva and it chugged along and rattled towards their house.

The evening air blew away any lingering thoughts about the morning incident from her mind. Tonight was Eileen's birthday and she was celebrating it with a few friends at her flat. The party was a short drive away, and it was in full swing when they rang the doorbell. Sita was glad there were some familiar faces from work.

'Hi doc, you look stunning. Green suits you,' said Andy, the young hospital steward.

Sita looked over at Ram. He was busy talking to the men, huddled in a corner near the beer cans.

'Ram, want to dance?' Eileen asked leading him on to the floor. He looked shy, but had a go. Sita enjoyed the disco music and dancing. Some of the young guys tried hard to copy John Travolta in Saturday Night Fever. Disco music blared on. Both were glad that they could enjoy the disco. It was a lot of fun. There were no formal moves like ballroom dancing where they would have felt embarrassed to try a few steps. This was a new experience.

'Could David and Laura not make it?' Sita asked Eileen.

'Oh, I didn't ask the docs. Thought they might be on call,' Eileen rushed off to fill someone's glass. 'What are we?' thought Sita for a moment. But, on reflection she was flattered that Eileen treated them as one of her own close friends. Drink flowed. Sita took a glass of wine. She was quite stunned by the amount of liquor consumed by both the men and women. Ram nursed his 'Tennents' lager admiring the models on the cans with the other guys.

'Happy birthday to you,' they all sang as Eileen cut the cake shaped like a nurse's cap. The buffet had only a few cheese and salad items that Sita could eat. Her vegetarianism caused quite a stir.

'Vegetarian? What can you eat? What do you live on?' said Andy, tucking into a ham sandwich, holding his plate, piled high with sausage rolls. 'Though you do look okay doc, not peely wally,' he conceded.

Sita laughed. 'Most of the world subsists on a few grains and vegetables. We're Brahmins so we can't eat meat,' she said smiling at Andrew.

'Aye, heard something about sacred coos.' He moved off to chat up the young nurse with bottle blonde hair.

John, Eileen's partner got out the guitar and they had a few folk songs. That was fun for both Sita and Ram. The entire crowd joined in a noisy rendition of the 'Wild Rover' as the party wound up. Clutching their afghan coats and trailing off in their flared denims most of the crowd left. Sita helped clear up the debris of the party. Later on as they sat with a cup of coffee, Sita related the racist incident to her friends.

'Come oan Sita, there's nae problem here. There's a lot of it doon in England' said Eileen, sipping her coffee.

'Naw, I think there's nae racism here,' said John.

'We've had to put up with a lot,' added Clare, 'My family was Irish. The Irish were abused and even to this day the term tinkers is used in the papers. My grandparents would have some stories to tell you!'

'Aye, sectarianism is rife. Look at the football games. Never changes eh?' queried John putting away his guitar.

'Look Sita, every immigrant group has gone through this, the Jews, the Polish, the Lithuanians, and the Irish. They're all integrated now. It'll just take time.' Ram joined in.

97

'Will our integration be so easy? Our colour will always set us apart.' Sita worried.

'Just ignore it. You've got us haven't you?' Eileen winked at her.

'True, I suppose good friends do make a big difference,' Sita said nodding in agreement.

They had a long discussion on the different groups that had settled in Glasgow, late into the night. When they were back home Sita realised that the coffee had still not made her fully sober. She was mellow with wine. Her pulses rose as she made love to Ram. Cuddling Ram, she fell into a deep sleep.

*

Lata had organised the first 'potluck' supper party. The six Indian families had managed to become friendly in the last year. They had met up occasionally and often commented that it would be good if they could meet up on a regular basis, and each one bring a dish so that the host would find it less strenuous to have a dinner for a large number each time.

The rows of colourful saris were arranged neatly in the wardrobe. She caressed the folds of each silky fabric, purple, lilac, red, orange, creamy ivory, a soft pink, a pale blue, from the brightest to the palest of shades. She picked the pale lilac with a silver border. She went over to the kitchen to check on the dish for the evening. The marinating sauce in the dish glowed amber.

'Sita, I love Ram's curries. Please bring my favourite, that 'madras poriyal,' Lata had said and they had laughed at the name given to the dish that Ram had concocted.

He set about making the dish.

'Take some rest if you want, I'll see to this,' he said.

The pungent aroma of onions frying, the spices added, and the flavour of the poriyal filled the house. Sita lay on the bed. Her tiredness of late had been more frequent. She was grateful for a short shuteye. Refreshed, she showered and got ready. As she put on her silver jewellery, the joy of wearing the soft silk exulted, the softness, the sheer luxury of it on her skin reminded her of festive days in Madras. The mirror showed a pretty, Indian girl, smiling back. The dark eyes were her best feature, bordered with lashes so thick that she did not need any mascara. She put some lipstick on, then a bindi to match her sari. Her hair was up in a neat chignon. Her tall, slim figure seemed even more graceful in the draping lilac silk.

Sita smiled. It made her think how well they were adjusting in this schizophrenic world. Only last week they were absorbing the new culture, wrapping the Saltire, discarding the familiar, now they wanted to retreat to what their souls hankered after. She remembered watching a chameleon, the brown bark of the creature turning to a bright leafy green as it had darted about on the areca nut tree, back in their house in Madras.

Ram's eyes widened a bit as he watched her put her slinky silver sandals on.

'Ready? Let's get there early. I need to ask Prasad if I can give these leaflets out,' Ram had a bundle of SNP material under his arm.

'Would anyone be interested?' asked Sita.

'I'll at least highlight how exciting these times are for Scotland,' Ram enthused. 'The Nationalist are vociferous in the Parliament. There is so much to talk about the devolution referendum. I'm sure everyone would want to read up on it to vote in an informed way.' Ram was carried away as he explained the rise of the SNP in Scotland. Sita was half listening, looking forward to a nice evening with friends who had common interests. They were the first to arrive. Lata was at her organising best. She had printed out the Potluck supper rules with a copy for each family. Nothing was left to chance.

'Right, we'll meet up every month on the first Saturday,' Lata began, relishing her important role as the self-selected stalwart of the newly formed group.

Immediately she was interrupted. 'We're all doctors, we might be on call. Not everyone can make it on the first Saturday of every month,' said Ron. There was a lot of discussion, everyone finally agreeing to keep the meeting for the first Saturday and all those who could make it would meet up. It was an enjoyable evening. The young families deferred to

Lata in the end. They appreciated the fact that she had the energy and interest to get it going. Rotas on dishes, children and how to keep them occupied, Lata had thought of everything. It was a success.

It was not just the food. The families took turns and met each month in their houses. The small houses were in Bearsden, Bishopbriggs and Milngavie, the little suburban utopias that the Indian professionals had chosen to live in. Most were doctors and their families who had worked hard as had all first generation immigrants. They specialised in areas they did not want to, like the unpopular Geriatrics. Some ended up accepting General Practice even though they had set their hearts on training for cutting-edge surgery, finding that their colour came in the way of career prospects. They had so many common problems that meeting up and airing them was therapeutic. They recalled racist incidents, name-calling, being stared at or not served in shops. Prasad remembered vividly one of the patients pointing to him out and saying loudly, 'I'm no' having any coloured touching me.' Most of them brushed these aside. 'If the white man could face the intense heat, disease, etc to get his empire perhaps we could put up with this ignorant prejudice. The Brits stayed in India for two hundred odd years we are only returning the compliment,' Ron commented. Working hard, paying their taxes and doing their best in their professions was more important. These meetings were a great way of reminiscing about their lives in India, keeping up with Indian politics and creating their own little society - a kind of extended family-so they no longer lived in a vacuum.

The host community was fine to live and work in but they could never get under its skin. The hard drinking, pub going, football mad culture of the Scots was not something that they could relate to easily. They were busy building a future, putting their roots down and a familiar form of relaxation was something to look forward to.

'Eat and talk. That's what we are all good at,' said Ron, glad that the evening was going well.

'Too bloody cold to do anything else, anyway,' commented Prasad.

'We could all join political parties and work for the common good,' started Ram.

'Where is the time? Working, paying the mortgage is tough enough and there is no domestic help here you know. It's not easy,' said Prasad.

'There are a lot of labour-saving appliances. At least read these leaflets. The Nationalists are doing well,' continued Ram.

'Well, look what's happening to the Referendum. Even the Scots aren't interested,' Prasad said as he smoothed his shirt collar round his heavy neck. Lata, his wife, cast a glance at his tightening shirt.

'It's not an important party, anyway.' Vijay brushed the Scottish political topic aside.

'Now in India, Mrs. Gandhi's hold is still going strong.' Ron quipped in.

'Yeah, people even talk of her contesting the election.'

'Dynastic power of Nehru and Gandhi's never fades.'

Comments and heated debate on Indian politics went on.

'Surely politics here is what matters to us.' Ram interrupted

'Devolution is not an important issue. Look at the disarray of the Labour Party, the infighting. The Tories are getting stronger.'

'As long as they cut the taxes I'm happy,' said Ron adding a frivolous tone that appealed to all. Most nodded giving him their approval. Some slapped their thighs and murmured a, 'yes, that's right.'

Ram had to pipe down. His interest was not reciprocated. He went back to being his quiet self.

'By the way I heard that Eastern Travel in London is offering a good price for flights to India,' said Prasad. The conversation moved onto other topics. How to buy a white Mercedes Benz car and get the best deals was discussed in detail.

'Not a single person is interested in the Scottish cause. I don't understand this lack of interest in the good of the country. They only think of lining their own pockets. Selfish, never getting involved with mainstream politics at all. All they care about is how to make money and buy the latest status symbol.' Ram's frustration and anger was evident.

'Not everyone is interested in the SNP,' Sita pointed out.

'No but they're not interested in what's going on here. What's the use of Indian politics? We're living here. This is what matters.'

Sita changed the topic.

'Ram how about us? Why don't you ever want to discuss our future?'

'What do you mean? We're happy aren't we?' Ram looked concerned. He could never find the right words. His mind was still on the Nationalist gains and the apathy of his friends to British politics.

'Ram you're taking me for granted. When was the last time you even looked at me properly or paid me a compliment?'

'Compliment! But…, you know I care for you. I pay the bills. I don't drink or smoke.'

'Ram when did you buy me a bunch of flowers?'

'What? Flowers? Why? You know… my dad didn't buy any flowers for my mum but he took care of her all his life...'

'Your mum and dad! Their young life was fifty years ago! Ram get back into the real world.'

She looked at his puzzled face. He made an awkward gesture, made as if he wanted to take her hand. His frown deepened. He clutched the car steering wheel, started the car.

'Oh what's the use?' Sita sighed. He drove for a while in silence.

She felt a sudden pain, a twitch. She clutched her stomach.

'Are you okay?' Ram stopped the car. With a look of deep concern, he touched her shoulder.

'Please, let's go home.' Her face contorted in pain.

She lay down when she arrived home. Ram fussed over her, worried about her health.

Chapter 11

The odd pain and unease she had felt had a reason. For a few weeks now, she had been aware of a change. Sita sensed a stirring in her being. The morning sickness in the next few days confirmed what she had suspected all along. A feeling of elation and panic gripped her. A baby to add to her confusing life? She herself was still grappling with her relationship with Ram. What was in store for a new life? Ram's grandmother's words came back to her.

'Having a child also brings a bond that holds the marriage together. Children bring a closeness that gets rid of our own egos. They give you great pleasure and pain, but life without one can be empty.' Would a baby bring about a closer bond between her and Ram?' she wondered

The tests later that week confirmed her pregnancy. She told Ram.

'Me a dad! How wonderful! This is great. We must celebrate.' Ram's joy was obvious.

'Isn't this all too sudden? We did not plan… are you okay with it?' Sita twisted her long hair.

'Of course I'm absolutely thrilled. My son will be …' Ram could not stop smiling.

'It could be a daughter Ram.' A slow smile spread on Sita's face.

'I don't mind, as long as it's a healthy baby. Aren't you happy, Sita?' He took her in his arms cuddling her closer, stroking her cheek. She was surprised by his spontaneous show of affection.

'I'm…I'm confused too, still in a state of shock.'

'Surely it will bring us closer.' Ram gave her a big squishy hug. Sita relished this sudden affectionate gesture, something she had always longed for. 'Maybe you'll stop asking me if I love you,' Ram teased her now.

'But how did this happen?' Sita was still turning this question over in her mind.

'Sita, I need to call both our families. This is fantastic news.' Ram was thinking of the next practical task.

She watched him as he pranced around, talking animatedly to his parents. She was surprised at the change in him. He was genuinely happy at the prospect of this new responsibility. Her mind was still churning. 'Was it that one night when the condom burst? Wish I had taken the pill and not worried about all the side effects.'

The parents on both sides were thrilled at the news. Her mum almost choked back her tears and was delighted. She tried persuading her.

'Sita, you need to come straight home. I'll pamper you for all the nine months.'

'Mum I've no idea if I'll get maternity leave…'

'You're not going to work after the baby, surely? Just resign.'

'Mum, I've not thought that far ahead, I'm just getting used to the idea.'

She had to share the good news with Lata. They came around the same evening, with some homemade Theeratipal, a full cream sweet to celebrate the wonderful news.

'I suppose you'll go home for the birth,' Lata commented as she dished out the sweet.

'I've not made my mind up, yet. I've just registered for taking the MRC in Paediatrics, studying hard for it.'

'Well you'll be dealing with a baby first hand. No need to look at books, right?' Prasad smiled. Ram opened a bottle of champagne.

'None for you though,' he said wagging a finger at Sita.

Later, Sita reiterated her thoughts on work to Ram.

104

'Ram, I've hardly been at the job and now this. I love my job. I don't want to give up my career before it has even started.'

'You need to take care of yourself first. You can always get back your career later.'

'Ram, I really need to think this through.'

'Of course, I'll support you if you do want to continue with your job but the baby and your health must come first.'

For the first time she noticed that Ram was really excited, willing to plan the future with her. Maybe the baby would bring them together. A feeling of warmth enveloped her as he snuggled into her that night. There was a new bud of tenderness emerging that she hoped would flower into fullness with time.

*

The small gathering of six couples and their children watched fascinated at the baby's naming ceremony. Sita's mum had made sure that a simple but important part of the rituals was followed. The baby was placed in the crib on the top of a glass table. Below the table on the carpet, she laid a clean sheet of foil on a silver tray. Her mum had traced the name UMA in Tamil with rice grains coloured with saffron on the foil. Flowers were kept and rangoli patterns were drawn on foil in other trays around the house. The room was decorated with little wick lamps beside a small altar of the family god. Her mum and dad read the mantras in Sanskrit, lifted the baby into Sita's arms, Ram stood beside her. The baby's name was whispered softly in her ear and then a tiny drop of sugar syrup placed on her tongue. Uma sucked the sweet taste and smiled happily. Sita, Ram and all the friends were given a sweet and the ceremony was over. The buffet lunch started and the people milled around the new baby and gave their blessings. Ram's heart swelled with pride. He loved all the fuss over his new baby. He chatted to the guests. Uma's birth gave Ram a new confidence. Ram proudly showed off the baby to everyone. His cheerful disposition was a complete change to the quiet Ram.

'The naming ceremony went off very well. You've such good friends here,' said her Dad.

'Mum, Dad I'm so glad you could come over to see the baby even if it is for such a short stay.'

'Sita, you know your Dad's work schedule. I'm so glad he agreed to take two weeks off.'

'Mum, I don't know how I'll cope with the baby on my own.'

'You'll cope fine. Everything is so easy in this country. You have the health visitor, both of you are doctors, and that friend of yours, Lata, is a real godsend. She is so supportive. You're lucky she lives so close.' Her mum seemed convinced of Sita's competence in looking after her newborn. It must be my tiredness after the baby that makes me feel so weak, thought Sita. She made her mind up to cope better and shake off the feeling of depression that clouded her outlook.

The parents' stay with them was over soon. As they were packing, Sita wondered how she would cope with the new baby. She often felt that she was suffering from postnatal depression. Her mum's reassuring words and competent handling of the baby took a lot of pressure off her. She had put on a brave facade, though her dad's positive attitude cheered her enormously.

'How kind nature is to this country. I love the greenery. Maybe in winter it's a bit cold and dark but I'm sure you have good summers,' her dad commented. He loved his first trip to Britain. Dad's short stay in the comfortably heated house, the general wealth of all the people made him happy. He chatted away about 'Made in England' being trademark for the best quality goods. His dealings with the British Raj gave him a different perspective to what Sita and Ram had experienced in Glasgow. An Englishman's word is as good as a promise. Fairness, justice these were the hallmarks of Britain in his mind.

'Mum, are you sure you can't stay longer. I really need you.'

'I wish I could Sita, I have to look after Gita. She has had a lot of problems with her pregnancy.'

'Mum, she has her in-laws and servants. I really am so scared of looking after the baby. I don't know if I can cope.'

'Of course you will! Your dad's blood pressure is not going down. I need to take care of him too. I must say I admire you. How well you've

106

managed to work and care for the house without any servants at all. Ram is great. The way he cooks and looks after you. Not many Indian men would do that.'

'Mum, it's not the same as looking after a baby.'

'Your Dad can't make a cup of coffee for himself. Why don't you come over once the baby is a bit older? You need to show her to Ram's family anyway. How about celebrating her first birthday in India?'

Sita understood that her mum wanted to get back home. Gita was her mum's favourite. Gita, being in Madras had become even closer to her mum.

'I would love to do that mum. I'll see how I manage the first few months with her.'

The parents had enjoyed their brief stay. They left Glasgow feeling happy that Sita was now 'well settled' with a kind husband and a lovely baby. Sita realised now that she was responsible for Uma. The huge responsibility weighed on her mind.

In their bedroom, Sita quizzed Ram.

'Politics seem more important to you than your own daughter's birth.'

'Well, Mrs.Thatcher, first woman Prime Minister is historic,' he accepted grudgingly.

'Oh, Ram, forget Maggie, think of Uma now,' Sita said.

Ram bent over the crib, touched the baby's cheek ever so gently and said,

'My little Scot Nat. Uma you'll need to fight for Independence.' Uma lying in her cot smiled sleepily. He hummed a lullaby, relishing his fatherhood.

*

The pub was busy. Jim was at his usual spot. Ram walked in with a packet of cigars, smiling happily.

'Heard the good news, dad eh. Well done, Ram.' Jim gave him a friendly tap on his shoulder.

'Help yourself to a cigar. I believe this is the custom here.'

'Absolutely right. Not sure why though. And a dram wouldn't go amiss.' Jim added.

'Of course. Same again for everyone.' Ram said to the barman.

'So how is the little one?'

'Oh both mum and baby are doing fine.'

'Must be hard, studying for your fellowship and sleepless nights.'

'I'll manage I'm sure.' Ram looked happy; nothing could spoil the special feeling. Not even Mrs.Thatcher winning the General Election. Jim and he discussed the implications for the SNP. Ram's Indian friends taunted him for espousing a lost cause. The S.N.P had decline, from eleven M.P's in 1974 to two. 'Why keep backing a dead horse, Ram?' Prasad teased him. Ram put on a brave front, his interest in the party never wavered.

At potluck meetings the debate ranged more on politics. The Iron Lady's agenda was radical departure from the centre ground of politics. All were fascinated by the new challenge. However, the politics that had shaped their youth engendered more lively discussions. Passions rose as articles from 'India Today' were argued upon. The State of Emergency declared by Mrs. Gandhi, her being thrown out of office, created more heated discussion. After Gandhi's return to power in the winter of 1979, the men joked at the women taking over.

'Ruled by two women who are more like men,' they said and laughed into their beers, some worried at the pace of change in women's position in the world.

*

'Yap, yap,' the ceaseless sound of Trixie the neighbour's dog came bounding in through the windows. Sita's sleep ravaged eyes shut tighter as if the sound would be reduced if she did not awaken. It did not work. She got up and opened the curtains as quietly as she could. The baby

108

moved in her cot. She looked at her, her breath getting faster, a huge suffocating sense almost choking her. She sat on the bed 'I can't cope. I'm not capable of looking after such a tender little thing.' Sita started crying herself. The pink nursery border on the wall spun around. She felt dizzy. Baby Uma whimpered. She jumped up from the bed, stared at the cot, stood still, 'I can't do it.' The baby started to cry. She froze, unable to scoop her up in her arms.

'Yap, Yap' Trixie's barking mingled with the baby's loud cry. Sita ran down the stairs opened the back door, got a lung full of air. 'Shut up you stupid dog!' she screamed. Her neighbours were both out at work. She felt so silly having stooped so low, screaming at a dog! The baby's cry grew louder. She ran back up the stairs and picked her up. She held her tightly, 'Sorry, sorry darling. Mummy will never do this again. I won't leave you ever.'

She had never expected this feeling of tiredness, not wanting to feed or look after the baby. Sita's bouts of crying, her unkempt look made Ram concerned. He came sometimes from work to find Sita in front of the TV, the neon light blurring her brain, the candescent light casting a shade around the room, her passive reclining form lying in a kind of stupor. He was worried enough to call Lata.

Lata, literally moved in to help her cope. She came every morning and left after Ram came home from work. 'Sita, you need to get help. You know you can't go on like this.' Lata picked up the baby, rocked her gently.

'Happiness is ephemeral, not a feeling that remains every day or all the time.' Lata talked as she fed the baby. Sita sat by looking listless, fidgeting with her hair.

'I know, I'm not stupid,' she retorted. Lata noted the unwarranted aggression. The helpless look of one not quite understanding showed clearly on Sita's pinched face.

'Being happy all the time is a fantasy, not reality.' Lata persisted.

'I know. You don't have to tell me. It's not my happiness at all Lata. I can't explain. It's more a feeling that I can't cope. My baby, I adore her and yet sometimes I could leave her to cry herself to sleep.'

'Sita, no one is perfect. You've gone through a lot. Not every woman comes out of childbirth able to cope with everything. Your mum being here maybe helped in the first weeks, but now that you've to manage...'

'That's what I mean, I'm hopeless...'

'No you're not hopeless at all. You're doing really well. I'm here to help you. Just lean on me. Don't hesitate at all. Think of me as your sister.' Lata was a tower of strength.

'No don't say that. You don't know Gita,' a smile spread faintly on Sita's mouth.

'There that's better.' Lata held little Uma, burped her and whispered baby talk to her widening eyes. The baby gave a toothless grin. She was enchanted. Sita looked on.

Months of Lata's unquestioning help and medication helped Sita able to get back to normal but her recovery was slow. When the clouds of her depression lifted, she looked at Uma as the best thing that happened to her. Her smile, Uma recognising Sita's voice and turning her head to find her, even the dribble of her milk on her tee-shirt made for a new feeling of being wanted and needed so thrilling. She played with Uma, talked to her and sang her lullabies in Tamil that she thought she had long forgotten. Now she could recollect them once she found the tune in her head.

Ram encouraging her to get back to part-time work helped towards her recovery. That was another goal. She had to get better to get back to work. The strength that she gained was more than the physical aspect alone. Becoming a mother was life-changing. Sita discovered more about herself bringing up the baby. The role of a working mother was challenging and new. Getting back to work, she realised that her career was something that she could not give up. Finding the balance between juggling the job and looking after Uma was deeply satisfying.

Gita's phone calls never changed. She moaned about her life as a mother. How restrictive it had become. Sita could detect a tinge of envy in her voice.

'How do you manage all that? Work, run a home and look after Uma! Sounds exhausting.'

'Gita, everyone does that here and Ram is fantastic, helps a lot.'

'Must be women of steel. I'm tired just shouting at their ayah. The twins really are so demanding. Ashok, you know is hopeless. He can't even bear to hear them cry.'

Gita complained about her tough life, not being able to get to her 'rummy parties' and the nights that she missed at the Lions Club and at the Gymkhana. Sita groaned inwardly. It made her think about the enormous changes that she had achieved living in Glasgow. Her economic independence, a freedom of the spirit from being beholden to no one but herself made her resolute.

*

The beautiful June sunshine streamed into the conservatory and lit up the potted plants. Uma was crawling around; Sita watched her intently making sure she did not hit herself or tumble down. Uma gripped the wicker chair and hauled herself up, but soon plopped back to the floor.

'Look, Uma is standing up. She'll be running around soon.' Sita looked at her proudly. Uma babbled and ran to Lata.

'Uma thinks you're her mum. I must thank you for all you've done. I don't know how I could have come out of the crisis without you.'

Sita turned around to see Lata, quietly sobbing. She tried to hide the tears from Sita.

'Whatever is wrong?'

'It's nothing I…' Lata mumbled. Sita put an arm around her shoulder.

'Surely you can tell me if something is wrong.'

The long held secret tumbled out. It was those words 'she thinks you're her mum,' Lata explained. Sita listened to Lata's story, shocked at her pain.

*

Lata looked across the wide-bodied jumbo jet. Their eyes met for a spilt second. She noted a flicker of recognition in the man's eyes. She looked away. Her eyes filled with tears, five thousand miles away from a home, a virtual exile. There was no other option. Her family had done the best for her. Last June 10, a year felt like an eon away. It was a date that would always be etched in her heart. The whole event was still like a dream, more a nightmare now. The tiny baby boy snatched away before she could nurse him once, a quick hug and kiss. That was all she was permitted.

A year in Delhi. Her parents had the whole thing planned perfectly. Even her closest friend was told that she was in Delhi doing extra work in the Sanskrit department of the University before her trip to take up her postgraduate degree at Edinburgh University.

It was the way he had recoiled when Lata told him that she was pregnant. She did not see him again. Being a different caste was not something insurmountable but his family obviously did not see it that way. What a coward! He had shied away from the most important thing in their life. How had she fallen in love with such a person?

This journey was strange. Lata, from Madras was coming over to study at Edinburgh University! Her whole being now was pining for the baby that she had to give up. Maybe her love of Sanskrit would help her get through this awful period.

'You need to go to Terminal One, madam, to take the flight to Edinburgh. There are free transfer coaches down below. Follow the yellow signs.' The ground staffs were helpful. She pushed the trolley towards the bay.

'Here let me help you,' he said. It was the man on the plane. He said, 'It's nice to see a familiar face. Were you not on the International flight from Delhi?'

She nodded a yes.

'I'm Prasad, going for my fellowship exams in Edinburgh. I'm glad to see an Indian face. Hope you don't mind me talking.'

She was glad of his company. Everything was alien, the food smells, the smooth coach even the English language that she was so familiar with sounded so strange. They sat beside each other on the plane journey to Edinburgh. He was so easy to talk to. She felt comfortable and relaxed.

112

Prasad and she met often in the café at the university, or at Kalpana, the Indian vegetarian restaurant on St.Patrick Square that became a favourite haunt. Being in a strange land brought them both close together. They had a quiet wedding, both families in India relieved that they had each other. Lata's secret remained with her. She did not have any more children. Every June 10 she said her own prayers and wept for the child she would never see again.

They moved to Glasgow and Prasad saw a new Lata emerging. Her childlessness made her bitter for some time. She lost her interest in her career. The vulnerable young woman, cried for the child she could not nurture and for her new barren life. He stayed in the background wanting a peaceful life. Their friendship and love entwined into a partnership of mutual need. As one of the oldest in the small Indian circle of friends, she quickly established herself in a commanding role. She helped all the newcomers whatever their needs. She gave up her research work leading up to M.Litt. She had lost her appetite for the hard work and rigour of carrying on with the research work. It had brought her here under such tragic circumstances. However, she never lost the love for Sanskrit and she kept her interest by collecting rare books and reading the books at her own pace. Getting her collection of rare books became a hobby that helped her cope with her loss. Her seniority gave her a new status that she revelled in. Seeing young women with their little children made her almost a surrogate older aunt, ready to help if they needed her. She had found her role in life. Yet she never became close to any one. She remained aloof but helpful. In Sita, she saw herself when she had arrived alone in this cold, damp country. Being from Madras and having so many cultural similarities helped to forge a strong friendship between them.

Lata looked drained. The secret that she had nurtured in her heart all these years had finally come out. A deep sense of relief followed a sensation of mild anxiety.

It was now Sita's turn to comfort Lata. The enormity of what she had related made her admire her even more. Lata must have gone through her own hell when she had helped Sita with the baby. The two women had come through much heartache together, their friendship now bonded in a web of painful experiences. June 10 took on a new meaning for Sita too.

113

Sita was in her debt. It was Lata who had helped her with her child's birth and the trauma of her post natal depression. Though there were other friends, she could never feel as close to them. The small tight knit potluck group of the six families were formed more out of a common need of the familiar than true friendship. Rivalries abounded. Aunty Lata became an extended family for Uma. Very few people were close to Lata. Sita was one of them.

*

'Ram I need to talk to you.' Sita said softly.

Uma was gurgling sleepily on his shoulder. Ram was carrying her around humming a lullaby.

He turned around so Sita could see the toddler.

'Is she asleep already? I'll put her to bed?' Ram carried her gently up the stairs. He came down whistling the lullaby still.

'Ram I know you're happy with Uma, so am I, she's perfect, but I don't want any more kids.'

'Why not? What about a little brother or sister for her? It's not fair, an only child...'

'Ram I am happy with just her.'

'What do you mean? What's wrong now? We're a family aren't we?' He walked away. She ran after him, forcing him to listen to her.

'All you care about is the bloody SNP. My life is ruined because of that.'

Ram's surprised voice interjected, 'It's only a few evenings of my time.'

'Stop going to the meetings. Uma and I need you.'

'What do you mean?'

'Paying the bills is not enough.' Sita's eyes narrowed.

'What?' Ram shook his head in disbelief.

'Spend more time with us. It's us the family or the SNP. You choose.'

'Don't be ridiculous Sita. You need to control your temper.'

'That's always your answer to everything, blaming me.'

Ram clammed up again, Sita's voice rose to another level ending as usual in tears. Ram moved to the kitchen. He checked on all the jars of spices, making a list of those that needed to be replaced.

The noise of the rattling bottles and the opening and shutting of the kitchen cabinets grated. Sita put her hands on her ears.

'Ram,' she screamed, again. He switched on the radio in the kitchen and turned up the volume. She slumped in the sofa pummelling the cushion.

Ram's face had recoiled as she had lashed out.

*

She recalled an old incident with the ayah now.

'Impatient, short tempered Sita Amma?' the cook whispered to the ayah. Her voice wafted over the chink in the window. Sita listened, her back stiffened, her body braced upright. She had never thought of herself in such terms. Her ears pricked on as she heard ayah respond, 'I would even say selfish. Being younger, she's thoroughly spoilt. Gita'ma is worse of course, the way she treats her maids.'

'She'll find it difficult to adjust anywhere else' said cook.

'Wonder how she'll settle down with a mother-in-law. Life is not sweet after marriage is it?' said ayah and giggled.

Sita was furious. She strode down to the veranda and shouted, 'Ayah,'

'Yes amma,' ayah came running over, guilt spread thick on her face. 'You called ma.'

'Why didn't you fold all the saris? My room is such a mess.' Sita was shaking.

'… But its done ma.'

115

Sita glared at her.

'… When you were on the terrace,' ayah tried to slide away quietly.

'Go on, you can clean the ceiling fan in my room. It's full of dust.' Sita stamped on a dried flower lying under her feet emphatically, gave ayah a look that sent her scuttling away.

*

She heard the kitchen door open. Ram came back and sat beside her. She held the cushion closer to her.

'Calmer now? Tell me what's bothering you.'

'You'll never understand.'

'Tell me what it is that you want.'

'I just wish we were closer to each other.'

'I just don't know what you want.' He moved away, took up the new Indian cookery book. 'Indian Recipes Made Simple.'

Sita took the dry clothes from the washing basket.

She crumpled the clothes that were in her hand. She twisted the end of her long hair then she brushed it back. Ram was busy studying the book. Sita went back to taking the creases out of the crumpled clothes then folding them.

116

Chapter 12

Sita felt guilty. She had neglected her friend Eileen since she had had the baby. Apart from phone calls or Eileen coming to see Uma they had hardly spent any time together. The book club, that they both belonged to, was still going strong. It was one of the few outings that Sita had managed to keep up with.

Eileen had sounded so excited on the phone. Now she was playing it cool. Waiting for Sita to get the coffee made, get Uma settled before the news was wrenched out of her.

The steam spiralled up from mugs of coffee. Sita put the tray down on the glass table, watching little Uma playing happily in her playpen.

'So Eileen what's this big news then?'

Eileen bit into her chocolate biscuit, took a sip of coffee biding for time.

'Come on. I can't wait. You sounded so excited.'

'I'm getting married.' Eileen's lips quivered, a deep red patch appeared just above the low neckline of her white blouse. She put the coffee mug down.

Sita ran over and gave her a hug.

'Congrats! John must be thrilled you've said yes at last.' Eileen shrugged off her hug. She held her arms tight against her chest. The words tumbled out slowly.

'No, it's no John.'

'What…, not John? You've been with him for ages.'

'I know but…'

'Who is it then? When did you break up with John? Why, I thought you were really in love and planning to get married.' Sita was stunned, the words rushing forth.

'Sita I'm marrying Faraz.'

'What! Dr. Ali, but he has just started work at …'

'I know…' Eileen fidgeted with the chain round her neck.

'What about John?' Sita gave Uma her toy, to stop her whimpering.

'It's nae use. My future is better with Faraz.'

'Why, I thought you loved John?'

'No, I've told you before…'

'Yes, that you and John were mates, 'nippin' him' since school you said'.

'Aye, but I also told you that I'll do anything to get out of Maryhill.'

'Eileen, you're not serious!'

'That's why I worked so hard to be a nurse. I want a better life. John will never get anywhere. He just plays in this no-hope band.'

'But you love him, you hardly know Faraz.'

'You'll no understand Sita, I need to do this. I don't want to end up like the rest of my family.'

'Eileen, how long have you known Faraz?'

'Long enough. He liked me enough to propose on our first date and I accepted.'

'Oh my God, but why Eileen?'

'Sita, I need to think of my future. I know Faraz is a wee bit strict about all the drinkin and things. I need to convert to Islam before the wedding.'

'Eileen! Think before you…'

'Cos, that's what I want, a good life.'

'Do you love him?'

'Och away. I'm being practical. I'm fed up of scrimpin and savin all the time.'

Sita was quiet for a moment. She lifted Uma, wiped her face and put her back in the playpen. She hesitated, then said,

'Do you know that Faraz is married?'

'He was. He's divorced noo. he disnae love her.'

'Eileen, you've been a good friend to me. Are you absolutely sure about this?'

'Aye, course I'm sure. Look it's nothing fancy. Just at the registry office. I am inviting Ram and you. We've not printed any invitations or nothing'. Just come on Friday night to the Shish Mahal for a meal.' She hesitated.

'Eileen, is there anything I can do?' Sita asked.

'I wondered if I can have a look at Indian dresses.' Eileen switched her accent when she was excited, Sita noted.

'Of course Eileen. Would you like to borrow one?'

'Mibbe, for a photograph, eh?' Are they dear to buy?'

'Depends. An elaborate one with a lot of embroidery or zari work will be costly and if the material is silk.'

'Aye, but I widnae use them later. Don't want to spend too much on it.'

'Come up. Let's raid my wardrobe and see if we can get you something nice.'

Sita picked up Uma and they went upstairs.

119

'I didnae realise you had such a collection, a wardrobe just for your saris?' Eileen exclaimed.

'This is the reality of my life. Everything is a bit of India and a bit of Scotland,' said Sita laughing. 'Red is the colour for weddings. I'm sure I have a sari, though Faraz may like a Salwar Kameez suit. I could ask Lata my friend. She has a collection being from Delhi. Most Punjabis also wear suits. I could ask at the Mandir.'

'Don't go to any bother for me,' Eileen's ponytail swung, as she turned her head to watch Uma on the bouncy chair. They chose a red sari. Sita found a petticoat, a blouse and some jewellery, and bindis to match and put them in a plastic bag.

'We need another cup of tea after all that hard work.' Sita fed Uma as the kettle boiled. Eileen looked for the tea bags.

'I know,' said Sita, 'my kitchen cupboards are another United Nations.' The spices left Eileen speechless. Cumin seeds, mustard seeds, bay leaves, curry leaves, garam masala, South Indian spices for Rasam and Sambar, tamarind paste, the shelves groaned under the weight of all them all. The other shelves had an array of supermarket tins and bottles; some tried once and never opened again.

'I didnae know there was so much to Indian cooking. Hope Faraz disnae expect all this.' Eileen looked worried.

'I'm sure you'll manage well,' Sita reassured Eileen.

'Just help me tie the sari for the photograph on my wedding day, I couldnae wear it all day. Probably trip and fall flat on my face,' Eileen joked.

They heard Ram's car in the driveway. Ram clattered in, a pile of SNP posters and leaflets hiding his face.

'Hi Eileen, how are you? This is a nice surprise.' He dumped the pile on the red sofa, lifted Uma and gave her a big kiss.

'Hi doc, I'm fine, I need to rush off, too much to do. Sita will explain.' She walked out of the door, feeling Sita's dismayed look.

Ram rearranged the pile of posters neatly and picked them up to take them to his study.

'Did you know that Faraz is divorced?'

'Faraz? Oh I've lost touch, you know since we left Law hospital…'

'She's marrying him.'

'Who?'

'Eileen.'

'What? I thought he was married to that young girl…'

She explained. Ram was surprised.

'I never thought that they'd be divorced so soon. She seemed awful young.' Sita wondered about Tasneem and her future. The young girl had looked so vulnerable when she had met her. Why do we follow our head and not our hearts? Sita wondered.

It was the first wedding in Glasgow that they were attending, the smallest that they had ever attended. None of Eileen's family were present. They could not get over her giving up the faith and marrying a 'Paki', as they regarded him. The hotel meal was for twenty couples. The evening was tinged with sadness, Eileen was emotional. She wore an ivory dress. Her blonde hair was piled high, a small corsage providing a sprig of colour.

'Why is she not wearing a white dress? Isn't it traditional? Sita asked Claire.

'Don't you know? She's up the duff.' Claire whispered.

Sita held her on to her wine glass, her knuckles wound tight round it. The print on the wall showed a Spanish matador triumphant over a bloodied bull. She looked away. The strip light above it highlighted all the bright colours.

The music started, and the mood changed as the tiny dance floor filled up. She took a sip of her wine, looked over at Ram. Their wedding had been so different.

The loud sound of a spoon on a plate broke her thoughts, the metallic thump ringing in her ear.

'A toast to the happy couple,' announced Andy. They all raised their glasses and wished Eileen and Faraz the very best in their new life together. Before they left the party, the photos were taken. Sita helped her put on the red sari. The photograph was taken just as Eileen had wanted. They looked happy. Eileen told her about the car that Faraz had given her as a wedding present. She was making plans for a new house, the nursery for the baby. Such giddying speed of their commitment to each other, said the others. Sita remained quiet. For all she knew this relationship would work out much better than one just based on love, she told herself.

Faraz and Eileen celebrated the arrival of Sofina, their baby by inviting Sita and Ram for a champagne meal. Sita gazed at the elaborate nursery that the baby had, everything coordinated, decorated by a design company.

'So life is perfect then?' she asked Eileen.

'I am so happy, Sita I can't ask for more. I'm already planning my next baby. Faraz wants a son.' The pink on her jumper reflected in her cheeks, Eileen looked a picture of contentment. She had started collecting books and tapes on Islamic culture. She was doing her best to learn and adapt. Sita admired the change in her friend, hoping that she would remain vivacious and not lose the crazy sense of humour.

Chapter 13

Glasgow 1980s

It was Diwali, the Hindu festival of lights. The North Indians believed it was the return of Lord Rama after his fourteen years of exile in the forest. The South Indians celebrated the victory of Lord Krishna over the demon Narakasura, the victory of good over evil. A deeper meaning appealed to Sita, that it was a celebration of the spiritual light within each soul. In Glasgow, it was perfect to celebrate a festival of lights in the days of dark winter, November nights being dark and cold. It was great to light up the house and have a joyous party.

Having Uma and inviting all their family friends with their children made a big difference. Even though Uma was young, the joy of getting her in a silk dress, preparing the sweets with a group of Indian ladies made it more meaningful. The temple had a series of activities. The children from the potluck exchanged presents. She felt a sense of community, a feeling of belonging.

Sita thought of her first Diwali in Glasgow. The 'thalai' Diwali, the first Diwali, was a special one for the newly weds. She had missed her family so much. The parcel had arrived just as her mum had promised her. The guy at the Post Office said a cheery, 'What's in it, home cooking from your mammy, eh?' 'I hope so,' Sita answered, not knowing if the Customs people would be strict about cooked food allowed into the country.

She remembered opening the parcel, the beautiful silk sari, and the diamond ring for Ram, and all the instructions for the first Diwali written out and posted with the parcel. Her mum's neat writing stared back from the page, as she tried to make sense of it through her tear soaked eyes. Ram and she followed all that her mother had written for their First Diwali. Somehow not having any family or friends at that time, it did not feel special at all.

Sita compared hers to Gita's 'thalai' Diwali in Chennai three years ago. The newly-weds, Gita and Ashok were the centre of attention. Ashok dressed in a new suit, and wearing the diamond ring that Sita's parents had given him as a Diwali gift. Gita was draped in a heavy silk sari with new jewellery adorning her neck and hands. The older members blessed them with prayers for a wonderful future. The families enjoyed a feast with various sweets made especially for the first Diwali. It was celebrated grandly, so that the young couple would remember it all their lives.

Every house would be lit up in India, for the Diwali celebrations, she thought. In her own house, Sita recalled that the clay lamps painted in myriad colours would be lit up and shed a soft glow with the flickering wicks. The oil would be replaced intermittently by a maid or one of the children. Their light would form strange patterns all over the steps on the veranda. The colour bulbs vulgar and bright, would add a brash cheer to the patterns formed on the doors and windows. The preparations for the festivities would last a whole week. Special sweets were made; savouries, spicy and delicious to snack on were made early and packed in airtight boxes. The trips to the shops were numerous, the silks chosen, the tailors harangued to make the latest fashions in blouses. A nostalgic scene of the activities of the celebration played on her mind now.

Everyone woke up before dawn. Sleepy and excited all had to go to the pooja room, prostrate in front of the deities, and look at their own face in the mirror and pray for a peaceful, prosperous life. Then her mum usually put some oil in their hair and they would rush to have a shower and wearing their new silks. The breakfast was something to look forward to as the sweets and special dishes were served. The fun with the fireworks would start straight after breakfast. The boys would not wait for the rituals and were often scolded for letting the fireworks off early. The rest of the day would be spent visiting friends and relatives. The kids would talk of all the fireworks and how brave they were setting them off. The parents would gossip about the price of all the things going up in the shops. The women would admire the silks and discuss the latest fashion.

Sita shook herself out of her thoughts. It was exciting in Glasgow now.

Diwali always came close to Guy Fawkes Day so plenty of fireworks were available in Glasgow. Ram loved to set the fireworks off. Sita and Uma watched the cascading light of the sparklers. The smile on Uma's face filled Sita with such joy. Christmas followed soon and the winter months no longer felt dreary and bleak.

*

Ram's despair was heightened by his lack of success in becoming an Orthopaedic surgeon. The series of interview left him in a despondent mood. Even little Uma's smile and the funny incidents at school that she related every day could not lift him out of his misery. He settled into General Practice, giving up on his ambition to be a surgeon.

He knew Sita was very different from him, vivacious, full of life wanting everything, deeply emotional. He did not fit the bill but he could not act differently. It was not in him. Her expectations of a romantic partner, talking of their dreams, buying flowers or perfume on impulse, doing things together was just not in his repertoire. He respected and loved her in a quiet way. He knew she was unhappy with their relationship. She stopped relying only on him, and concentrated on her work and built up her own social circle looking for fulfilment from others.

His work and his politics consumed him. Glasgow or Madras, it was immaterial to him. His life was clearly structured, a series of obligations and duties to be carried forward without any questioning or emotion. His order of priorities was always on the practical side. Looking after the family home, paying bills came first, a duty and an obligation that was important. The job was the core of his life. He had not reached his ambition. That frustrated him for a while, but the compromise of becoming a GP did not irk him. He was able to provide well for his family and that satisfied him. Sita and now Uma brought out a deep primal sense of needing to protect them, an emotion that he had never felt before. He wondered if his parents ever felt the same. They had never been demonstrative. He had spent most of his life farmed out to relatives. Ram had little experience of a close family life. He hoped his and Sita's lives would go on an even keel. He preferred a quiet peaceful life. Good food, a beer or a glass of wine, friends, dining out, the simple pleasures of life and he felt complete.

It was Jim on the phone.

'I need a wee help from you, Ram.'

125

'Yes, what can I do for you?'

'I need to find a home for a wee kitten. My mum's cat's had kittens. She has managed to give them away, just one left. Would little Uma like one?'

'Great idea, I'll keep it secret. When can I collect it?'

'How about the weekend? Saturday okay?' Jim was relieved, to have found a home for the kitten.

Perfect, thought Ram. Uma would have some company. He decided to surprise her on Saturday. Mr.T, the scrawny kitten became part of the family.

Chapter 14

BB was still large in their lives.

'You take me to the Garden Festival, no? Lots of seeds and vegetables to buy there, no?'

'Garden Festival is over Balvinder. It was only for a short time.'

'Why, why, it was so good.'

BB's interest was infectious. Sita saw another side to her. BB loved gardening, not flower beds, tubs or even the lawn. Her interest was solely on growing vegetables. She had green fingers. Everything she touched in her little garden came up roses, well cabbage and greens actually.

'Family back in Punjab live in village, cows in house,' she said proudly. 'I milk them when I was little, arre, arre what difficult life but I miss it now.'

'Did you work in the fields? What did you grow?'

'Everything we need for house, onions, greens, garlic. No supermarket there you know. Now everything here comes in plastic, no taste.'

BB often walked down the road to Sita's clutching little plastic carrier bags of her home grown veggies. Sita loved the fresh, earthy smell and flavour of them. Ram enjoyed washing and preparing the vegetables. He had an eye for the fresh herbs like mint, coriander, green chillies that BB managed to grow in her garden in spring and summer. The greenhouse kept her busy during the cooler months. She gave up her hobby only in the depths of winter from the time of Diwali in November to February or early spring. The winter months she went full swing preparing delicious north Indian sweets, rich in milk, cream, ghee. Ram's interest in learning them from her brought the two families closer.

BB was having a special havan for her daughter's graduation. BB bustled about her kitchen. Sita and Lata had both offered to help her with some of the dishes to be prepared the night before for the big meal at the temple next day. Prasad and Ram accompanied them and helped pack the heavy pots, bags of rice and parcels of sweets for the big event. All of Glasgow's Indian community would be there. BB was pleased. Her thirty years of living in Glasgow, getting the temple off the ground had given her a wide circle of friends. She felt important. Some would come because they could not refuse her invitation. They knew very well that she would take umbrage later at them for not attending such an important event in her life.

Bollywood music was playing loudly on the hi-fi in the kitchen. Lata and BB were mouthing the words over Lata Mangeshakar's voice as they cooked. Sita washed up after them.

Suddenly the lights went off.

'Arre, aree, not good light going off,' BB's voice showed that she was upset.

'I'll check the fuse,' Ram offered. They crowded around the candlelit table.

'Bad omen. This should not happen on an auspicious day,' said Lata very quietly hoping BB would not hear.

'Why?' asked Sita.

'At any auspicious event lights should not go out. Even in the days when they had wicker lamp if it goes out, it is a sign from God that something is not right.' Lata patiently explained to Sita.

'Bollocks' said Prasad, his round face creased with scepticism. 'Just means that safety checks have not been made, always a human error. People need to getaway from all this mumbo-jumbo.' He was already worried that the Sunday lunch that he relished, would be cancelled. BB might decide against the meal. He paced up and down reassuring BB that it had happened the day before the event; she was not to worry about a bad omen. He loved the lunch at the temple, where Lata could not restrict his food intake in front of others. Lata kept a strict tab on his intake at home to help reduce his sugar intake and keep his diabetes from getting worse. He had no will power whatsoever. Sweets were his favourite food. The more syrupy and creamier, the more he ate.

The fuse was replaced. Prasad's face lit up with a smile. The cooking in the house continued. The door bell rang.

Prasad saw a young girl standing at the doorway. A short, stumpy white girl with multi coloured hair, nose rings, ears with lots of pierced jewellery, smiled hesitantly. A tattoo showed through the neckline of her tee shirt. She lifted a heavy bag into the hallway.

'Hi, I'm Liz. Is Kelly in?'

'Come in, Come in.' Prasad opened the door but his smile turned to a puzzled grin as he queried, 'Who's Kelly?'

'Kulvinder, I call her Kelly,' she added shyly.

'Ah, a nice short name for Kulvinder.' Prasad opened the door wide. 'Come in, dear.'

She hesitated then walked in. 'Thank you.'

'She must be in the kitchen helping her mum.' Prasad walked over to the kitchen. BB saw them nearing the kitchen, preceded by Prasad's booming voice 'Kulvinder your friend is here.' The colour drained from BB's face. The big ladle with which she was stirring the dhal held aloft, froze for a moment in midair. She made her way quickly over to the young girl.

'Liz beti,' she croaked, then recovered quickly, 'No, no Kulvinder no here, up her room,' her voice turned harsh.

'Why I saw Kulvinder here earlier,' said Prasad, his voice loud enough for the two ladies in the kitchen to look up from their various tasks, making the chapatti flour, cutting vegetables and making the gravy.

BB gave him a withering look.

'Go beti, wait up there. I tell Kulvinder to come.' she said firmly, going back to stirring dhal.

'Mrs B,' her eyes pleaded. She hauled the big bag from behind her, 'I have nowhere to go.'

BB dropped the ladle, wiped her hands on the cloth beside her and walked over to the girl.

'What you mean?' she whispered, moving close to the girl.

'My mum's thrown me out.'

BB dragged her out of the kitchen with such a quick movement that all were perplexed.

'No, no stay here. Not in my house.'

She took her to the stairs, just as Kulvinder came out of the toilet.

'Kelly, thank god.' Liz ran over. She hugged and kissed her, trying to kiss her on her lips. Kulvinder saw the expression on her mum's face and quickly avoided the telltale disaster.

'What are you doing here?' asked Kulvinder moving her away and holding her at arms length. BB interrupted.

'I too busy here today. Go. We talk another day go, go upstairs or outside,' she hurried both the girls; her face twisted in a strange mixture of anger and shame and bundled them both up the stairs. 'Go upstairs, very busy now, take her beti, and talk there no here.' Fast words and she hauled them up the stairs.

BB hurried to the kitchen, straightened herself and declared in a loud voice,

'These gories, always trouble at home, fight, and fight with mum' She bustled about. 'Now we have too much to do for pooja tomorrow.' She was trembling as she turned on the music louder. The Bollywood music filled the air.

'Poor girl,' Prasad started, saw Lata's warning look and moved back to the safety of the lounge.

The atmosphere changed in the kitchen. Lata and Sita wondered why BB was so inhospitable to the young girl. It must be the way the girl was dressed they discussed in whispers, drugs maybe? 'Very unsavoury-looking girl, even at university they can get into bad company,' said Lata, not having seen the entire drama out in the hallway.

Sita was busy in the kitchen and only heard the gossip from Lata as they made their way to the temple early next the morning. Prasad had described all that had happened. Ram as usual had little to say. Sita felt sorry for BB. Here was something over which BB could have little control.

The next day, the havan at the temple went off without a hitch. Kulvinder arrived late, with a red blotchy face, but maintained a sullen silence until the ceremony was over. The boxes of syrupy sweets were distributed and all the aunties and uncles congratulated the young girl on her achievement.

'Very good, you need to look for an educated boy now, shopkeeper will not do,' said Manpreet looking at BB with envy.

Two days later BB was at Sita's door, with a big bag of fresh green peas. She took her into the conservatory.

'The havan went off well. What a big crowd!' said Sita to BB wondering what else to say?

BB looked down, picked the bag and said,

'Yes.' Then after a pause she continued, 'my garden very good this year.'

The huge bag of green peas in the pods lay beside them. The autumn sunshine cast a golden hue on the wicker set. The fuchsia plant trailing its pink flowers was a contrast to the green potted plants and the huge Yucca plant that stood to attention in the corner, in the conservatory. They squatted comfortably on the floor, a newspaper spread in front of them. They worked through them, getting the green peas so fresh and small, prising them out of the pods into the large plastic bowls.

BB looked resplendent in a bright green salwar kameez. Uma wandered in looking for Kulvinder, and then went on to watch some TV in the lounge, disappointed that the young girl was not there. Kulvinder had been a great babysitter. Sita had relied on her often when Lata was busy. The extra money was most appreciated by the young student. Uma looked up to her like the older sister she did not have.

'You're sure this will be okay?' BB was not convinced about freezing the peas. 'See last year I gave some to local shop, some I threw away.'

'You've had such a great crop this year. I'll blanch them, cool them quickly in the ice, and then freeze them. We can use them all year.' They cleared after the task was completed. Sita made a pot of tea and they settled down for a chat.

BB lived with her husband Pavan, owner of a huge cash and carry, son Aman, and young daughter Kulvinder. The husband and son worked long hours at the cash and carry. They had very little time to socialise. Pavan was a quiet individual who worked all hours and kept in the background.

'I came from Punjab, sixteen years old, married to him, family friend. Whole family had small shop. We all worked very hard. All lived in small house.'

Sita listened fascinated, to BB's struggle with the in-laws, the difficult birth of her son and the loss of her two babies before she gave birth to her daughter. She told her about the success, jealousies in business. And, finally, how the in-laws moved to their own house, not having any more to do with them.

'Money always breaks up families,' BB pontificated.

'I suppose it can.' Sita agreed.

'I lost babies because fight, fight all the time in house.'

'I know that stress can be awful at that time.' Sita agreed sympathy showing on her face.

'Much later, only when they move, Kulvinder born. Not here, in Punjab. Prayed to all gods. I make sure she no die. She my rani, my princess.' BB's eyes had a glint of tears. She hesitated for a while then a small sob came out of her throat. Sita looked worried,

'Are you okay Balvinder? Can I get you something?'

'No, no just my heart broke,' she sobbed. Soon the tears flowed as she recounted the shocking news of her daughter, dabbing her eyes with her bright green duppatta.

'Sita you must help me. I must have done bad things last birth.'

'Come now, you are fine.'

'You promise, not tell anyone.'

'Tell what…?'

'She …Kulvinder is not okay…'

'Not okay? Kulvinder is a lovely girl…'

'She only likes girls, says she won't marry … My in-laws don't know…'

'What do you mean…?'Sita was confused.

'I need help. How I get her married? That Liz lesbian or something.' BB sobbed into her duppatta. Sita sat stunned.

'We tell no one. You doctor, help me please, give some pills to change her, no?' The vulnerable BB implored. A new side that Sita had never imagined that she would ever witness emerged.

'There is no pill to help this Balvinder.'

'What you mean? You won't help me?' Balvinder's eyes hardened, the steely tone set in her voice.

'No, this is not a medical condition. I can't cure her of it.' Sita tried to explain.

'She must have got from someone.'

'No Balvinder, it's not a virus, not that simple.' Sita was racking her brain trying to find a simple explanation.

'You don't want to help me, you just laughing at me.' Balvinder's demeanour changed. 'I'll never help you. You, no good doctor. You no my friend.' She pointed her finger at her and banged the teacup on the table and rose. With that she rolled out of the house, anger and sadness so clear on her face.

The next few weeks seeing her at the temple, BB cast some cool frosty looks her way. It did not last long. Just three weeks later, she came back to Sita's house with a big bag of spinach, apologising and reinstating her friendship.

'I, so sorry, please. I no understand that day, too much sadness in my heart.' said BB.

Sita nodded.

'Now, Kulvinder, she gone, away to London. May never see her again.' BB's face crumpled in pain.

Sita felt sorry for her. Kulvinder, her princess had left her. She understood why BB had been distraught.

'I can't help you with this. Some people are born that way.'

'You sure there no medicine you can give me for her? It's not right. It must be sickness. Why you no help me?'

'As I said some people are born this way. You need to accept it.' Sita wondered if there were any booklets on female sexuality and then realised that even if there were any, none would be in Punjabi.

'No, no way to accept. It's a shame on my family. Don't tell no one, please,' BB pleaded.

'Of course, I'll not tell anyone, Balvinder. I understand.' said Sita patting her hand in sympathy. They heard the door slam. Uma ran in.

'Mum did you see this 'Glasgow is miles better', oh, hello aunty,' Uma skipped in and unfurled a poster.

'What are you on about?' Sita gave her a hug.

Uma had a huge yellow Mr. Men's smiley face on the poster that she had been given on her school visit to the museum.

'That's quite a clever idea. I do think Glasgow's miles better,' Sita paused, 'except for the weather. Now if only they could sort that out.' They all laughed. Uma ran up the stairs to change out of her uniform.

Sita turned back to BB.

'Balvinder you can be sure that I'll not tell anyone about Kulvinder. Your secret is safe with me. I'll help you in anyway that you want.'

'What use? She gone away. I lost my daughter now.'

It was a weary BB, the weight of her unhappiness crushing her spirit who shed some more tears before she left. Sita felt sorry for her.

Chapter 15

'Mum, I'm not coming. It's so hot, so boring.'

'Uma it's your grandpa's 60th birthday, 'Shashtiapthapoorthi.' It not only celebrates longevity but people say it is good to get the blessings of the couple who have lived and experienced life together.'

'Mum, why don't you and Dad go. I'll stay with Emma.'

'You do that for school holidays like Easter, already. No this is an important function. You can't miss it.'

'Mum, my exams…'

'We are only going for a week. You're coming.' Uma knew once Sita had made her mind up it was no use trying to change it.

*

The ceiling fan was circulating the air around the room. The air conditioners were on all day as it was summer. June was the worst time to visit Madras. They had always come in summer due to Uma's school session, July or August was the tail end of the summer. It was unbearably hot.

'Uma, the tailor is here with your pavadai. Try it on to see if it fits,' her grandma called Uma.

Ram and Uma's Grandpa were reading the paper.

'Oh, she's won again. Prime minister for the third time.' Ram commented on the British General election results.

'A lot of people admire Mrs.Thatcher here in India. She seems a very strong person, bit like our Indira Gandhi,' said Uma's granddad.

'People in Scotland hate her. She'll introduce the poll tax soon. People are fed up voting for the Labour Party in Scotland and getting a Tory Government to live under.'

'Our Federal system is not any better. Congress Party seems to be set for life as our rulers.'

'Amma, look, all they talk about is politics.' Sita said to her mum. Her mum was admiring Uma in her new skirt.

'Doesn't she look beautiful in the Indian dress, Uma come here let Grandpa see you.'

'Mum, I feel like a Christmas tree.' Looking at her face Uma quickly changed tack, 'I just prefer my jeans. They're so comfy.'

'Lost all our culture. They forget their roots so quickly.' Sita was annoyed at Uma's rudeness.

'Well, when you were growing up all you did was listen to Cliff Richard and Elvis. You loved everything western didn't you?' Her mum reminded Sita.

'You look lovely Uma. That'll be perfect for the ceremony' Grandma gave her a hug.

*

They were resting after the ceremony.

'Mum the ceremony was just like a wedding. Grandpa and grandma looked so nice. I'm glad I didn't miss it.'

'Dad, why did you make it so simple? I thought you'd have a grand one like Judge Mani Iyer,' Sita asked her dad.

'Sita, why waste money on grand parties? I just wanted to follow the rituals. I've decided to mark my sixtieth birthday instead by starting a charity.'

'Grandpa that's fantastic. So cool! Who're you going to help?' Uma queried.

137

'Tomorrow we'll all be going to 'Muthal Padi' (First Step).It's a foundling home for abandoned babies.'

'Dad, that's wonderful,' Sita agreed.

First Step was a tiny building; only half a dozen babies were looked after there.

'I'm starting small and hopefully will be able to help more babies in the coming years. I want to get it right,' said her dad.

The babies were in a clean small nursery. Sita and Ram talked to the doctor in charge and the staff and were impressed. The whole outfit was simple, clean but provided the necessities.

'Dad this is such a great thing, Sita cuddled a tiny undernourished baby, a scrap of humanity. I'll do all I can to raise money in Glasgow too.'

'Mum can I hold her, please?'

'She's so tiny. Be careful Uma.'

'Jai, your brother will be overseeing the whole charity. As a doctor he'll have a good input too. Both your mum and I'll be here most days of the week. We have a good goal to work towards. The temple, now this home will keep us busy in our old age.' Sita's dad had worked it all out. She was pleased for them.

*

They were watching a TV programme on the Ramayana. Uma fidgeted. She preferred her walkman and pop music. She got up and made a plea.

'Mum that's enough for me. Can I eat a ladoo? We never get these south Indian ones in Glasgow. Let's all pig out,' Uma ran into the kitchen.

'She's turning out to be a lovely girl,' said Sita's dad.

'Dad, she is stubborn, has a temper. Grandparents only see the nice side.'

Ram nodded, agreeing with Sita.

'So Sita, you're happy with the GP practice, both doing the same.'

'Yes Dad, but not in the same surgery and I'm part time as you know.'

'The British National Health service is the best. See how much we have to pay for doctors here,' her dad praised Britain.

'It's all changed. In two terms, Mrs. Thatcher has ruined the NHS. Soon it will be privatised completely,' Ram commented.

'Ram, the people have voted for her. She's so popular,' Sita said absentmindedly, watching the scene on TV.

'Not in Scotland. Most people vote for Labour, and all they get is a Tory Government. An Independent Scotland is the only way.'

'So, are there a lot of SNP M.P'S in Parliament?' dad continued.

Ram looked sheepish, 'Actually there are only two M.P.'s now in Westminster but there are a lot of voters who will vote SNP. I'm sure, if they get away from the English dominated system that Britain is still clinging on to.'

The maid brought in some fresh sherbet. Sita changed the topic, away from politics.

'By the way, Dad, remember Sridhar's son Anant? The one who did his MBBS with me. I met him recently. He's working in St. Andrews.'

'Oh, I didn't realise he was there. I heard that he'd gone to Scotland for his Fellowship. I thought it was Edinburgh.'

'He was in Edinburgh but moved to St.Andrews after he finished the exams.'

'St. Andrews? That's where the famous Golf course is.'

'You're right, 'The Open' held every year is world famous.'

'That's where Madras College is I think. Did you know that Madras system of education was founded by Andrew Bell after seeing a student writing the letters of the Tamil alphabet in the sand on our beach here? Poor kids sitting around him learning to write watched him tracing the letters with rapt attention. Bell was inspired by the idea and the monitor system… well you're living in Scotland you'll know about it. '

'Actually, I didn't know that, Dad. There are so many connections between Madras and Scotland but there is very little that we are aware of. Tell me more. Hold on, Uma come here and learn a bit of history.'

'Mum, I've had enough for the day. Give me a break, eh?'

'She's not interested. Once the walkman goes on the ears she's lost to the world. Pop music addiction.' Sita looked annoyed.

'Don't force her. She's just a kid.' Ram smiled at Uma.

'Ram, she really does twist you round her little finger,' Sita chided. Ram smiled happily.

'So Dad, what was that about Madras College again?' Sita pursued the topic.

'Andrew Bell a Minister was asked to provide education for orphans of British soldiers. He had no money to pay teachers for these orphans. He was walking along Madras beach when he witnessed the scene I was telling you about, a young boy tracing the Tamil alphabets on the sand. That gave him the idea that what was needed was not qualified teachers but a bright student who could teach the basics to the young. Andrew Bell wrote papers on it and the monitor system was born. Many educational establishments paid for his idea. The money that he made from publishing the monitor system helped establish the Madras College on the Fife Coast in Scotland.'

'I never knew. I had heard about Yale, the Ivy League College funded by the money that Elihu Yale made by trading in Madras, but this is amazing,' said Ram

'How little we know about the strong connections between our countries,' wondered Sita and added a mental note, 'I must tell Jyoti, to add to her 'Scotphil' collection.'

*

'Ram you must go, of course you must visit your classmate. Is Mani not the close friend you still keep in touch with?' Sita insisted.

140

'I know but he is a politician now, probably too busy.' Ram hesitated.

'He wouldn't have invited you if he was that busy. Go on, give him my apologies, I have to attend Aunty Parvati's pooja or she'll never forgive me.' Both knew that Aunty Parvati was a force to reckon with.

A crowd streamed out of the Taj hotel's 'Mysore Function Room' as Ram made his way in. Mani came over straight away. A small group were at the top table. Ram recognised her immediately.

'Ram, good to see you. Where is the family?' Mani, the young man with loud shirts transformed to a politician with an enormous girth, was wearing the Congress party white shirt and a Gandhi cap.

'Sorry they had to attend a pooja.' Ram's eyes strayed back to her.

'This group offers a free mobile eye clinic to the poor areas of my constituency. I think you know some doctors here. Do you remember, Vidya, Kumar and Lal? They were in our class at Jipmer?' Mani asked Ram.

'Yes, I do.'

They reminisced about their days at Jipmer.

'Remember the young guys who were in the group that 'ragged' you? Well two are consultants at our biggest hospitals,' said Kumar. They laughed at their days of cramming for the exams.

He managed to get a few minutes with Vidya at the end.

Ram came back home, shocked that feelings that he had forgotten about had resurged. Was it because she looked forlorn as she said that she was widowed, he wondered. Ram remained more withdrawn till Uma's new experiences and her reactions occupied him.

*

'Jackfruit, that's a funny name. What is it? Uma grimaced at the funny shaped bulbous fruit hanging heavy on the bark of the tree in the garden.

'Jack fruit I know is a strange name for an Indian fruit. 'Chakka' was the original name but the Brits could not pronounce it so it became jackfruit and thrust its way into common parlance.'

141

Uma looked at the fruit. She was not sure if she would like to taste it. The tree was rich with fruit. They hung like little hippos on the huge tree. The fruit, often bigger than a watermelon, was ugly to look at. The green mottled skin had bumps like tiny hills on its outer skin.

'You'll love the taste. The fruit inside is delicious.' Ram was trying to convince Uma to try it.

Uma watched as the cook and the maids, gathered around to deseed and get the luscious golden yellow sumptuous fleshy fruit. Cut in half, it revealed an intriguing design that an artist would want to paint. The pungent, aroma hit her first. Strong and sugary. Uma was not sure if she would try it. She screwed up her nose. The white shiny sticky sap had to be removed, the fleshy seeds prised out. Hands were dipped in oil and water to work at the delicate work. The seeds were huge, covered in a brown chest nutty coat. The fruit was eaten, with honey. Uma refused to try it.

'Yuk, it seems weird. No way! I'm not touching it,' she said and ran away.

Uma loved Madras beach. The blue water stretched as far as the eyes could see. The horizon was visible in the distance. Nature, displayed a tremendous show on a permanent stage for all to enjoy. The huge waves bellowed like thunder. The exhilaration of watching the white foam as it approached, its ferocity as it rose high and crashed down, the soft waves lapping against her bare feet made her want more. She screamed, 'I'm getting dragged away.'

'Don't worry I'm holding you tight,' Ram shouted back. They stood as the waves lashed on.

Uma she wrote her name on the sand with a twig and shouted in excitement as she found the waves erasing her name in seconds. The sandy grit between her toes, the shells, the detritus left by the tide were treasures she collected. She ran to the car, her sand-crusted legs bare, carrying her sandals and wiping her salt sprayed face.

'I must take you to Elphistone's Ice Cream Parlour,' said Sita, 'It has the best Chocolate Delight ice cream that you've ever had.' Sita remembered her own childhood haunts and took great pleasure in getting Uma to enjoy the same.

They visited Jyoti. Her kids and Uma howled with laughter listening to their mum's schooldays. Sita recounted tales with Jyoti giggling like a young girl as they reminisced together.

'Did you actually stand up and wish your teachers 'Good morning Miss,' and not speak until you were spoken to?' Uma laughed so hard her tummy hurt. 'Sounds like the Victorian classroom that I saw at Scotland Street Museum.'

'Well our school did give us a sound foundation for life,' said Jyoti in a serious tone.

'So that's why I became a doctor, and your mum now lives a life of luxury in Madras, while I'm slaving away in Glasgow, 'joked Sita to Jyoti's kids.

Once they were back in Glasgow, the routine took over. Sita relished her new role fundraising for her dad's foundling home. It fulfilled her in ways she could not imagine. The photos and letters of the progress of the tiny babies made her feel her life had an important purpose.

Ram kept a tenuous link, to Vidya's life through Mani.

Chapter 16

Sita had heard of a book launch at her library and invited Eileen along to it. They had not seen much of each other recently. Children and work kept them both busy. They had both arrived at Brookwood library in Bearsden, on time. She was a bit surprised at Eileen wearing a scarf, but said nothing. Eileen looked haggard, tired, not her cheery old self at all. They entered the beautiful blonde sandstone building with its automatic door. It was nice, warm and quiet. The librarian at the door welcomed them and showed them to the back of the library. As they walked over to the seats, Eileen stopped and chatted to two women who huddled in the corner as they looked for a place to sit.

'Hello Sadie, Aggie, whit're yous doin here?' Eileen gave them both a big hug.

They looked at her strangely at first, and then one of them said 'Oh its oor Eileen. How are you hen?'

'Oh Sita, meet my old neighbours, Sadie and Aggie from Maryhill.' She introduced them.

'Less of tha' old bit, mind,' said Sadie laughing. 'Hello hen,' she said to Sita

'So what's wie tha' scarf an aw?' asked Sadie, straight to the point.

'I need to wear it noo, I'm a Muslim, married Dr.Ali,' said Eileen.'

'Och aye,' Sadie said with a puzzled look as she pulled her anorak tight over her expansive belly. The fleece jumper made her sweat, her face red with the walk up the stairs to the library. Aggie checked her wee purse and then put it in her trackie bottoms. Her thin wiry body shook with a racking cough. She pushed her dyed blonde hair off her face and gave a hoarse, 'how are ye?' to Sita. A Laurel and Hardy pair, thought Sita, one obese and the other thin as a rake. Sita noticed that Eileen switched from proper English to her dialect when she spoke them. 'Bit like me talking in

144

Tamil with my parents or family and then switching over to English when I need to,' thought Sita.

'Eileen, so whir hav you been hidin? Hav'nae' seen you fur ages. You're lookin good though.'

'Aye, I first moved into they nurses' flats at the hospital, but noo I'm away over on the Southside in a nice wee hoose.'

'Och aye, guid, you did so well at thay nursing course. Though, you married, ah cannae believe, hen.'

'Aye, well done, Eileen,' added Aggie. 'No many of oor kids' dae much with their schoolin like you did Eileen. Look at my Darren,' said Aggie. 'So dae you know Morna who has written this book then? She's oor tutor noo.'

'Naw, just Sita dragged me oot here. She wanted to buy the book. She's read her last wan. Did you say that Morna is your tutor? Whit are you learnin then?' asked Eileen.

'Just they adult litraracy thingummyjig,' murmured Sadie, 'she's learnin us tae reed and writ better, aye so she does.'

They were distracted by a loud laugh. Two smartly dressed women talking about Morna's book, walked to the row in front of them, one still stifling a laugh.

'Have you read the extracts of her book Kay? They're so realistic,' said the first woman, flicking her well cut hair with the palm of her hand.

'Wonderful, I could picture each of the scenes in my mind.' The other woman replied

'Oh the dreariness of the life in the peripheral estates, the deprivation was so well drawn.'

'Not sure about so much of the expletive deleted.' They both laughed and took their seats in front of Sadie and Aggie.

Sadie wondered about their words.

'What are thay oan aboot?' She whispered to Aggie as they took their seats. Two rows of blue cushioned chairs were arranged in a semi circle

145

near the Scottish section of books. They chose to sit in the back row, close to the door. The author's book was displayed on a table beside two chairs facing the public. Biscuits, muffins and tea were laid on a small table at the side of the enclosure.

Sadie whispered, 'I could dae with a wee cuppa, but no one else is going near it.'

'Ach let's wait and see eh?' Agee wished she had smoked a fag before she took her seat. She was thinking of the pleasures of a lit cigarette, and taking a long satisfying draw. Sadie looked around the small gathering of twenty women. None of their mates from their class were there. The two ladies in front of them were talking quietly. Sadie looked at the woman sitting in front of her and took in her £200 boots and the costly winter coat lying carefully draped on the back of her chair, her costly haircut, the nice perfume and more importantly her confident style. She was perfectly made-up, her hair and skin glossy like a model whom one would see on magazine covers. Even the woman's posture, made Sadie feel awkward. She shifted on her seat, embarrassed for staring at her. They heard a bustle and Morna walked in with the head of the library services. The three librarians also followed them and sat down facing the crowd of people.

Morna smiled at Sadie and Agee in recognition. The head of library services introduced Morna. He spoke of work that she had done before, the stories set in bleak estates in the periphery of Glasgow. Then he asked her to do a reading from her book. Agee and Sadie felt as if they were at a school meeting. Morna was such fun in class. Here it was all formal. The book was entitled 'A Life in a Day.' After the reading the people were given time for their questions. The lady in front of Sadie asked a question immediately.

'So these feral children that you were writing about, how can society cope with them?'

'Feral children, what dis she mean?' Sadie whispered to Aggie.

'I need to go oot for a fag. Its way oe'er ma heid, all tha reedin an tha.' Aggie excused herself and went out. Other people asked more questions.

'The main character, the social worker, why did she swear so much, I mean she is a graduate isn't she?' Eileen asked.

146

'Why did you use such foul language? Was it to sell more books?' The lady with the expensive dress asked her.

'Your book has no answers to any of the problems depicted, does it?' Eileen asked and waited for an answer.

Sadie marvelled at how so many were able to ask Morna all the questions and the calm way she answered them. She was dying to ask her why she had written only bits that showed the worst of Maryhill. She did not have the nerve. Sita and Eileen seemed so confident too. Aggie came back in time to have the tea. Morna came over to say hello to them. Sadie rustled up all her courage and asked her.

'Could ye no have said sumthin aboot us tryin to learn things? All you says sounds like its dreadful roond aboot us.'

'Do you know my mum came from Maryhill? I managed to move away but I never forgot my roots. This book is to show the authorities how much needs to be done to help the area. I am with you. This is a book that I hope will inspire people to campaign for the improvement of the area,' Morna said. She touched Sadie's arm, with a warm smile as she spoke more about the ideas that she had for helping their area.

'Surely there's mair to oor area than jist problems hen, ye know that.' Sadie tried. She wished she could speak posh, clearly, like the others. Morna was called over to the other side to sign the books for those who wanted to buy her book.

'I'm sorry I need to go,' said Morna. I'll talk to you later. At the class next week maybe,' she said and hurried away. Sita and Eileen stood in the queue to buy the book. They waved to Sadie and Aggie, and watched them leave the building.

Back on the bus, Sadie remarked, 'She's dun well fur herself, that wee lassie, Eileen. Don't know aboot that scarf an aw, married a doctor tae.'

'Aye, she had her heid stuck in thay books, guid fur her.'

'Nursin, tha's a great joab, lookin after the sick an aw.'

'Pays well tae, but she hasnae changed, at aw.' added Aggie, pulling a cigarette from the pack.

'That wisnae fair, that book.' Sadie's face crumpled in anger.

'Aye, but it's the truth though.' Aggie was lighting up.

'All she wrote aboot is the drinkin and thieving, gangs an that.' She thumped the stick in her hand on the floor. People in front of her turned around.

'Maryhill is sum place eh.I'd leave it tomorrow if I could.' Agee worried for her Darren.

'I mean why write the same old thing? Everyone knows about these things. Why not about oor class, how we're trying to learn new skills? I mean look at thay computer classes. Are they no all full like?' Sadie was still angry.

'Aye, but it's oor kids isn't it? They hav'nae changed, huv they hen?' Aggie was thinking of the kids that Darren was hanging around with.

'Nothing much changes here eh. Need mair jobs fur oor men.' Sadie shook her head.

'Wha' men? Neither of us managed to hang on to oors.' Aggie gave a cigarette-ridden cough that sounded like a metallic drum in her throat. She lit another cigarette, drew on it deeply. She was glad to get out of that stuffy place.

'I don't know if I'll go back to tha adult learnin class again,' remarked Sadie.

'Och away, its good fun to get oot of the hoose once a week. We're learnin to writ better aren't we?' Aggie did enjoy doing something different when Darren was at school.

'I suppose it does help us think a wee bit,' Sadie agreed reluctantly.

'Mibbe we should write oor ain book then.' They laughed again. The bus wound its way round the dark streets. They got off the bus.

'See yous at the Bingo the'morro then? Aggie helped Sadie get off the bus.

'Aye, Darren's away at his gran's.' She hurried back to her son.

148

Groups of youths were hanging about near the 'offy.' A burnt-out car was the centre of attention for the younger kids. Dogs were also running about with the kids. They shouted and swore as Sadie walked slowly back home.

An empty bottle of buckie skittered past her.

Eileen stayed back at Sita's for a coffee and a chat.

'Can you understand why I wanted to get out of Maryhill?' said Eileen to Sita. 'They're good folks but that's what I would have ended up if I had not got my head together and done my nursing course,' she shuddered.

'They seemed okay to me. Trying to attend the adult learning class can't be easy for them at their age.'

'I know. That's what I mean. It was a struggle for me too. There was no one to tell me what to do after school. Thank God, for my English teacher who gave me the best career's advice. She literally filled the form for me.'

'You've done well, Eileen, I really admire you. Don't know if I would have been as determined as you.'

'Come on, can't have been easy going to medical school in India either. Are women not way behind over there?'

'We have real extremes. We have a woman Prime minister, women in all walks of life on the one hand, and then on the other we have women who are treated as chattels, killed for not having the right dowry.'

'Anyway, this evening was different, I enjoyed the reading. Don't know if I'll enjoy the book though.' Eileen crushed the tissue in her hand.

'Why won't you? Surely you have a better view of life in Maryhill, and you can even challenge the author if you felt she'd portrayed it in a bad light,' Sita commented.

'I know. It's just that I'm fed up with writers always showing our areas in a bad light. We do have many success stories too.'

'Let's read the book first then we can make all these judgements, eh?' said Sita pouring another cup of the coffee from the pot.

Eileen had changed. Sita had seen a slow transformation in her from a bubbly, vivacious young nurse to a quiet withdrawn wife and mother. Their meetings were infrequent. Eileen was often unable to attend their book club meetings. Whenever Sita rang her, she could get only short answers. She was intrigued. Eileen was her one close friend who had made Sita's life bearable when she had arrived in Glasgow, naïve, scared of the challenges of starting a new life in a strange country. Eileen had been her link to the host culture. They had clicked from the outset. She was quieter now.

'Eileen how are you getting on? How are the children? We've hardly had a chance to talk.'

'Nothing much to say. Everything is just fine.'

'When did your mother-in-law come over? You never told me.'

'She'll be with us now, permanently. She's has got no one back in Pakistan.'

'Do you get on with her?' Sita persisted. Eileen shrugged and got up and picked up Uma's new photo from the mantelpiece.

'Look she's grown so much, a young lady now.'

'Eileen is everything okay with you?' Sita put an arm round her.

'I'm fine.' They both heard footsteps.

Ram came clattering down the stairs,

'So, where did you two gallivant to today?' he asked.

'Ram, I told you we were at the library for a book launch.' Sita's face had a pinched expression, knowing well what his next comment would be.

'Not another one of those novels is it?' he snorted.

'You like histories and biographies. Why can't I enjoy what I like?' Sita retorted.

'At least you learn something from the past or from people's lives. What use is pure fiction?' Ram gave a mocking laugh.

'Ram, you'll never understand,' Sita turned away.

Eileen looked at her watch.

'I better get back home. Faraz's mum's not too keen on me going out at night.'

'I suppose you better get back then, but we need to meet up more.' Sita followed her to the door.

'Yes, I'll call you soon.' Eileen waved her goodbye from the car. Sita locked the door and came back to the lounge. Ram had already brought a tray to take the coffee things back to the kitchen.

'Ram, I'm bit worried about Eileen. Did you see the change in her?'

'What change, oh the scarf. Quite a lot of Muslims have started wearing it now.'

'No, there's something troubling her but she's not telling me, I just know.'

'Did you ask her?'

'I tried but she kept avoiding the subject.'

'Maybe you're imagining things' said Ram. They stacked the dishwasher together in silence. Sita had an uneasy feeling about Eileen.

Chapter 17

Uma was a bright child who came up with top marks without much of an effort, good at sports, an all-rounder but extremely demanding in every other way. Sita found her stubborn behaviour a challenge. Even as a tiny child, Uma would throw tantrums. Sita remembered the embarrassment of it all. The terrible twos were just that, Uma lying on the street outside Fraser's store screaming until Sita bought her the horrible Cabbage Patch doll. She knew that Uma's teenage years were not going to be easy.

'Get that music down. It's too loud and get ready quickly,' Sita shouted. Uma didn't bother. She hated going to the potluck meetings that her parents had every month. The six families got together, as the adults tried hard to recreate a little India for their offspring. There were fun bits when they were younger. As none of the families had any relatives in Glasgow, the potluck families got together over the festive season. They had presents, games and lots of company whether it was Christmas or Diwali. The children were fed up with potluck. They had voted with their feet as soon as they were teens and parents could not force them to come. Uma, just turned a teenager, was dragged along. She had argued about it all the way in the car with her parents.

'It may be okay for your generation but it soooo boring mum. Why have such a meeting at all- just to eat? I hate it. Everyone gathers so late, and you're greeted with that awfully tangy fresh orange juice, though the men always seem to manage a whisky or a beer. Wouldn't mind it if we kids could have a snifter.'

'Now Uma! Stop that nonsense and come on let's go. It's good to meet up with our kind. Once a month is not too much to ask surely?'

The surly teens and the 'not -quite –teens' were fuming, ripping the niceties of these monthly meetings to shreds. They had their own school friends, and their interests were changing. Some longed to get a bit of their independence and planned for courses in Universities away from

152

Glasgow. Nothing that parents did was cool. They hated their parent's insular lives. The world was full of exciting things that they wanted to explore. The girls in particular hated the intensive scrutiny that they were subjected to by the 'aunties', always wanting to know their achievements in school, and at University. Were the children tall, fair? Did they study well? Did they behave properly, and did they get too familiar with the local permissive society's liberal mores? The pressure on the kids was unrelenting. They had to be model kids, study well, get into a good professional career, and marry, preferably an Indian professional. Most of the educated aunties were liberal and accepting of the impact of the west on their growing youngsters, but there were a few who belonged to the traditional clique and their tongues never stopped dolling out the sharp comments that could not be ignored. It was the bane of their teen lives.

Some had arrived early at Aunty Reena's house. Uma walked in with a fixed smile on her face. After the usual pleasantries, the young ones went over to the conservatory. They listened to the latest music and chatted politely. When the food was served, they trooped back into the dining room half-heartedly. The girls in particular were now conscious of their figures.

'Look at the huge platters of deep fried starters like pakoras and samosas, with rich chutneys. Don't know why they bother with the little bits of salad. Maybe to salve their conscience, I'm not touching it' said Uma. The other girls did the same. The boys ate with gusto.

The meal was another gluttonous fare with each family trying to outdo the other in rich creamy sauces, reliving all their food experience in India. There was lamb curry, chicken in a rich cashew and cream sauce, many vegetable curries, dhal raita, poppadoms. The list was endless. The girls took small bits of meat or salad and nibbled delicately. The fashion magazines were full of anorexics. These were their role models. When their parents were growing up in India, their role models were different. The Bollywood stars were well endowed, a sign of wealth. The directors chose an image, more a fantasy, pandering to the masses in the poor country.

The sweets were even worse, deep fried in ghee or sickly sweet, and syrupy. Gulab Jamuns, Laddoos. Ice cream and other local desserts were also offered. No wonder the Indians were heading for diabetes in such

153

big numbers thought Uma, shaking her head in disgust. The health conscious girls hardly touched the sweets.

Ram was in his element on their way home. 'Not a single person interested in the Scottish cause, all kow-towing to Maggie. I don't understand this lack of interest in the good of our country. They only think of their own pockets. 'Better with Maggie, less tax for me' is all they can talk about. Selfish, never getting involved with mainstream politics at all. All they care about is how to make money and buy the latest status symbol. The stock market, making a quick buck or the latest Mercedes Benz or BMW models seem of more interest to them,' Ram fumed as he drove them back home.

Somehow, BB had inveigled herself into the group. Being a neighbour she had often gate crashed when it was Sita's turn. There was no way that the families could keep her out. The motley crowd of three South Indian and three other North Indian families became friends. BB was never asked to join in but she appeared as often as she could.

'Mum, Aunty BB was interrogating me about my friend Padma. 'What she is doing at home? Why no here? Is she study hard for her exams? She have boyfriends, you tell me beti,' she said dragging me to sit beside her.' Uma imitated her. 'Trying to get me to grass on her, I hate that woman.' Uma made a face. 'That woman is unbelievable, the nosy bitch.'

'Uma! Don't be so cheeky, have some respect for older people,' Sita tried to stop the ranting on both sides from Ram and from Uma.

'I'm never going to go to another marathon session of eating and gossiping. This is the last one,' Uma protested as they headed home.

'Uma! Stop talking about Aunty BB! What's wrong with enjoying getting together and relaxing over a nice meal? Better than getting drunk in a pub,' said Sita again. It fell on deaf ears, Uma was determined that that was the last potluck for her. As each of the kids left to study at university or moved away to take up jobs, potluck for the kids came to an end. It had run its course for them.

Uma, the teenager was going through the period of testing her parents to the limit. If it was not her outrageous clothes, it was her hair dyed a bright red. The arguments had become a daily feature. It was wearing them down. Their own childhoods had been one of meek obedience. If they resented what their parents foisted on them, they sulked but never challenged them in such a flagrant manner. They found Uma's teen traumas very difficult. The generation gap was evident. Neither Ram nor she had any idea how to handle her defiant behaviour.

'Mum, meet Danny,' she had said one evening. Sita looked at the strange creature in front of her, the blusher on his cheeks the orangey clothes, the pigtail and an effeminate wee boy grunting a short hello. Before she could recover, Uma had taken him up to her room to listen to the latest Boy George records. When questioned about the boy, Uma, said 'Mum you know nothing about retro fashion. Just chill.' The language, the attitude irritated Sita but she kept her calm.

After constant arguments with little resolution, both Ram and Sita realised that the only way forward with their child was to concentrate on the big values and ignore the trivia. The dressing up and the loud music were outward vestiges of defiance, more a way of asserting her independence, of striking out on her own. Yet, often when she needed them, Uma turned to them both. That was the crucial thing. The talk at the potluck dinners was often about the difficulty of raising children in an alien culture that gave so much importance to individual rights. Most of the parents concluded that as long as they led good lives, did not get into the drug culture or neglected their academic work, they could afford to give them some laxity to enjoy their youth. Some disagreed. BB was always around to keep her beady eyes on any misappropriate behaviour on either the parents' or children's part.

'Look at the Muslims,' she would harangue them, 'such good discipline, strict with their girls, learn Koran, even got schools for them. We no good, too soft.'

BB would look accusingly at the group of parents, none of whom would argue with her. They did not agree with her views but said little to defy her. They made their own rules to suit their children.

*

'Uma turn that noise down right now.' Sita's voice was high.

'Oh, God,' muttered Uma, turning it down but banging the door shut.

155

Sita's hand trembled as looked at the mounting paperwork on her desk. Just neglecting a few days work, now she was fazed just looking at it. She made her mind up to tackle it and get it completed. She worked steadily for an hour and a half. The strings of Bach's sonata came from Uma's room. She heard Uma's footsteps coming down the stairs.

The door was flung open, Uma's face peeked in. 'Mum,' she said quietly.

'Yes' Sita put her pen down, got up stretched her hands over her head.

'Mum,' Uma was standing beside her, 'sorry I banged the door. My Highers... I am so nervous.'

'I'm sorry too that I shouted. It was too loud though.'

'Well, rock music needs to be played loud.' Uma frowned.

Sita gestured towards her paper pile, 'I was stressed too.'

'Yeah, I know.' Uma came and stood beside her.

Sita pushed the curl back on her forehead, and gave her a hug.

'I didn't know you liked Bach.'

'I do need a change occasionally. It's lot easier to study with that in the background.' Sita nodded.

'Want a cup a tea?'

'I could murder one, ta.' Uma linked her arm and walked to the kitchen. 'I'll have it in my humungous mug,' she said bringing out the mug that had a tiny cat on its rim and its four paws decorating its sides. 'Mum thanks. This masala chai will pep me up.'

Uma put her feet up on the old red sofa and bit into the chocolate biscuit. The mug swayed dangerously then steadied as she took it in both hands and took a sip.

Sita looked at Uma. She had so many of Ram's mannerisms. She looked like him in many ways, that curl that endeared her, the dimple on her chin and the curve of her lips was so like Ram when he smiled. Sita slumped beside her, her mug of tea sloshing up the sides about to spill.

156

They both laughed as she managed to right it in time. Mr. T the cat hid under the chair wondering at their sudden outburst of laughter.

Ram's work for the SNP became more intensive. 'Funny how our own identity seemed to follow the same struggle as Scotland getting its own Parliament,' Sita pondered as she and Uma filled innumerable envelopes to help Ram during the elections. Their family life had taken on a comfortable, contented normality. On the radio Shirley Bassey was belting out her famous Bond film song 'Diamonds are forever.' The commercial jingle jolted her from her thoughts. The diamond on her finger sparkled. She caressed it. It was the ring that Ram's old grandma had given her. The blue Jaeger diamond caught the light again, a myriad little shapes danced before her eyes. The colours ranged from blue to a prism of the brightest yellows and pink, the facets had revealing layers of cuts. From a rough piece of carbon formed by a rock the diamond had been prised out by man and caringly restored to its inimitable glory. Each cut had revealed its beauty. The craftsman had spent hours to get it to this perfection, a gem to be treasured. Waves of love for Ram that had been suppressed came out. She felt their relationship was like the uncut diamond slowly revealing its brilliance now.

Chapter 18

The few days off stretched nice and long in front of her. Sita lay on her bed pulling the duvet closer, cozying into its warmth. There was no need at all to rush out headlong into a busy day with work, or other stress. Even Ram's lack of affection retreated into the distance as she dozed for a bit. She luxuriated in having the whole bed to herself, closed her eyes and dreamed lazily of having a 'me day.'

She made up a vague list of having a long soak in the bath, getting into her jeans, not her work clothes that demanded some effort to look smart. She also decided on a breakfast at Little Italy on Byres Road with real coffee and a croissant. She could already smell the coffee, the roasted coffee bean aroma teasing her, making her smile. She would buy a gift for Lata's fiftieth birthday and then treat herself to the perfect dress with matching accessories, something she never had time for during her hectic working day. Maybe even get her hair done.

After a light lunch, she would head to the Botanic Gardens, read the book that she had started. If the weather turned, she would walk into the Kibble Palace, a place she had often frequented when she first arrived in Glasgow. The sight of the tropical plants such as turmeric, chilli, banana plant and the coconut palm in the lush humid glass enclosed Kibble transported her back to Madras. Those little bits of greenery had given her snatches of happiness.

She opened her eyes. The pale light streaming through the pink curtains cast a lovely glow on the bedroom walls. She flicked the radio on and quickly changed from Radio 4 where John Humphreys was haranguing a politician. Classic FM was just right; the strains of Mozart's violin concerto filled the room. She hummed happily as she had a bath in the en-suite. She got dressed, ready to start her carefully planned, blissful day.

The phone rang. She looked out of the window as she reached for the phone. The call was one of those awful cold sales. She frowned and banged the phone down. The weather at least was promising, late autumn turning the leaves russet, burnished with gold as the sun came out from behind the clouds.

After the breakfast and a read of the paper, she strolled over to the antiquarian shop, the impecunious browsers' paradise, Voltaire and Rousseau in Otago Lane. It was a place of infinite joy for Sita. She often went for a browse. Trevor, the ginger cat, was sitting on his usual chair near the pile of foreign language dictionaries. The sun just glinted on the chair. Trevor must find it warm and soothing. He seemed to know the most comfy place in the shop, like all cats do. Sita loved old books but she was here to look for something special for Lata. Giving up the Sanskrit masters at Edinburgh University had not stopped her love for the language and researching old scriptures or reading any work in the language was an interest that Lata still pursued. Just week ago, Sita had seen the book but the owner said he had kept it for a special customer. 'Come again next week. Maybe she won't buy it,' he had said.

Browsing around, Sita noticed another lady whom she had seen before. She smiled at her and moved on. The lady was talking to the owner about a set of three heavy books which she had presumably just bought. As the owner started packing, she came over to the shelf that Sita was at.

They both reached for the same book.

'Sorry, I should have waited,' said the lady in a very proper accent.

'No, it's my fault,' said Sita.

'It is a rare find. Are you interested in Sanskrit'?' said the lady as she clutched the book. It was the hard-bound copy with a gold spine, the Sanskrit book she had wanted to give as a gift to Lata. It was the same book that the antiquarian shop owner, had refused to sell her last week. Sita stared at her, as curiosity got the better of her. The lady held the book closer to her chest as though she would not part with it. She was dressed in a classic way, a heavy woollen coat, lovely paisley patterned scarf, a well used but good leather bag. The hair was well-cut; grey going on white, high cheekbones, an aquiline nose but it was the eyes that were arresting. The deep blue pools ached with sadness.

'I was going to buy that as a gift for my friend's birthday.' Sita mentioned, hoping she would somehow convince the lady to part with the book.

'Oh, would you like it then?' she said, 'I'm so selfish; I have a collection of them.'

'A collection? How wonderful. I never thought that these books would be of interest for locals...' Sita hesitated, and then continued, 'I'm so sorry that was a silly thing to say.'

'No, you are perfectly right. Not many of us are interested in old books let alone one in an obscure dead language,' she smiled. 'I'm Mary Armitage by the way.' She held out her hand.

'I'm Sita Iyer.' They both shook hands and Mary handed her the book.

'Oh I can't take that. Your collection might be ruined,' Sita was embarrassed.

'I insist that you have it. Though, you can also do me a favour,' she said, 'I have all these books that I have bought. Will you help me carry them to my place? I live just around the corner.' she pointed to a pile of thick books lying beside the cash register.

'If you are sure.' Sita was pleased that she had got the book.

They walked over to Mary's house. The grand house was in Hillhead. The sandstone building was set far ahead of a long a driveway on an incline. The garden in front had old trees that gave shade and privacy not seen in new houses gardens. One of the rowan trees had bent low almost to its roots on its right, to get at the sunlight. The shape was very unusual. The tree seemed to have survived despite the lack of sunshine and fought its way up. Laden now with red berries, it looked defiant amidst the strong well- trained trees with abundant green foliage.

The house was dark inside. The enormous hallway had rich wooden panelling with a huge stairway right in the middle. They put the books in the drawing room which was almost a library, with a heavy bookshelf lining an entire wall.

Mary offered her for a cup of tea. They sat at the dining table. The cruet set that was on the table was made of silver. It was not polished;

and the dull blackened silver with the oxidised effect gave it a nice homely feel. 'I use it all the time, I only polish it occasionally,' said Mrs. Armitage as she brought out the sugar bowl. Sita was surprised to see that it was a smaller version of her own powder bowl. The silver powder bowl had been her grandmother's. It was one of the pieces which her mum had polished and presented to her for the wedding. Along with the Chandan bowl for the sandalwood paste, the kunkum cup holding the red powder for bindi and the silver dinner plates were part of the silverware for her wedding. The pooja trays, the panir chombu, in which fragrant rosewater was poured on special occasions, panchpathram and uthrini, the traditional tumbler and spoon that was used at all religious ceremonies by Brahmins- the silverware that were part of her dowry, now she was looking at a bowl that looked familiar.

The powder bowl had a special place in her heart. It was an heirloom. Her mum had put talcum powder in it. Sita remembered it had a huge pink fluffy powder-puff in it. She had seen it lying on her mum's dressing table. The smell of Cuticura powder wafted in her memory. She would play with the powder puff, lifting a huge chunk of the talc and put it all over her face, the grey clown-like face in the mirror would get her into a fit of giggles. Still clear in her mind was the haze of powder falling on the dressing table's dark mahogany creating a grey film. She would trace funny doodles on it. The servant maid would come over, dust it off and give her a row for making her clean the dressing table all over again. She had held it up and looked at it more carefully. The silver bowl had scenes of an Indian village etched on it. There was a palm tree, a small hut and even the silhouettes of a farmer and his wife tilling the fields of paddy. So much detail worked into the bowl by the silversmith. It had been on her dressing table, and just as she had played with it, Uma had done the same. Some family rituals were to be treasured.

The bowl in Mary's had scenes of a croft on the sides. She examined the bowl and related the similarity to Mary. There were so many influences during the British Raj that had seeped into each other's cultures. The photograph of her mum and dad had the same rigid pose and similarity in dress as the British one she saw at Mary's. Sita's dad had posed sitting on the chair, dressed in a smart suit, the highly polished shoes and ties just right, his hands clutching the arms of the chair. Her mum stood beside him in a beautiful silk sari, with a puffed sleeve blouse embroidered with little rosebuds, an obvious British fashion that had been borrowed. Her arm was touching her dad's shoulder lightly. The

161

sepia photograph that she remembered now, was so similar to Mrs Armitage's parents' photograph that was hanging on her wall.

A Siamese cat with gracious markings walked in, purred and rubbed his soft fur on Sita's legs. She smiled and caressed the cat. They chatted away, learning about each other and their love of books. Mary was a specialist in linguistics. Languages had always fascinated her. She had been to India, though not to Madras. Reminiscing about the trip to India made her sad.

'It was my husband's sudden death. It was a heart attack, and I loved him dearly...' Her eyes glazed again, the pain still evident.

'Oh, I'm so sorry.'

'We had a love that needed no words. We were just one,' she added softly.

'Do you have any family to help you?'

'No, he was my world. I find it hard to keep going. Books are my friends now.'

'You mean you have no one at all?' Sita felt sad for her.

'I have a nephew, Neil, who comes down occasionally. He's a doctor in Aberdeen, coming down to Glasgow I heard.'

Sita was embarrassed; felt she was intruding, yet the fact that she had opened up to her, a complete stranger, made her feel responsible.

'I'm so sorry I had to buy the book. It's Lata's fiftieth birthday. She is a very special friend.'

'No dear, that's perfectly all right, I understand.' Mary explained how she was a regular at the antiquarian bookshop and that they held any book and gave her first refusal before they put it out for general sales.

'It would be the perfect gift for my friend's fiftieth birthday,' Sita said hesitatingly.

She thanked her politely for the tea and left. The sad life of a wonderful lady, living in a huge house with just a cat and books for company, made Sita imagine a life without a partner. The rest of the day turned into one of deep thought.

Chapter 19

Glasgow 1990s

The spa was perfect. Stobo Castle knew how to pamper its clients in every way. The fluffy towels, the Belgian chocolates on the bed, the champagne on arrival, were oodles of fun stuff in the bathroom. The sheer luxury of it all made Sita tingle with pleasure. She stepped into the Jacuzzi the bubbles floating, massaging her back with warm spurts of scented water. Ram had picked the perfect spot of indulgence for their anniversary. Making such a wonderful gesture was so out of character for him. Was he changing at last, was he becoming sensitive after years of her trying to instil some romance into their marriage? She wondered as she luxuriated in the warmth.

Later at the delicious dinner, she asked him. 'When did you plan all this? It's fantastic.'

'Oh, I didn't. It was Uma's idea. She got it all booked,' he said sheepishly.

She was crestfallen for a moment, and then she checked herself.

'It's great anyway, an anniversary I'll never forget.'

It was a romantic night that she made a special effort for, determined to make it an evening to treasure. The champagne helped. She chatted away happily, even if Ram' answers were in monosyllables at times. Back in the room, Ram switched the TV on as they got ready for bed. The success of the Scottish Parliament's referendum results were blaring. The newscaster's excitement was evident. 78% of the Scots have voted yes, 'Scotland is on its way to its own Parliament after three hundred years,' he declared. Ram rubbed his hands. A smile lit up his face. The Scottish Parliament was a reality now. A future Independent Scotland was edging ever so close, he thought.

*

164

Glasgow revealed a newfound confidence. The city becoming the European city of culture had made a huge change. Blonde or red sandstone buildings hidden under layers of century old soot, when cleaned unwrapped like a butterfly winging itself out of a cocoon of darkness into graceful beauty. Sita marvelled at the work in the galleries.

'By the way, Ram, Jyoti and family are coming over soon. It will be lovely to see her after all these years.' Sita was excited and happy that her friend was coming to visit them.

'Good, I can try some of these recipes then.' Ram was looking at the new book by Madhur Jaffrey which accompanied the BBC programmes.

'You're not on call are you? We must show them as much of Scotland as we can. It's a once in a life time trip for them.'

Jyoti, Suresh and the two youngsters arrived in the spring, the summer holidays in Madras for them. Glasgow was at its best this spring. The spring flowers were in bloom, the emerald green of the lush lawns and the amethyst and diamonds of the narcissi vied for attention. The golden daffodils were in abundance on all the verges. The green foliage of the trees and shrubs glistened as they thrust against the blue skies. Even when it rained, their guests appreciated it as a welcome relief.

'Just to get away from the 'agni nakakshatram', the hottest period in April is such a relief,' said Jyoti, no longer the slender friend that Sita used to know. She had the mumsy figure, fuller, like most Indian middle-aged mums. They sat in the bedroom, and Sita watched Jyoti brush her hair and pin it up in a neat chignon.

'I see that you've cut your hair short. Suits you' said Jyoti and turned around from the dressing table mirror to face Sita, 'and you have maintained your figure. I'm envious.'

'I find it easier to manage the hair short.' Sita patted her hair.

'Can't twist the end of your plait like you used to,' giggled Jyoti. They both laughed.

'Uma is a lovely young girl,' Jyoti continued.

'Thanks. She has given us both such a focus. Ram is a wonderful dad.'

'So the cold war is over, no more hankering after a Mills and Boon type of hero?' Jyoti's mischievous eyes were dancing with mirth.

'Don't be daft. I'm happy.' Sita gave her a hug.

They sat up as loud techno music assailed their ears.

'Uma, turn that racket down!' Sita shouted. They looked at each other and said at the same time.

'We do sound like our mums, don't we?' and laughed again.

The two weeks ended all too soon. Sita helped Jyoti pack for the trip home. It was emotional. Sita got the case out from the attic, dusted it, and cleaned it inside out. How did dust get into the case when it has been locked and put away? The labels from the last flight were stuck on the front. She pulled them off and wiped the glue off them. The cases had to be packed meticulously. Twenty-three kilos and not a kilo more. The airlines were always strict about this rule.

Jyoti had piles of clothing stacked neatly on the top of her bed. She asked for and lined the cases with a thin polythene sheet, just as a protection for the soft-sided cases. The monsoon downpour in Mumbai could ruin the clothes. The petticoats went in first, black, white, red then a couple of other shades. Saris with their matching blouses, the silk ones neatly covered in their little muslin bags came next. Underwear, nighties and all the toiletries were stuffed into little corners. They had gone overboard and bought too many gifts for the family. So difficult to find things that people wanted, expensive, and often too heavy to carry. The shirts, some toys and electrical goods were in the case. Shortbread, chocolates, medicines went in the hand luggage. The books, the books that were so much liked were always a problem. Too heavy to carry, she had to leave some with Sita.

'I'll just buy what is available at the airport.' Jyoti's disappointment showed up in her voice.

The suitcase contained diabetic strips and a glucose meter for Suresh. Just forty years old and he had a chronic disease that affected his lifestyle completely. Sita touched the packets thinking of the young family. Packing over, they joined the others in the lounge, the last evening before they left.

166

'I wondered if Glasgow would be all doom and gloom, dark, cold, damp, but we've had a great time.' Jyoti sipped her glass of wine.

'Well, I'm glad you came now. Glasgow has changed beyond recognition. The urban regeneration during the European Year of Culture has been a roaring success.' Ram was waxing eloquent.

'I agree,' Sita concurred. 'The buildings are so clean. I'm glad you came. We wouldn't have seen the beauty of the city. You know what it's like when you live in the place.'

Sita had looked at the Victorian sandstone buildings as they had gone round the city with new eyes. The rain had washed it. The beauty had taken her breath away. She wondered about the lives of the people who would have lived there hundreds of years ago in the grand buildings. It must have been an upstairs downstairs world of servants and the rich. She had felt a thrill at the beauty of it all and a deep sense of pride. She had said to Jyoti, 'this is my home now, I just realised that we have lived here longer than in Madras.'

'So Scotophil, which was the best part of this trip?' Suresh asked Jyoti.

'Obviously just being with Sita and family.' Jyoti gave a warm smile.

'That's understood...'

'Mum, tell us, the Burrell, the People's Palace, Rabbie Burns's cottage in Alloway?' Vivek butted in, listing all the places. 'I loved the Electric brae. That was awesome. The car went up the way when it should have been rolling down.'

'Just an optical illusion,' said Suresh leaning his ample body back on the red sofa.

'It was real to me,' said young Vivek. His eyes were back on the hand held Nintendo game. 'And I loved the motorways, the speed, the cars, many models that we don't see in India.'

'Motorways? That's strange,' said Sita. He did not answer, was engrossed in his game.

'The Burrell, surely,' said Ram.

'No, actually, I preferred the People's Palace. That display of Wright's Coal Tar, Pears soap, the Bakelite radio, Vim, took me back to mum's time,' said Jyoti. 'I also enjoyed the ceilidh. That was fun, trying to dance to all the Scottish tunes.'

'You've collected enough stuff for your hobby I hope. I can't afford another trip,' Suresh teased Jyoti.

'Of course I have. Thanks for a great silver wedding anniversary present,' she whispered, her eyes glowing as she looked at Suresh.

'Silver Wedding! How did I forget?' Sita's eyebrows lifted up a fraction.

'We're all getting middle-aged now,' said Suresh looking for some more cashews in the little dish by his side.

'Yours won't be far behind. Two or three more years?' Jyoti asked Sita.

*

'Things could only get better' the New Labour Party song rang in her ears often. There was a feel of freshness, that anything could be achieved. Uma was growing up. She would leave the nest soon. She had turned out to be a bright young girl following their footsteps by becoming a medical student. The years had flown in quickly. She moved over to the kitchen. She cut the okra that Ram had brought from the Indian shop. She washed and dried each one carefully. Topped and tailed them. Holding a bunch of three, she chopped them into tiny perfect rounds. The sticky resin oozed out. She wiped it with a kitchen tissue and continued with the rest. She heated the wok and added a bit of oil and as soon as it was hot she put in a teaspoon full of mustard seeds. The seeds spluttered, and then she added a spoonful of urad dhal adding a few curry leaves and finally the okra. She turned the heat down letting them fry slowly in the pan till they turned up crisp, just the way Ram liked them. She was still a bit hesitant about cooking the karela, the green spotty, ridged gourd which contained a bitter taste that was hard to like. She left it and moved onto other dishes she felt confident enough to make.

On Radio Four Scotland, the newscaster explained the process of the referendum on devolution and traced its sorry history, from when it was introduced the first time in 1979, Sita remembered as Uma had just started school that year. The 40% rule he described in detail. The Scottish

168

electorate found the process so difficult to understand. Sita took more of an interest now than when the event actually had taken place.

She continued making the rest of the meal of plain rice, sambar and a raita. How much of Ram had she absorbed into her own life? Cooking, she now realised was therapeutic. They had grown together. In a few months she was going to be forty. She shuddered. Forty- only a number maybe, but she still felt like a twenty year old. She called Ram and Uma for their dinner. Ram was still busy with the newspaper. Uma came down the stairs. She had something on her mind.

'Mum, I'm moving to student digs and that's final.' Her steely voice said it all.

'Uma, that's madness. Dad drives you down everyday. He won't be happy.'

'That's his problem.'

'Uma!'

'Mum I need to use the library all the time and I want some independence. Surely you can see that. I've done it for four years, that's enough.' Uma tossed her head defiantly, looking straight at her mum.

'Your friend Padma managed okay. Why can't you? And it's your final year'

'I'm not Padma okay?' She stood her ground.

*

The excitement of being in her own flat was sweet. Uma relished it. It was a perfect compromise. She could go home when she felt like it, needed the bed linen washed or needed a bit of home cooking.

Sita had to get used to the empty nest syndrome. She was glad of her career. She wondered if she should take up a full time job now. Yet, now she could indulge in her love of books and maybe even get Ram to travel with her. Sita started planning too. They joined the rambler's local group and enjoyed the shorter walks at the weekends. Ram and she grew closer doing things together.

*

Lata and Sita had a quiet afternoon.

'Did you hear the Varma's have had a new baby girl?' Lata said.

'Don't tell me and they have named her V …something,' giggled Sita.

'You are dead right. They are calling her Vandhana. All four of them. The V family and you know what is so funny we Indians find that letter of the alphabet quite hard to pronounce. It often becomes a W. It will become   Wiwek Warma, Warsha, Warun and Wandhana'

'True, but have you noticed how the French accent and mistakes are considered sweet? 'Zee's so deeficult' by a French guy is cute, but an Indian accent is considered too primitive. 'These Pakis never learn it right, do they?' is often flung at us.'

'Did you hear that the Home Secretary is introducing English lessons for citizenship to help the immigrants integrate? That's a laugh. I wonder how many of the 500,000 Brits in France or Spain learn the lingo to integrate when they buy properties, and move up there.'

'Have you seen the 'A Place is the Sun', TV programme? I wet myself laughing. This couple had sold everything in Glasgow to settle in Spain. They wanted to go up the hills, not near the place where there were all these Brits. They claimed they wanted the true Spanish idyll. The programme showed them miserable, wondering why they were unhappy and wanting to get back! When the presenter asked them why, they said that the locals made no effort or concessions that they could not speak the language. Had they attempted to learn it? No, they said. It was too bloomin' hard! They felt too isolated. What did they expect?'

'I love the way the Brits see everything from a narrow euro perspective. The French frogs are lovely, tinged with jealousy at their rich heritage, the Italians – only ice-cream, fast cars and the fashion is good. The Spanish? Well, they were good for providing a tourist paradise for a holiday. They don't really matter. Of course, don't even mention the Germans. The smaller western European countries are tolerated but only just. The Scandinavians are looked up to. They are blonde and blue eyed, their physical traits to be aspired to, but they are too few so they don't

170

matter either. The rest of Europe, Greece, Eastern Europe are unimportant as they are all considered inferior.'

'Two hundred years stay in our subcontinent was only to plunder the riches, but there was no connection with the people at all. They did little to integrate then but expect the incoming migrants to transform themselves immediately. Remember the Madras Museum still has photos of the British troops in their woollen uniforms. How many died from heat strokes until they adapted and wore topis and safari suits. The Gymkhana clubs in some major cities in India retain their Sunday lunches, roast beef and Yorkshire pudding. It's funny to see the old retainers from the Raj, look down their noses if you pick the wrong glass or place the fork and knife the wrong way.'

'Of course we have now colonised them with our food. The chicken tikka masala beat fish and chips as the national dish is proof enough.'

'So much for integration, eh! Curry in every home, school and in every supermarket?'

'We sound worse than the locals now! Enough of the racist gripe. Let's get on with the serious bit of gossip. So is it true that lesbianism is the in thing in London amongst the Asians? God help us, at least Scotland lags behind in all this kind of lewd behaviour. Kids seem to be worse in the South.'

'Don't tell me you've suddenly turned homophobic now?'

They both laughed aloud as they realised that they had started to sound like aunty BB.

Chapter 20

Sita and Ram attended Namita's wedding. Namita, the bride looked gorgeous; the dull gold work on the pale ivory dress looked beautiful. The dress was a superb blend of eastern and western fashion. David the groom was looking nervous and handsome in his Nehru suit. They made a lovely couple. The wedding theme had all the Indian, Scots and Irish bits to it. Irish to show David's family roots. The little cakes on each of the tables had been decorated with tiny Scots, Indian and Irish flags. After the 'Pundit', the priest had finished his rituals and the bride and groom had exchanged their vows in Sanskrit then David and Namita exchanged their rings.

The evening reception was fun with chart music interspersed with bhangra music. Namita's friends Jodie and Gemma had come dressed in Bollywood style dresses. The whole atmosphere was one of a meeting of minds, cultures and genuine happiness. 'This is the new Scotland,' Uma thought to herself.

The aunties were gossiping as usual, liberal tongues but the narrowest of mind. Sita paid little attention to them. Still she could not miss their loud comments on the dresses that the girls were wearing. The strappy dresses were too much for the oldies. Some were wishing that they had such good figures and had the nerve to wear the stylish dresses instead of the heavy silk saris. They sighed with envy as they fed their ever-spreading love handles more sweets, helping the expansion of their girth.

'No modesty no, showing everything. Arre, arre, why dress like goras?' BB's voice reigned supreme.

'These Bollywood designers are disgusting. They are now spoiling our traditional dresses. It's not just the midriff, now the whole of the top is on show. Leaves little to the imagination,' agreed Reena, fingering her new jewellery set that BB had yet to notice.

'I blame the mums, no control of girls, bad, very bad,' BB shook her head in despair. It was a lost cause. The young girls seemed not to care and gyrated to the music, oblivious to her catty remarks.

Her beady eyes now fell on Reena's glittering gold set.

'Now where you buy this? How much you pay, tell me?' Reena was pleased. She recounted the purchase in detail. the weight of the 22 carat set and described the intricacies of the filigree work, how she had to get the matching earrings and bangles.

'But how much you pay?' BB needed the important information.

'Three hundred pounds only. He gave me a good discount,' Reena's pride was short lived.

'Chor, Chor, that thief, he charge too much. I get you cheaper.' BB explained that her jeweller would give her a much better bargain. Her eyes moved back to the young ones dancing. She did not want to miss any untoward behaviour that she could swoop on. She trooped along to the ladies, to watch the make up rituals of the young.

Uma had managed to avoid aunty BB all morning as BB was busy with the rituals and dominating the proceedings in her usual style. It was the evening reception that was her gossip-collecting time and Uma was not lucky this time. She was just coming out of the ladies when Aunty BB cornered her to get the latest news. BB wanted a personal bit of news.

'Uma dear, a wedding always make me so emotionful.' She touched her heart. 'Now tell me all. What you doing, any plans to get married?'

'I'm fine aunty.' Uma looked around for an excuse to leave her side.

'Why, you looking away? No want to talk to old aunty? So long time no, we not see each other? I like speak to you. I remember you as little girl.'

'Yes aunty, I'm busy working now. How is Kulvinder?'

BB's eyes misted over, 'I no see her ever nowadays. She gone. London.'

Uma knew this was dangerous territory; she was so relieved when aunty Reena interrupted them to say that the DJ wanted to play a special old

173

Indian hymn tune just for BB and would she be kind enough to come over and bless the couple. Uma ran over to the young girls' side some 'eyeing up the talent' and others like her young married friends enjoying the music and having a drink. Uma danced with some of the girls and had a fun time, enjoying the music, both the chart toppers and Bhangra tunes.

Alice and Nihar had come to the wedding from London. Their son Alan, now a teenager was with them. 'Alan, hey you're taller than me. What are you studying now?' asked Uma and gave him a big hug. She remembered him as a baby.

'Doing my A levels this year, a lot of pressure, I want to be a media hack,' he replied. Uma spent a lot of time chatting to them at the wedding. Their daughter Bina and Uma had been at University together. Bina was working at a teaching hospital in England and Uma wanted to hear all about her. Bina was doing neonatology and they had a lot in common. Uma had a good time reminiscing about the university days. She was listening to Alan's new interest in hip hop music when they were rudely interrupted; Mr. Raj Singh came over and asked Alan right out of the blue, 'How do see yourself Alan, an Indian, an Irish (his mum Alice was from Ireland) or an English guy, now that you live in London?' Alan said without batting an eyelid, 'I regard myself as a human being. Nothing more'. That phrase that the seventeen year old Alan used stood out for Uma. What a simple way of rounding up all this labelling and putting people into little compartments of race, colour, religion or any other factor!

*

Sita and Ram's return from India came at a hectic time for them. The enormous changes at the surgery with the new computer systems, the constant directives from the new Labour government made their working lives more stressful. The new healthy eating drive involved the G.P practices. Sita was aware of the fact that the Asians were five times more likely to suffer from heart disease than the host population. She approached BB to ask for the Mandir as a place where such information be relayed to the people.

The ladies were meeting to discuss the preparations for introducing a 'Health Week' promotion at the Mandir in a month's time. BB had

174

suggested having tea first to give everyone time to arrive and settle down for business. As usual, she had hijacked the event for her own purposes.

'The engagement is off? What both girls still not married? Oh, dear! What a terrible thing to happen! Meena must be desperate now.' Reena's eyes lit up with this news, almost as if she had woken up from a dream. She now listened with interest. BB's last half hour had been the most boring diatribe on her ailments. Diabetes, blood pressure, colds all had to be described in detail. The medications for each one and the side effects had also to be entertained. Reena was about to take leave when BB came up with the juicy bits. This was more interesting. BB relished spreading the gossip. Sita and Lata continued sipping their tea. 'Poor Meena! When did you see her? I've tried so hard to phone and talk to her but she seems to shy away from our groups,' Lata added.

'Well can you blame her? It's not easy when you have two well qualified girls, not willing to settle down.'

'How old are they? Once a girl passes her thirtieth birthday, that's it. She is left on the shelf for life.'

'I think both are past thirty. The older one was at nursery with my Sarla so she must be thirty-two and the younger one was only 18 months younger.' Reena calculated, her brows knitted in concentration.

'You know this is becoming a big problem for our families. How do you convince our girls that they need to listen to their parents? When we choose the boys for them, they refuse point blank. There are fewer of our Indian boys and some seem quite happy to go back home and get a 'virgin bride.' Look at Meena's own boy, did he not go home and get that beautiful girl? They seem quite happy too.'

'Have you forgotten, Ashish your son, Reena? You made sure he got a 'virgin bride', from India. 'How is the little poppet, Tina, your granddaughter?'

'She's gorgeous, crawling already. By the way, are you coming to the 'rummy' evening next week?'

'Never miss it.'

Reena and BB spent some time analysing the problem of Asian girls and their inability to settle down. Tea and jalebis made the gossip even tastier. As soon as Rita the latecomer arrived, they finished their tea session. BB was so pleased her own girl was 'well-settled' in London, at least in the eyes of the Asian community. She was not going to reveal her daughter's problem to all and sundry. That was a well-kept secret and she made sure it remained so.

The programme for the Healthy Week was discussed. Sita suggested that the local Health Board would be willing to bring specialists such as a dietician, perhaps some consultant specialists in heart disease, nephrologists would be asked to contribute short talks to explain the health problems in simple terms and preventative steps that could be taken. There were some worries about getting a dietician who would have in-depth knowledge of the Asian diet especially the vegetarian one. They pencilled in the duties for each of the members to carry out and left the temple.

Sita drove home with Lata.

'They will desire to utter many words, who do not know how to speak a few faultless ones.'

Lata said them out aloud. 'Remember this from the Thirukurral?' she asked Sita.

'Why are you quoting Tamil scriptures now, given up Sanskrit have you?' Sita's eyes were on the road, the sniffling rain made it hard to keep the windscreen wiper on. She had to keep turning it on and off. It annoyed her.

'Her venom never stops does it?' said Lata

'Who? BB?' asked Sita.

Lata nodded.

'She has nothing else to do with her life I suppose. As long as it is harmless and people are not hurt,' said Sita.

'But why don't people tell her to shut up? I feel like doing it myself. It's so malicious, uncalled for. If only people knew of Kulvinder.' Lata grimaced. Her thin shoulders heaved.

'I know, but why spoil the child's life? Being a lesbian is not something the girl can help. Live and let live, I say,' said Sita.

'I know. It's just that BB has been getting away with her awful behaviour now for years, no one challenges her. She's going to ruin someone's life with her stupid tongue wagging.'

'Have you noticed that Reena is becoming her clone now?' said Sita.

'I know, but we need to do something about BB. I can't understand her vicious mind at all.' Lata shrugged in despair.

'You can't change people's habits can you?' asked Sita, driving carefully.

They stopped on the way to get some Indian groceries from the Indian shop at Woodlands Road. Back home, BB called. Sita took the receiver reluctantly from Ram. She thought of the questions that would pour out. Now it was BB's constant worry about the menopause.

'Why so hot me all the time?'

'Why my temper goes up down?'

'I sleep very so little. Give some tablets no?'

BB's demands were tiresome. She steeled herself, and greeted her politely.

'Hello Balvinder, how are you?'

'Sita, I no need you anymore.'

'Oh?' Sita was smiling but sounded concerned.

'I now have a Punjabi lady doctor. She talk same like me so…'

'Balvinder, that's so good, have you registered with her then?'

'No, No you still my doctor. She help even if I no go to surgery.'

'That's good Balvinder, but you must get registered for house calls. I'll talk to Margaret at the surgery tomorrow.'

'No worry. She just see me just like that. I'll still see you at temple no?'

'Of course Balvinder. You are also most welcome to come over any time to our house.'

'Yes, Yes, but I come also to potluck supper, no?'

'Sure you're more than welcome.'

Sita put the phone down, relieved. Maybe BB would feel happier with the new young doctor who could talk to her in Punjabi, she thought and hoped that she would not be harangued by her phone calls again. It was still very strange that BB chose to keep her as a doctor and have another Punjabi doctor to help her.

Chapter 21

The Friday night madness continued at the Accident and Emergency. Uma was doing a locum to help cover for a friend. She had forgotten how crazy a Friday night could get in the A&E in Glasgow. The usual run of stab wounds, drunk and drug cases were all being dealt with. She was run off her feet. Ewan Mc McLeod, her old flatmate, was wheeled in. He was in pain, but on seeing her, he gave a sheepish grin. She did not recognise him for a minute. It was such a long time since she had laid eyes on him.

'What's wrong then?' She asked in a kindly voice.

'I was installing a new power shower in my flat when the drill slipped and fell on my foot,' explained Ewan. The wound was deep, needed a few stitches. They got talking and he told her that he would soon be in charge of the IT Company that was contracted to her hospital. She asked after Lucy and they laughed at the memory of the awful student digs that they had shared. She had to rush off to another case but she took his phone number as her computer was playing up and she could do with some advice from someone she knew. He took her number too.

He called her a week later and the computer problem was not the only thing he helped her with. She found to her surprise that geeky, nerdy Ewan was pleasant, nice to talk to, clever, witty in an unassuming way deeply interested in philosophy and comparative religion. The friendship developed slowly. She enjoyed discussing and arguing with his views. It was a change from medicine and nice to relax with someone so patient and quietly determined to argue his point of view with absolute conviction.

She got to know him better when he introduced her to hiking- his passion. She had done her Duke of Edinburgh gold badge at Glasgow High, had hated the fifty-kilometre walk so much as she had not prepared for it in any way. The miserable weather, the cold, carrying twenty-kilogram backpack had spoilt it all. The bitchiness of her schoolmates was something she wanted to forget, but this was completely different. Going on a few mile hikes, walking on the Campsie brought a great sense of the outdoors and got all the endorphins going. The gym was good for the body but the outdoors touched her soul.

The friendship slowly turned into a deep love, Uma felt she could rely on him totally. He was caring, considerate, always wanting to be with her. He encouraged her career ambitions and the days with him were idyllic. She did notice that he was focussed on her totally. She loved the idea of someone who cared for her deeply. She needed constant reassurance of his love for her and he gave her that without any question.

They decided on a quiet engagement and wanted to marry as soon as possible. With everyone's work commitments, the earliest date that was suitable to all, was three months away. They bought a house and on Ewan's insistence, Uma reluctantly agreed and they moved in together. The Asian community was horrified that the young couple were 'living in sin.' Parma and her mum tried to reason with Uma. 'Waiting three months is not long if you both love each other,' but Uma was totally smitten. Stubborn as usual, she went ahead with Ewan's idea. The disapproval from all the community was palpable. Even their close friends made comments that showed their anxiety in confronting change. The traditional way was always more familiar and easier to cope with. The potluck supper members were obsessed with what they perceived as a new threat to their culture. Their children were not only 'coconuts', brown outside and white inside, as it was pointed out, but were now marrying into the host community.

'Mixed marriages don't work.' Reena was clear and equivocal about her view on this.

'How can you make such a sweeping statement?' Prasad was incensed. 'Some times we mouth things without understanding at all.' His jowls shook and he vented his fury by banging the marble coaster on the table. Ram moved quickly to rescue his good crystal glass from getting too close to the offending coaster.

'There are enough problems in marriage even when you marry within our own culture. Surely they'll face even more, 'added Reena.

'What about when they have children. Maybe they'll be confused about their heritage.' Ron joined in.

180

'It'll never work,' said BB emphatically. 'Too different, no same anything. Why our children go off like this? All parents too soft, that's why.'

'I think the local boys marry our girls hoping for fidelity, a person who is more pliant, not a feminist and ambitious career type,' said Reena again.

'I agree,' said Ron again. 'There are a lot of men going to the Far East to get young wives who do to their bidding.'

Prasad face reddened. He angrily shouted over.

'You have all such small minds! Why believe the sensational trash that you read in the newspapers.' He glared at Ron. Ram steered him quickly out of the room, 'Let's cool down Prasad,' he said taking him out of the room. They sat in the conservatory, drinking quietly.

'Uma and Ewan are very happy you know,' Sita said gently to those in the room.

'Some mixed marriages do work really well,' added Lata in support.

BB did not like to be challenged in any way. She moved onto admiring the new necklace that Reena was wearing.

'You bought from same jeweller? What you pay this time? He's chor, too costly. I get you better price,' she said. The supper ended, some happy to discuss issues, others with their entrenched positions never to be changed at all.

Chapter 22

Glasgow Late 1990s

That one meeting with Neil had transformed her life. Sita came home from the surgery oblivious to the grey skies. The whole world was shining bright. The rosewood furniture gleamed, the kitchen was sparkling, Mrs.Chalmers the cleaner, had given it a thorough going over. She was a stickler, one of the old school of cleaning, the skirting boards, and the windows given a shine without Sita ever having to say anything. Humming a tune, Sita placed the flowers she had treated herself to in the vase.

For the first time in many years, she started dressing with care, subtle changes, choosing younger styles, a softer hairstyle, and new shades of make up. Uma noticed straight away.

'Mum, you look fantastic, I'm glad you're not letting yourself go. Forty is the new thirty. Good on you, mum.' Uma was happy for her.

'Dad, don't you think mum looks great?'

'She always does,' said Ram, a bit embarrassed.

'Dad, you never notice, do you?' Uma teased him.

'Uma, stop making a big deal of it,' said Sita, flicking her hair.

It was the little things. Working in the same room brought Neil and Sita together. It was unavoidable, flame and cotton as her grandma used to say about attraction. Brushing hands as they handed patient notes to each other, leaning over her desk when he asked her about a patient, sitting beside each other at staff meetings or drug company presentations. There were many opportunities. Sharing the coffee break, gave her little glimpses of his life. His crazy humour with the one-liners, wry, self-deprecating, made her smile. Neil's daft wee notes on patients that he left at her table made her laugh aloud. Their first meeting when they had discussed their 'odd' patients became their own little private joke. Innocuous and yet the underlying need to communicate with each other,

182

he would ask her teasing question, 'Guess who was referred to the VID, the Verbal Incontinence department?' Then, he would answer it himself, 'Yes, you've guessed right, it was Mr. Know it all.' Looking very busy and important he would enter the room, discuss a patient's notes and often they would both end up convulsed with laughter. Work was now exciting, the place she wanted to be all the time. She got all the news about Neil. The receptionists' gossip at the tea breaks was useful this time.

'He's moved down from Aberdeen, Pat, his wife, left him, too much heartache because they could not have children,' Margaret the secretary mentioned as she sipped her coffee.

'How do you know so much Margaret?' Sita asked. 'I mean such personal details.'

'Well, you know my mum still lives in Aberdeen. Pat's mum and my mum go to the same church. It's a small world, isn't it?' said Margaret with a twinkle in her eye.

'Wow, he's quite a dish,' Julie the other receptionist lowered her voice and twiddled with the reading glasses lying on her ample bosom

'Leave him. He's all mine' Margaret laughed as she brushed back her grey hair.

'Don't you think he's gorgeous, Sita?' Julie glanced over. Sita spilled her tea, but recovered and nodded, 'Yes, I suppose so.' She tried hard not too look interested but she was desperate to find out more. Was he still married, divorced? The questions raced through her mind.

As if on cue Margaret continued.

'He's free, divorced. I can have him. He's a good catch.'

'He can be my toy boy any day,' added Julie They started laughing out loudly.

'Hey, what's the joke?' Neil walked in and helped himself to a coffee.

Margaret teased him. 'Right, you need to choose now. Who would you have Julie or me? We both fancy you.'

'What do you mean?' Neil looked embarrassed. He glanced over at Sita. She blushed and looked away.

'Just joking. Don't need to look so shocked,' said Margaret. Neil smiled.

Sita got up to wash her cup. Neil's eyes followed her. She could feel them.

She found him easy to talk to about anything at all. His passion for hiking, his love of rugby, and his love of books, the interest in fiction was one that bonded them straight away. Sita had joined the book club at Brookwood Library. The monthly meetings helped in her love of books, but they were set books. Deconstructing them, arguing the structure, the prose, the style was good, but she wanted to read books of her own choice and talk about them share a beautiful line or a scene that appealed to her.

She missed Eileen, their shopping forays for books and the coffee mornings when they had long chats about the books that they had read. Eileen had become busy with her own life. Their meetings were often hurried ones. Between picking up Eileen's kids and pandering to her mother-in-law's health problems, she had little time for Sita. They had phone conversations and had the old 'blether' as Eileen put it, but discussing fiction was rare. Lata was wonderful but her interest was confined to an in-depth study of the Indian epics and her love of Sanskrit was something that Sita could not share to the same extent.

'No, no too tragic, should not read that one,' Neil joked as she put her book down.

'Why ever not?' Sita looked serious.

'Kills herself for a true love that she never finds. Maybe there is no such thing as true love.' Neil winked. The kettle boiled noisily. Julie made the tea as Neil put out their mugs.

Margaret and Julie both sighed.

'Aye, you're right there, Neil. Where is he, my true love? I'm still waiting, nearly sixty and no sign of him yet,' Margaret giggled.

'I think its one of the best books I've ever read. Emma's character is so well written.' Sita looked even more serious. The last chapter always made her tense, yet she loved every part of the book. However many times she read it, she felt it affected her deeply.

'I was only teasing. It's a long time since I've read it. Maybe I should have a go again.' Neil's voice was a bit more placatory.

'I'll lend you my copy if you want. I'm almost at the last chapter,' said Sita, flicking her hair, conscious of Neil's eyes on her.

'See you two, don't you read any new ones? Why go over an old book again?' Margaret laughed. 'Life's too short and there are lots of great new ones to read.'

'I prefer my magazines any day. 'People's Friend,' now you can't go wrong there. Every story ends happily ever after. I love it, gentle, talks about the good old days. It makes me feel so much better. Give me that any day,' said Julie.

Both Neil and Sita nodded and smiled at her and at each other.

It was her old favourite 'Madame Bovary', which brought Neil and Sita together. The simmering feeling of love and lust overpowered them, but both trod the paths very cautiously. They got closer. Discussing books, talking about the patients, were opportunities that brought them together. They did not need to seek or be surreptitious about it. The relationship moved on from one of a colleague to one of a close friendship. Margaret, the secretary commented on it in a jocular fashion to Sita, 'Leave my toy boy alone, I want him all to myself.'

'I see that you've seduced my aunt too,' said Neil to Sita when they were on their own.

'Your aunt? I don't know anyone related to you.' Sita was surprised.

'Mary, Mary Armitage. I believe you know her.'

Sita remembered meeting her at the bookshop

'She would like to meet you.'

'Meet me! Why?'

'I was just teasing you.' Neil brought out a Sanskrit book from his briefcase that she had given him for Sita.

They heard the familiar voice of BB coming from the reception. BB was arguing. Julie had put on her receptionist visage, a stoic look and asked her, 'Who's your appointment with Mrs.Bhal?'

'No, no appointment, I see Sita now.'

'Sorry, Dr. Iyer is with a patient. I'll give you an appointment for next week.'

'No, I see her today. Oh, Raj, beta, you work here?' BB hobbled over to the young trainee doctor. Julie was not pleased.

'Hello aunty, I'm doing my six months training here.'

'Good, you see me now.'

'Sorry Mrs.Bhal, Dr. Sharma has other patients now,' Julie butted in. 'If you could take a seat please. I'll tell Dr. Iyer that you are here. Maybe she would see you at her tea break.'

All the efforts of the staff at the surgery to stop BB coming often and without an appointment were of no avail.

Sita and Neil engrossed in conversation walked into the reception to collect the patient's folders. BB sprang up from her seat and hobbled over quickly to Sita.

'You see me now. Oh! Such pain, my knee.' Her eyes were measuring Neil at her side. Sita moved a few inches away from him as BB shook her head in disapproval. The tight set of her lips was discernable.

'You need to wait a bit Balvinder. Patients with appointments first. I'll see you at my break.' Sita smiled to placate her. Neil winked at Sita. His face relayed the words without saying it, and 'this is one of our hypochondriacs.' BB did not miss the wink. Sita watched her eyes widen and knew that she made a mental note of the scene.

BB, the bane of Sita's life, was someone she could not avoid.

'I help you lot many, many years ago. I always care for you. You treat old BB now.'

186

Every time she spoke to her, BB reminded Sita of her first time at the mandir, the centre of the Hindu community. BB's frequent visits to the surgery and her nosiness unsettled Sita. There was bitterness to the old woman since her daughter left for London. Her gossip took on a more sinister edge. Sita wondered if BB wanted to pass on her hurt to someone else. Her way of coping had taken a turn for the worse since her onset of menopause. The mood swings and depression now made her reckless to the harm she was doing to the victims of her vicious tongue.

Sita drove home, feeling the stress of BB's visit slowly making her panic. The metallic silver hugged the road. The black tarmac slithered dark in the rain. The windscreen wiper whooshed on high speed, the scenes of the motorway verges, raced by. Nothing registered, the sound of the droplets on the windscreen making its strange patterns comforting, yet scary in their own way. The drive offered an exhilarating freedom. Freedom to think as one wanted, have a sense of gay abandon. She listened to the music on the car radio. Cocooned in the metal box warmth, she felt nothing could touch her. It was a safe and private place, a haven at dark times. The endless stretch of road, made no demands, a straight path to race, or set one's own pace, to gaze at the views that whizzed past the windows of the car.

Sita dreaded going back home, when she left after the innocent coffee that she had had with Neil. Ram would be back later in the day and she did not relish the guilt that was swelling up like a tidal wave in her. The constant guilt made her tired and depressed. She did not have time to think of a way out of it. She needed 'me' time, the last thing she could find in her hectic life.

Her mind seething with too many conflicting thoughts, the car, almost a weapon, she had stepped on the accelerator. Glancing at the speedometer doing maximum 70 mph was the last thing she remembered. As she headed towards the merging motorway she recognised the slight curve of the road, then everything happened in a flash. She was lying upside down, still held back by the seat belt. She had hit the crash barriers. She undid the belt and slowly eased herself out of the driver's window. The glass had shattered completely, giving her a way out. It was a miracle. She was in one piece. The car was a write off.

'Are you all right'? People from the cars behind came rushing over to help. One of them dialled 999 and before she knew the emergency services had swung into action. The little cut on her shoulder was cleaned. The paramedics wanted her to have a check over at the hospital.

'No I'm a doctor, I am fine, and I don't need to go to the hospital. Yes, I'll sign the form,' she added. The traffic police took her home. She called Ram and explained. There was not even a whiplash injury though she felt her neck sore for a few days.

'A miracle! No doubt, someone is watching over you.' Everyone's words echoed the same relieved and surprised reaction.

Ram was wonderful, loving, pampering her. He persuaded her to drive as soon as she was well again. She was not happy to get back in the car and she was grateful for his gentle persuasion.

They both realised how much they loved and needed each other. The whole tension in their relationship shifted. 'Why does it have to be such a traumatic event to bring us back to our senses'? thought Sita. 'I am going to be more patient and work harder at the relationship. If only he could change a little bit.'

She booked a holiday just for the two of them. Ram was surprised but wanted to help her get over the trauma of the car accident. It was a weekend away at Pitlochry, the gateway to the Highlands. Things could not have been better. They were happy together again.

The fresh air, the long walks made her relax. Her silly crush on Neil as she thought of it was still in the background but she pulled herself out of such thoughts.

Chapter 23

'A journey to find himself,' thought Neil. The week had been a confusing mess. Thoughts of his life with Pat had come crowding in. He could not believe his passion for Sita was overwhelming and taking over his life. He looked around the room. The slight whiff of disinfectant, the patient records piled high on his table stared back at him. He could not concentrate. The paperwork could wait. Emotions played havoc with his life. Pat and he, how could it end so suddenly?

Life was messy. How does one cope with a broken heart? He walked along the beach the cold wind almost comforting his wounded heart. The grey coastline of Aberdeen, the harsh stony beach, the pebbles that he stepped on were like a reminder of their life together. How could such a deep love turn to nothing? Pat had been his friend. She had helped him with his first job after medical college. They had worked together at their careers. Her nursing skills had been an asset to him as a young doctor. It was on this beach that they had planned a future together, a friendship that had slowly turned to love.

The blue of the border tile was what he remembered. Against the virgin white bathroom, the Greek design stood proud. Pat was sobbing her heart out. The pregnancy test tube lay on the floor. The thin strip of blue that she desperately wanted eluded her again. How many times had he comforted her? He tried to hold her. She jerked free, rushed to the bedroom and flung herself on the bed. The sobs he heard were almost inhuman, racking coming from deep within, the sound of her soul breaking into little pieces. This was her last try, her fifth attempt at the IVF treatment. The three embryos that had been inserted were no longer the dream babies that she had longed for. She clammed up. Neil could do nothing to comfort her. The emotional impasse was dreadful. She just upped and left.

She never came back. Each night he returned to an empty house. The tiny pebble that he had given her was lying on the bedside table, the pinkish veins on a grey stone made a strange pattern. He found no way of contacting her. He could not throw her things away. He boxed her things, all the things that had been part of their lives. He boxed their lives, sealed and left them in storage and moved on. He left the details with Pat's mum. He tried working all hours, heading towards a breakdown. He stopped the downward spiral. He had to cope.

His life with Pat for seven years had been whittled away by her obsession to have a baby. Though he wanted that equally, he had to come to terms with the fact that Pat's love for him had changed radically. Each attempt of theirs to have a baby that failed plunged her into deeper despair. Nothing he said or did mattered anymore. They had gone through all available options. Their relationship had turned sour and she had left. Neil had always believed that marriage was for life. He was bereft.

It was the last thing he expected. Love at first sight! How could he fall madly in love with a married woman? He told himself repeatedly it was love on the rebound. However the feelings were genuine. Each time he looked at Sita he wanted to take her in his arms, be with her always. He felt so alive with her, even if it was only for a few hours at work. Talking to her about patients or the boring health-board administration work still felt like stolen moments of pleasure. She had slowly opened up to him about Ram, his obsessive political activities that took a lot of his time. He was confused. He could never break up a marriage. Working with her each week made it so painful. They had become close, working together. His whole being wanted to express his love for her. How? When? He did not know the answers.

Sita behaved impeccably but he had noticed how she stole glances at him and how she scrupulously avoided being alone with him. Instinctively he knew she liked him, as lovers all over the world recognise the frisson that happens between two adults in love. After a lot of thought, he decided that he could not destroy a marriage. He would do nothing and remain just a good friend and colleague.

The morning surgery was busy. Neil lifted his head from the prescription pad and looked at the patient. He had not been concentrating as Mrs.McNally was recounting her usual problems. It was a routine check-up and a repeat prescription. His mind was distracted, every sinew straining wanting to be with Sita. The feeling was overpowering. He heard Mrs. McNally's brolly clattering on the floor and saw her removing her cardigan to get her blood pressure checked.

'Warned her doctor but she is so keen. Young ones these days! She wants to go for it.'

'Yes Mrs.McNally, let's see how the blood pressure is. 120 over 80. That's good. You are taking care then with your diet? Just continue with the medication. Anything else?'

'Doctor so can I ask Jodie to bring in her application?'

'Application?'

'For the job experience. The receptionist said I need to have a word with you.'
Neil felt quite foolish.

'Jodie?'

'Well its only for a couple of weeks work experience from the school. She's set her heart on nursing and the practice nurse here is willing if you approve.'

'Of course Mrs.Mcnally. I'll have a word with Janette the practice manager. I'll remind her about your granddaughter.'

'Oh thanks doctor I knew you'd agree…' She rattled on about Jodie as she put her cardigan back on and collected her umbrella.

'Bye'

Margaret came in with the mail and coffee.

'Neil, there's a conference in Perth next month. Dr. Forsyth said that you might be interested in it as it's on Rheumatology. Shall I book you in for it?'

'What dates are they on Margaret?'

'It's on the 13th and 14th of February.'

'Ok, go ahead and thanks for the coffee, I need it.'

191

'All of you work too hard.' Margaret smiled and added, 'Sita will also be attending the conference as she's doing research for the firm on rheumatology; you know, the one that's sponsoring the conference.'

Neil looked up sharply, 'Oh that's good I'll have good company then.' He tried to sound casual. All his good intentions and the decision that he had just made flew out the window. His heart raced as he thought of time that he could have with Sita alone. This would be his chance to open his heart out to her on Valentine's Day. He could not have planned it better. 'Stop being so soppy' he scolded himself. The cloud had lifted. All his self-doubts were away and a new determination came in. He must make his feelings known to her. If she turned him down, he would have to accept it, but he was not going to give up without even trying.

It was a week before the conference; One of the drug companies held a presentation evening. The drinks flowed freely. Sita was dancing with Neil when he planted a kiss on her cheek first which ended up a full-blown kiss on her lips. She kissed back, then pulled herself away, guilt spreading fast making her heart beat crazily. Then Neil blurted out his feelings for her. Sita was stunned. Elated yet fearful, she joked that it was the drinks talking. Neil did not allow her to shrug it away. They sat in the corner away from their colleagues. They talked for hours. Sita was hesitant, veering between wanting to agree with him, reciprocate and yet her marital vows were too sacred for her. Neil pressed her hand. They kissed again. She knew, she knew now. It felt right. It had happened the way she had always fantasised. Someone whom she felt was a soul mate, a person with a sense of humour, who needed her, wanted to be with her. Someone she could talk to for hours, share her love of reading. She had expected it since her very first meeting with Neil. Her skin tingled and she giggled nervously at the absurdity of it. She, at forty years of age, married and settled with Ram, after all these years had now found her soul mate.

The taxi brought her home. She was still in a daze. In a few hours, her life had changed from one of simmering, doubting love to one where she had to make a choice.

Later on that evening Sita spent a restless time, flicking magazines, half listening to the endless chatter of political news on the TV. She tried hard to concentrate, gave up and snuggled into bed. There were some papers on the rheumatology research she had to read before the conference. She put it aside and reached for her novel. Reading her favourite 'Wuthering Heights' again she drifted off. Ram came in, took the book off her, kissed her lightly and turned the lights off.

*

Sita sneaked in the Valentine card and put it in Neil's surgery in file. The romantic note was to pour her heart out to him. Love like theirs was something that did not happen to everyone. They had been soul mates from the moment their eyes met for the first time. She felt almost one with him. They were like two peas in a pod. That familiarity, that ease of being with him was something she had never felt with Ram. His gestures, his voice, his touch enraptured her. She blushed, the colour rising in her cheeks as she thought of how Neil would react to her words. This was the first time that she had written about how strongly she loved him. She wanted to be with him, to rewrite her life so she could be with him forever.

Neil made sure it was a Valentine night to remember. They slipped out of the conference room. Neil did not say a word. They held each other as soon as they were out of sight of their colleagues. She walked into his hotel room, heart thumping; feeling elated that at last they could be together. He was gentle and impatient at the same time. They ripped off their clothes and made passionate love. As she snuggled in the crook of his shoulder, Sita felt this was where she wanted to be always. Neil kissed her hair traced her nose and said, 'I love you more than ever.' Sita turned and hit her hand against the bedstead.

She woke up, shocked at the dream. She was in her bed beside Ram. She glanced at the watch that she had not removed before going to bed. Her heart stopped. Ram had given the watch her for her fortieth birthday. Guilt spread like a hot rash as she realised what she had done. Ram was sleeping soundly.

What an awful dream! She was ashamed that she had dreamt so vividly of committing adultery. Ram stirred beside her. She jumped out of bed and rushed into the bathroom as she heard Ram muttering 'It's awful early, what's the hurry?'

The shower cleansed her guilt. She stayed under the pulsing jets of hot water, vainly trying to wipe the thoughts that kept racing back. She kept herself busy all day.

193

Chapter 24

Eileen's phone call was disturbing. Sita could hardly make out the words.'
I need to ... I need help... I...,' she had sobbed, words slurred,
worryingly so.

'I'll come over straightaway,' Sita made sure that Eileen understood
that she was coming over to be with her.

The driveway of red chips of the huge semidetached stone house
crunched as she parked the car. The brisk wind lifted her skirt as she rang
the doorbell. Sita straightened her skirt, waited in the porch. The door
opened. It was Eileen, much calmer. She ran out and gave her a big, a
hug so tight that Sita felt she could hardly breathe.

'Where are the children?' she asked, the quiet of the house felt so
strange.

'They're at friends. I....I can't stay with him any longer Sita, I'm leaving
him,' Eileen broke down again.' I tried so hard, I did my utmost, but, I
can't take anymore.' Eileen explained.' We're too different. Our culture, I
mean, I can't take it anymore.'

The change had been gradual. Faraz had become more involved with
the Moslem community after his mother arrived. His father's death had
made her a dependent immigrant. She took charge of the household.
Sofina, the teen, Eileen and Faraz's daughter had constant battles about
dress, times, going out. Eileen found it wearying, caught in the middle.
As the years went by Faraz seemed to have reverted to strict Moslem
norms. More so since Sofina had started secondary school.

They were in the big drawing room sitting on the heavy brocaded sofa.
The huge bay windows let the light in. The curtains, heavy red velvet tied
up with plaited cords tight round them gave an air of grandeur. The
swags and pelmet gave a rich elegance to the room.

Eileen looked vulnerable, the blonde hair with tiny flecks of grey, thinning now and sparse. The bubbly, vivacious personality was subdued. A face stricken with anxiety and misery looked back at Sita.

'You can't leave him, after all these years.' Sita was trying to get her to reconcile, if possible at all.

'It's the children who have kept me here so long. I'm just at the end of my tether.' Eileen patted the cushion that she had hugged, and then tugged at the tassels hanging from the cushion. They talked for a long time. There was no easy answer at all. Sharing her worries seemed to make Eileen feel a bit better.

'I'll make us a cuppa,' said Eileen going to the kitchen.

Sita looked at the photographs of happier times arranged all round the room. One of the photos showed Faraz, Eileen and the two kids, Omar and Sofina looking happy at a picnic by a waterfall. Others were different. Eileen in a salwar kameez, the scarf tight round her face, taking the children to the mosque, another one showed her with his family a huge group, the matriarchal mother in the centre looking important. There were many others of visits to Pakistan and family gatherings, weddings and Id celebrations.

She got up and followed her to the kitchen. One of the kitchen cupboards was open. Sita remembered Eileen's amazement when she had first seen all the spices in her own kitchen. Here was a shelf loaded with the same. How well Eileen had tried to change her life to accommodate such a huge cultural change. She had given up her life style, her freedom, observing his traditions and even accepting his mother's orthodoxy. She had worn the scarf, kept his religion alive, and brought up the children in his culture. The feisty young nurse had become a happy bride and mother rejoicing in her new found happiness with a man to care for her and protect her and her children. Now she faced a life that was alien, hard to adjust to. It affected her more as it was Sophina, her daughter was made to cut herself off from the dominant culture and become a recluse. She remembered her own carefree teens, the freedom that she had had going to discos, enjoying life. Now her daughter was asked to restrict her life to study and religion only. She wanted Faraz to remember that their daughter was a product of both cultures and not to impose such a difficult choice.

As she left her, Sita remembered the words from the Bhagavad-Gita. 'Mud is the truth in all the pots.' Its ancient words rang true five thousand years later. Its philosophy could even give answers to some problems of today, she thought. The numerous discussions that they had at potluck suppers and at the Sanskrit evenings at Lata's enlightened them on so many of the problems in their lives. The Bhagavad-Gita had answers to some of the modern twists in life. She thought about the various views that were argued about ferociously! But in the end most had accepted this particular quote from the ancient book. She went over the conclusions that they had all reached after long debates and recognised the universal truths that- 'one's origins become stronger as the energy, the lust of youth fades. The subconscious brings out the earliest feelings. From suckling at our mother's breast, every cadence and sound of our mother tongue remains in our subconscious. The first sounds, the lullabies, songs, nursery rhymes, imprints on our soul. When another subsumes one's own culture, the veneer of the new culture and the experiences are happily absorbed in the process of growing up. However, the onset of maturity changes that. It is replaced by a yearning for the familiar. That veneer is sheered off by age and is reinforced by memories, taste, sounds of our birth and childhood. When young and settling down the survival and importance of work, providing for one's family takes precedence. The birth of a baby revokes the old deep-seated values and the urgency returns. The urgency to pass on our own set of values to the next generation becomes important. They all had as young immigrants, experienced the same. Having adjusted to their host's culture they had adapted and foundered their way into a culture that they felt comfortable in. In some ways, Eileen's enormous change was even greater. She had willingly given up her culture and basic freedom for the peace and harmony of her family.

Faraz's religiosity was rekindled by his mother's presence. Maybe her influence reignited all that was familiar. His rejection of his own culture and imbibing the new of the last fifteen years was a mere blip. Now he had matured and wanted to get back to his familiar culture.

Sita felt a deep sense of helplessness. Eileen had helped her so much when she had needed her, but now Sita could offer very little succour to her. Where would Eileen go after nearly twenty years as a housewife? Her skills as a nurse would have to be relearned. Sita drove home, worried that her friend's life, and that of her children, was going to be traumatic.

196

Chapter 25

Sita was grateful that it was her turn to host the monthly potluck. She had no time to daydream. Household chores helped her move on to getting the house ready for the friends. They arrived on time, the ladies in their lovely saris and the men comfortable in their casual wear. The dishes were left in the kitchen, some to be warmed. Others like salads and the desserts were left on the dining table. Lata and Prasad were there early, followed by Padma. Sita was busy in the kitchen when she heard the doorbell.

'Will you get it for me please, Padma?' She shouted across.

Padma answered the door to Uma. She giggled and whispered 'It's the PIGGGS (Potluck Indian Glasgow Gourmet Graduate Society) tonight.' They both laughed at the acronym they had given to the Potluck supper evenings that their parents group enjoyed every month. They were going to escape up to the bedrooms, but Sita opened the lounge door. 'Say a quick hello to all, ' she cast a pleading look to Uma.

There they were, aunties in their finery, all in bright saris like Christmas trees decked with glittering gold jewellery.

'Have to wear these grand saris to potluck. What use are they in the cupboards all the time? Our children are never going to use them,' one of the aunties said loudly. The others nodded in agreement. Then all the eyes were on the girls as Sita ushered them in. 'Uncles,' some dressed in their sober suits were busy discussing the stock market and how it has ruined their investments. One in particular, Uncle Randir, always reminded Uma of Captain Mainwaring from Dad's Army with his tight suits ready to burst forth and his double chins shaking every time he spoke to her.

Uma looked in and saw that she was in the direct firing line of Aunty BB. Bigger than life in every sense aunty BB held court as always. Aunty BB wasted no time.

'How are you Beti? Heard all about bad, bad Dilip. See, I told you, better with someone mum and dad choose. You big educated girls get all these ideas. They all wrong. Now you happy with Ewan, a gora! Come here and tell me all about it.'

BB moved her bulky self and patted the space beside her on the couch. She was desperate for any morsel of gossip, so much better from the horse's mouth and she could always spice it up a bit more for use later. Uma made her excuses and ran up the stairs.

The aunty network immediately set to work overtime. Sita went up to the bedroom to talk to Uma.

It was prime time for the invective in the lounge to resume.

'Look at these girls! They don't even want to talk to us. Look how she ran upstairs without even saying hello properly to all of us here. No respect for elders at all,' Aunty BB remonstrated shaking her head vigorously.

'Poor Uma. She has such a busy job, maybe tired,' said Aunty Reena in a placatory tone.

'We work all time, and in kitchen. No, just no respect,' tutted BB.

'What about poor Divya, got divorced I heard ...'

'Who, who divorced?' BB demanded. She had missed the name momentarily distracted by the Bollywood video that Lata was showing Reena. No one gave a name.

'Terrible time for our poor girls. They have big jobs but no common sense. How they going to live? Who take care of them? When they have children? Aree, aree the Kaliyug is here already!' Aunty BB relished holding court.

'At least our boys are sensible. They happily marry girls from home or the ones chosen by the parents, but our girls, they are all becoming Bridget Jones,' said aunty Reena.

'Who is Jones?' chipped in Uncle Prasad.

'You know, they are looking for Mr. Darcy, the perfect guy , tall, dark no, no not dark we Indians like tall, fair, rich doctors, only professionals,' Reena continued. 'Yes, we introduce them to eligible guys, but do they even look?'

'No! They are all wanting to find them on their own, fall in love and live happily ever after,' intoned Aunty Reena with a faraway look in her eyes imagining life with a Mr. Darcy rather than thin and wheezy Vijay, her husband of thirty three years.

'What happens in reality?' Prasad winked at Ram.

'They all end up divorced, depressed, or like Sushma?' BB butted in.

'Why what happened?' asked Reena.

BB was happy to fill in the details.

'You know that girl now 34 years old! No body marry her.'

'Sushma? She is very bright. Has she not just become a Consultant?' Prasad came in with positive news, happy that the youngsters were thriving in their jobs.

'What's use becoming a consultant when all you can come home to is a cat'? Aunty BB dropped the juicy gossip about Sushma, which she was dying to share with the others.

No one commented on this new gossip. Some felt sorry for Sushma. BB looked disappointed.

'Settling down in time is so important. If they get to their thirties, who will marry them, and when are they going to have children? Our girls are all going to end up as lonely old spinsters. They come to all these gatherings until they are teens and then they reject it,' Reena continued.

'Yes, yes then the local culture takes over. They think they know better. They will only realise when they become like all these British couples, divorce, divorce all the time.' Ron rolled his head to emphasise the loss of the culture that their age group was familiar with.

'Half the marriages end in divorce here and yet the people are still looking for love. I dread to think of our kid's future.' Aunty Maya at last

199

got her view in. They heard the footsteps hurrying down the stairs. Sita came through to the lounge. The conversation took a sudden change.

'I saw that Preethi, yesterday in her controvertable,' BB was quick to rise to the challenge of starting another topic.

'You mean the Merc convertible?' Uncle Prasad piped in.

'Never puts the roof down I heard, doesn't want to get dark you know, we Indians get tanned too quickly.'

'Why spend £25,000 if you are not going to use it'? Prasad was puzzled.

He got a frosty look from Aunty Saroj. 'We do like fair girls, in fact I just told little Nisha today, 'Drink more milk beti. You will become fair like Aiyshwara Rai.'

'Bloody racist,' muttered Uncle Ron under his breath.

Padma had listened to the conversation standing at the vantage point of the hallway. She had come down to help herself to drinks. She shook her head in disbelief at the aunties' chat. Something's never change she told herself. She ran up the stairs to tell Uma. They both laughed at being privy to the conversations. Women usually spoke endlessly about saris, films, and often about food and recipes, their children and their achievements in school and university. They recalled that the men had more fun, making self-deprecating jokes of their lack of machismo in Scotland. They were aware that they were beholden to their wives some times. The women of late had become obsessed with the matrimonial exploits of each family much to the amusement of the younger generation.

Chapter 26

Driving early in the morning at 6 o'clock, to get to the hotel, Sita witnessed a wondrous sky its darkness lit by the rising sun. Ram was driving, deep in his own thoughts. The sun, an enormous ball of orange was eerie to begin with, covered by a veil of grey cloud with streaks of black running like veins through it. She asked him to park the car in the lay-by to take in this sight. She thought that if an artist had painted the sky, people would shrug it off as his flight of imagination, unreal colour of the sun. A camera would have been so useful to have recorded it and revisited it. However, she knew that a picture like that of nature would stay with her always, locked in her memory. The extraordinary darkness lifted slowly as the sun rose. They moved off the lay-by and drove back onto the road. The temperature gauge showed that it was minus two, a bitterly cold morning. Some of the cars that overtook them on the inside lane bore a film of frost, like a lacy throw over their various hues. The frozen dew lent a silvery white sparkle to the grass; a carpet of chilled life edged the road. They reached their Highland idyll. The roofs were sloping, the slates or tiles in shades of grey, green or terracotta, shaped and designed to shake off the rain, dripping down constantly on the green grass below. The grass that grew lush with the moisture, a landscape of deep green, a vivid colour against the purple hills, heather-ripe and often a cloud laden grey sky, was the incomparable beauty of the Highlands.

Sita wakened to the sound of church bells ringing, a dog barking and somebody playing the bagpipes. She stirred at the strange sounds, and then she remembered they were in the highlands for their colleagues wedding and obviously the piper was tuning his pipes. She stretched lazily. The wine had gone to her head so she was nursing a slight hangover. Ram was ready and tackling some breakfast as they had ordered room service. After the shower, she was packing her case when the phone rang.

'Hi Uma, how are you? No, can't be true!' Her heart seemed to stop beating.

Ram took the phone from her to get the details. She was pale, sitting on the hotel bed, her knuckles showing as she held on to the edge as if her life depended on it. 'A heart attack.' 'Bypass.' The words swirled round as they drove back to Glasgow. Why was she in the remotest part of the country? Why was she not in London? She could have boarded a plane and reached home faster. Everything flashed by a jumble of thoughts. Poor Uma was studying for her exams. She had to convey the news to them from Glasgow. Ram tried to ease everything for her.

The phone call about her dad's heart attack still felt unreal. She could not take it all in. Prasad was waiting for them to offer any help that they might need. Ram took her in his arms. Her tears flowed silently as they walked back to the car. As the car pulled out of the house and headed towards the airport, Ram looked at her, took her hand and squeezed it 'He'll be ok.' She choked the sob that rose in her throat, wiped her eyes and said in a whisper, 'I just spoke to him last week. He was fine. Ram, Did they say how serious it was?'

'No, just that he is still in the ICU and recovering.'

'Ram I need to be with him.'

'Of course I've already called the travel agent.' Prasad interjected.

'Thanks. Can I get a flight tonight?'

'Well, there are flights leaving everyday from London. I've booked you on one. The tickets will be at the desk for you to collect,' said Prasad. Sita had not absorbed all the practical details of her journey. She kept asking questions about her dad and about the trip. Until she was in the seat and the plane winged its way back to Madras, her mind churned distractedly, imagining the worst. The trip back was a nightmare. Sita's mind was going over the scenarios. Heart attacks occur in twos or threes. He could have a massive one within a few days. She could not concentrate on anything. She prayed hard, all that she could do. She felt guilty.

The heat of Chennai and the bright sun almost mocked her grief. She wanted to curl up in a dark place, not cope with the rumbustious life that hit her as she got off the plane. On the drive from the airport, she tried to get as many details as possible from Jai, her brother. She ran into the hospital. Her mum was sitting beside the hospital bed. She hugged her silently. 'Thank God, he has pulled through,' she whispered. Sita sat close beside her dad. He was lying there, a tired weak person, not the laughing strong dad that she always looked up to. She took his hand 'Dad you'll be fine. You'll be home soon and we'll all take care of you.' He smiled weakly. 'You need to get better soon.' She tried hard to look brave and not cry in front of him.

The hospital bed where her father lay was unbearable for her to look at. She, of all people should be inured to this. Hospital beds were her everyday things. She had never looked at them before with such horror. She wanted to ease him away from it, take him away from the misery and pain. She wanted to rip the ventilator stuck down his throat, make him comfortable. He moved, pressed her fingers. She sobbed, inside. Memories of him heaving her on to his shoulders teaching her to ride a bike, her first tennis lesson, walking with him on the beach came back to her. the trip to the bookshop, his tall body bending down to read the comic with her at Higginbotham's, the old colonial bookshop on Mount Road that they used to frequent. She could not accept this helpless wreck of a man, kept alive by technological wizardry. She ran to the toilet where the sickening smell of disinfectant and the air freshener made her feel worse. She came back quickly to his bedside. Seeing her mother's gaunt face, she wiped her tears. I must be strong for her she told herself.

At home her brother and Gita sat around, stunned by the enormity of what had happened. Dad was the head of the family, someone they had thought would be there always. Now a new reality faced them. He was a weak person, some one they need to take care of. The roles had reversed. As was the custom in India her older brother Jai and his wife Mala would take care of their parents. Sita was relieved. All the family in India were close to her parents and ready to help. She was the only one in UK. The way they all rallied around made her realise how important family was to everything. It was the foundation stone of life.

The consultant confirmed that her dad's heart attack was serious. He was lucky to be alive. The visits to the hospital were fraught with worry. Within a few days he had come out of the Intensive Care Unit and was off the ventilator, stabilised but weak. He would recover and get his strength back slowly.

The family sat quietly on the veranda, each deep in their thoughts. Sita's aunt, put down her prayer beads. Ten years older than her dad, she was the closest to him. She had removed her dentures. The gums showed pink as she sucked in her cheeks. Tears glistened as she said,

'He has led a good life. Just as well he started the charity on his sixtieth birthday.' They all nodded in agreement. 'Seize the day. One never knows what's round the corner,' she said as she wiped her eyes. Then she started reciting some slokas. They found the sounds of prayer soothing.

Many frantic phone calls, friends and relatives visiting and enquiring after his health, made for a hectic week. A kind of routine was slowly established. Hospital visits played a major role as they all took turns to be with him. Ram and Uma called every day, the distance making things so much harder.

'Sita, has he stabilised? What's the consultant saying?' Ram was concerned.

'He is out of ICU thank God. He is recovering slowly. It will take months. How is Uma?'

'She's okay. How are you coping?' Ram asked after her now.

'I am busy visiting him in hospital. I'm so glad I'm near him.'

'Good. By the way, all your colleagues were asking for you.'

Sita's hand shook. She took a deep breath, and said, 'that's nice of them. Ram, I'll need to stay for a couple of weeks, at least, till Dad gets home.'

'Of course, I'll tell Dr. Forsyth. You take care and give all the family my regards.' Ram rang off.

The fortnight passed so quickly. Leaving her dad weak, seeing him so unlike what she had known all her life was difficult. Her dad called a family conference to advise them of the will that he had already written before she left for Glasgow. None of them wanted to go through with the awful business, but her dad insisted.

'We have to do this today as you're leaving soon, back to Glasgow, and don't know when you'll be back again.'

He would not listen to her protestations that there was no need for the reading of the will at that moment.

She followed her mum as she went to get the will. Her mum opened the Godrej, the steel bureau that was part of all Indian family's furniture, something that was solid and kept all valuables safe from prying hands. The lovely smell of Mysore Sandalwood soap wafted out. Her mind went back to days when her dad came out of the shower and filled the whole room with the smell of the special sandalwood soap. She wiped back a tear. The Godrej had neatly folded saris, rows of matching blouses, and petticoats beside them all coordinated. Heavy silks and brocades were on the top shelf. Just below the top shelf was the locker cabinet. Inside jewellery, money and documents were kept. The thought of going through her dad's documents made her feel like she was intruding upon his life. Dad to her was still real, the fact that all this had to be laid bare and discussed with the family made the whole thing surreal. The documents were in perfect condition some left in a bank vault, like deeds of the houses, the foundling home and the will.

'Have you found the will?' her brother Jai asked, as her mum brought the box with the documents.

'Yes, it's here. I'm sure the lawyer will have a copy anyway.'

Sita was more distracted by all the memories that the contents of his Godrej had brought back to her. Her dad did not wear any jewellery, but had kept his father's pocket watch, a monocle on a solid gold chain. Her father had shown it to all the children when they were little. Tears ran down her face.

'Jai, you know I'm not bothered about the will. It feels so wrong to read it now,' she sobbed.

'Sita, this is something that we all need to do. All of us are feeling dreadful like you.'

Her mum took the parchment out and handed it to Jai. He sat behind the ebony desk where her father used to work. It looked the same as always. Sita took dad's pen and held it close in her hand.

Jai read out the will. The properties and the foundling home were divided equally amongst all the children with special provision made for the care of their mum. Later, Sita decided that she would use her inheritance to open a clinic to add to the foundling home. This was the best way that she could use her father's legacy. Her dad seemed relieved once the contents of his will had been read out. Sita stayed a few more days.

The return plane trip was as emotional as the one when she had rushed over to see him. Glasgow's grey cloudy skies were a relief. They echoed her feelings. She got back to her working routine. Work became a means of keeping her mind from preying on her dad's illness.

Chapter 27

The red sofa, stripped bare, the springs showed years of use. Time to dump it but it had been part of her life for a very long time. From the first moment when she chose it in the furniture store, lovingly put it in her lounge, their lives were imprinted on it. The days spent flopping on it, lying in its cavernous cushions covered to the neck with a soft blanket or a duvet when one of them was ill and feeling poorly. Baby Uma had grown up on it, jumping on it as a wee girl. She would lie on it wanting to be hugged and comforted by Mum when callous young boys broke her heart. It had been relegated to the family room. Each time the idea of getting rid of it was broached, it was quickly brushed aside and reprieved. The old faithful. Sita stroked the cushion, still soft, the pattern starting to fade. They had recovered it so many times, restored its springs and renewed it. The hardwood base was still perfect. Twenty odd years' use had dented it very little, the scuff marks only visible if one looked carefully.

'Aye, they don't mak'em like this anymare. Solid.' One of the guys who had come to repair it, rattled on. Sita brought the two men mugs of tea.

'It's as old as me or older but its guid stuff,' he joked, pointing to his baldhead with a few grey hairs forming a perfect crescent moon shape around his head. The young guy with him, laughed.

'Wullie, you're fifty going on twenty, man.' The young man thwacked him with the gloves he had on him.

'Aye, it's had a guid run. Is this not the third time I've been here missus?'

Sita nodded. He slurped his tea. They both left the empty mugs on the table then put their gloves on to lift the heavy sofa. She watched as they struggled down the path. They hauled it into the back of the van.

'Will give yous a call when it's ready then,' he said. Sita thanked him and shut the door.

She had taken another week off work. Dr. Forsyth was most understanding. Ram was baffled at her erratic behaviour, often saying if she went back to work, she would get over her dad's heart attack faster. Sita's confusion raged on. She was hesitant about going back to work, seeing Neil again. She thanked God that she had missed the conference. Just the acts of dreaming about Neil, committing adultery in thought made her feel uncomfortable. Her emotions were raw. She felt too vulnerable and she was worried that she might make a fool of herself if she did see him again.

To accept loss of the love of her life forever was however impossible. Loss of property would be much easier. Sita was facing a dreadful choice, Neil and the life of love with him or her family with Ram. Her quandary was harder than she had imagined. Every fibre in her body wanted to go with Neil, live the life she had always wanted.

Her heart warmed to the idea of a love that was perfect. Her head told her quite clearly that her duty to her daughter was important. Now, after her father's heart attack, she realised more than ever the need for family support. How often she had to hold her hand and comfort her. How could she desert her now?

Going away with Neil would be a final break with Ram and her life with him. There could be no compromise. The community would make it impossible. Leaving her daughter was too much of a sacrifice. Uma was an adult. But would she understand?

Ram had been a kind man, giving twenty odd years of his life to her, the father of her child. How could she rupture the family to fulfil her needs? What a selfish act! She tossed and turned. Living with Neil, she could lose her family forever. Could she live like that? By the end of the sleepless night she had made her mind up. She had to tell him.

In the cold break of dawn, the task was terrifying. She was panicking now.

How was she going to break the news to Neil? She was quite clear in her mind that she was not going to have anything more to do with him. Seeing his heart broken would be horrifying, but she had to do it and do it now. She took a deep breath and called him.

'Neil I need to see you…'

'Sita darling, you know I've been waiting to see you. Of course tell me when.' His intense love made her choke back the tears.

'How about this afternoon, after lunch? 2.30 okay?'

'Oh, I've a house call; make it four, at our usual coffee shop?'

She walked in, nervous, striding determinedly but her legs felt like jelly. Neil came right over and gave her a hug. She withdrew quickly and sat down. He took her hand. That spark, that frisson that ran through her whole body was still there. Her heart beat fast. As she tried to wriggle her hand free from his grip, she saw the ring that Ram had given her. The token of his love, stared back at her. The beautiful yellow gemstone, the Tiger's eye glared back at her accusingly. How could she have led Neil on so foolishly?

'Darling, you look wonderful. I missed you so much,' Neil whispered. The waiter hovered for their order.

'Just a mineral water for me please,' she said.

'A cappuccino. Thanks.' Neil added. 'Something wrong?' Neil's eyes were questioning. He took hold of her hand again. She tried to wrest it away from him.

'Well,' she hesitated

'You've gone through a lot, I know but these weeks only made my love for you even stronger. I can't live without you...'

'Neil, don't make it harder!' she cried.

'What do you mean? I know that this is not the time to tell Ram or Uma, but we need to think of our future too. We can't live this life of lies. I need you. I want to wake up beside you. These snatches of time are not enough.'

The waiter brought the coffee and the water. Sita's hand shook as she took the glass, the ice tinkling and the piece of lemon floating on top toppled out of the glass.

'Steady on sweetheart. Your dad's heart attack has affected you more than I thought. I'm sure he'll be fine now that he's had his bypass. Sita look at me.' He put his finger on her cheek and softly traced it and smiled lovingly at her. Her heart was crumbling into a thousand little pieces.

'I'll take care of you I'll shower you with ….'

'Neil please, I need to say something…' The ring on her finger caught a glint of the light and flashed at her. She wanted to say so many things. The words just were stuck in her throat.

'I … we can't see each other anymore …'

'What? Sita what are you saying? You're still not yourself. You're thinking of your dad…'

'Neil I've made up my mind. This won't work. I can't leave my family …'

He looked stunned. She left hurriedly, tears stinging her eyes. Neil followed her; he tried to hold her hand. She moved faster. 'Why was the car parked so far?' she thought, hurrying.

'Neil, please leave me alone,' she pleaded as quietly as she could. The crowd on the road slowed her. She wanted to flee.

'Sita, listen, we need to talk this through.' Neil held onto the car door as Sita got in. 'Just take your time. You're just back from India and still worrying about your dad. I'll wait.'

She sobbed, 'Neil you're making this so difficult.'

'Don't let's throw away something so good.' He gave her a look that made her heart flip again. She could not wait any longer.

'Neil please I can't do this. Let me go.'

He stood aside. His face turned ashen when the car moved on.

She drove for miles. She had no idea where. After an hour or so, she found herself at the banks of Loch Lomond. She got out but not even the soft twilight or the gentle breeze could soothe her aching heart. Perfect peace, the sound of waves lapping on the golden sand was calming. The air seemed freshened by the mist, almost rising from the Loch. She could have a completely new life, if she wanted.

She walked back to the car. She sat in the car thinking. She turned the ignition and the radio came on automatically. On Radio Scotland political experts were discussing the exciting details of the setting up of the Scottish Parliament after three hundred years. All these years of Ram's extolling of the SNP cause made her conscious of these new beginnings for Scotland. She let the programme flow over her. One of the panel members, a sceptic, was giving his viewpoint.

'Aye, a Parliament, devolution is neither here nor there. We will still be stuck with Westminster. No real power, just another talking shop. Still in limbo.'

She switched the radio off. Meaningless. Everything in the world made no sense at all. Not now. Nothing made sense. She remembered her grandma repeating some words told at her birth. 'Coming upside down does not bode well! She does have pretty features, but an upside down life I'm sure for this one.'

Was this her upside down world? Her mind in turmoil, she wept more tears. As darkness fell over the loch, she realised it was not safe to stay. Hours of sobbing and thinking had made her mind numb. She had made her choice. She felt nothing as she drove home.

Ram came out of the kitchen.

'Where were you? I made a nice new halva. I'll get you a piece.' He went into the kitchen again. She ran up the stairs, locked herself in the bathroom to sob her heart out.

'Must be PMT again,' muttered Ram as he helped himself to the halva. He picked up the paper. The coverage of the new Parliament was extensive. He read all the supplements given with the papers, with interest. The red sofa was back from its repair for the umpteenth time. He sank into its comfort.

Chapter 28

The dark October had turned into a darker November. The fact that one had to put the lights on in the car to drive to work in the morning and arrive home in darkness made the month dreich. The nine days of Navrathri, Halloween and Guy Fawkes Night were all over. Diwali was the next celebration, the festival of lights. Even Glasgow's non-Hindu population was aware of it and joined in the celebrations. People were more tolerant of the fireworks. The colourful lamps in some houses, on windows or doorsteps on the day no longer looked incongruous. It was a bit like Christmas had come early. The shops were full of lights and Christmas things. The Indian sweet shops were laden with ghee-rich ladoos, gulabjamuns, jilebis, barfis and every kind of sweet possible.

Sita saw Prasad getting out of the car. He lumbered slowly along the driveway to the front door as she opened it.

'Come in Prasad. Nice to see you.' Sita welcomed him in. She called out to Ram.

'Just came to collect the posters for the Diwali,' said Prasad as he sat down heavily on the sofa. His weight seemed to be climbing up despite his health problems.

'That's a lot of cards,' Prasad's jocular face scanned the mantelpiece looking at the cards with interest.

'It was our wedding anniversary last week.' Sita said as Ram walked into the lounge.

'Why didn't you say? We could have had a party. I could do with some good food. The wife starves me because of my diabetes. No ladoos for me.' Prasad's eyes glazed over. 'By the way, congratulations. Sita and Ram, the perfect pair from the Ramayana.' Prasad looked at Ram and said with a guffaw, 'Hope there is no Ravana to whisk your lovely Sita away.' Prasad always made a joke of everything.

'No chance of that. I'm lumbered with her for life.' Ram retorted comforted by the age-old custom that marriage was for life.

Sita smiled. Her mouth widened but her eyes were cold. Sometimes words said in jest can be closer to the truth. Did he know something she wondered?

'Would you like a cup of tea or some juice?' Sita asked as her hands twisted the duster she had in her hand.

'No, I'll just collect the posters and be on my way. My raksashi, my witch, will be waiting with the dinner ready, an awful salad or one chapatti and a spoonful of dhal. See what I am reduced to?' Prasad laughed at his demonising of his own wife.

'Good that she's looking after your health. I'll get the posters for you,' said Ram and hurried away to get them.

In the awkward silence between them Prasad was talking, twittering away about Diwali.

'It's a very important social event in Glasgow's cultural calendar. We've invited some councillors to a programme of dance and music. I'm looking forward to the sumptuous meal.'

Sita eyes were on the stairs. She tapped her fingers on the half moon table, moved the little ornament on the table. Could he sense her discomfort?

'So, Uma, is she doing all right?' Prasad made small talk.

Sita nodded, 'Yes, she's fine.' Prasad continued asking other questions that Sita answered without much thought.

She sighed with relief when Ram came down with the posters and handed them to Prasad.

'We'll probably see you at the Mandir on Sunday,' said Prasad and left. Ram switched the TV on. Sita stood looking at the pile of library books that she had placed on the table.

'You've not read any of them? What is up? Are you feeling all right? Not like you to stop reading fiction.' Ram looked at her. Sita was

213

twiddling with the ornament on the table, eyes darting about. Ram tried again.

'Sita, are Uma and Ewan coming over for the Diwali function?' Sita shook her head and moved away to the kitchen.

'Was that a yes or a no?' he shouted as she went away up the stairs.

'Women and their hormones,' thought Ram. Sita was in a world of her own. He had noticed that recently her behaviour was erratic but as usual, Ram assumed she would get over it. She was distracted, forgot simple things, and seemed to lie in the bed or mope around a lot. He settled comfortably in the sofa to watch the local news.

Sita sat on the bed feeling a bit sick. She hated this feeling of guilt for something that she had not done. She kept telling herself that she had not committed adultery, only fleeting thoughts and a few months of infatuation. She knew in her heart that the decision to be with Ram was the right one for her. Yet every time she met people, even an innocuous remark gave her a jolt. Work was even more difficult. It brought back memories. She decided to speak to Ram about leaving the surgery and take up her research on a fulltime basis, maybe work with the drug company and a hospital. It would give her a break from the surgery. Neil had taken time off. He had swapped his summer holidays with one of the other partners. The break was long enough for Sita to organise getting away permanently, if she wanted. She had a preliminary meeting with Dr. Forsyth, who was most understanding. He assumed that Sita wanted a change since her father's heart attack had been so traumatic for her. She felt better that she could get back to her life as it was before. Although the hurt would be inside her forever.

Chapter 29

The temple had moved. As the number of people increased, the need for a bigger place had become a necessity. The Hindu community had managed to raise the money for the new Mandir. It was now in a huge converted building near La Belle Place, near Charing Cross. They walked down the steps to the big hall where the deities were placed under a colourful altar. The smell of the incense sticks, flowers, the kitchen aromas all mingled to give that unique temple ambience. The wisps of camphor smoke rose gently over the worshippers. Some had their eyes closed. Women were in their finery in saris or salwar kameez suits, and the younger ones in jeans and the latest tops straddling their identities of the twin cultures. Streaks of copper, blonde highlighted the hair of the young, their hair and makeup copied assiduously from the magazines. The older women had hennaed hair or deep black dyes. Some had the grey determined roots loudly demanding attention at the parting, or escaping in curly wisps at the back. The hair scrunchies and jewelled hair slides did nothing to hold the grey back. There was now a row of chairs for the older and infirm members who could no longer sit on the floor. Most of the congregation sat on the floor, white sheets rolled out on top of the thick carpet, men and women on each side but most families sat together. There was no strict code restricting the sides to each sex.

Ram rang the bell. They prostrated to the gods and sat on the floor. BB gave Sita a knowing smile and a tiny wave. The hymns, or bhajans were over and the priest had started his sermon He read a verse from the Ramayana. For the next twenty minutes he quoted this particular line from the verse and explained its significance. 'As birds are made to fly and rivers to run, so the soul to follow duty.' He elaborated on the importance of doing one's duty and pointed to the special role of a wife and mother in life. The story of Sita as she followed Rama to the forest, the difficulties that she had to put up with was quoted. He explained how being a faithful wife and doing one's duty to family is the foundation of a moral life. A mother is a role model, not just for the family but for the community as a whole. Sita was uncomfortable. Her mind wandered. She noticed BB holding court, in the row in front of her, now on a chair as befitted an older member. The priest continued about the significance of Sita's purity and her selflessness and her love of Lord Rama. BB listened intently, occasionally turning around and darted glowering glances at Sita. The priest elaborated on the reason for Sita's disgrace. He quoted from the Ramayana, Lord Rama's words.

'How should my home receive again
A mistress soiled with deathless stain?
How should I brook the foul disgrace,
Scorned by my friends and all my race?
For Rávan bore thee through the sky,
And fixed on thine his evil eye.
About thy waist his arms he threw,
Close to his breast his captive drew,
And kept thee, vassal of his power,
An inmate of his ladies' bower.'

Lord Rama loved his wife deeply, but it was the society's scorn that he cited for being unable to accept her. The priest explained in detail Goddess Sita's enforced stay with Ravana. The morality of woman had bearing on the community at large, he said. BB shook her head in agreement, turned back and nodded to Sita as though she affirmed all that the priest said. The priest moved on further to extol how Sita proved her chastity, her purity, by throwing herself on the fire and coming out without a blemish. That purity is what all Hindu women should aim for, he claimed. Sita's mind was all over the place. 'Why is BB giving me such looks?' she wondered. She caught the last quote that the priest was reciting, the one where Lord Rama accepts his wife and she is restored at his side.

At the lunch that followed, BB started the sniping, she made sure that she would be within hearing distance of Sita and Ram.

'Morals, all good in books no? Living like Lord Rama and Sita, very difficult nai?' BB said in a loud voice.

'What do you mean?' Reena was all ears. A juicy bit of gossip was always welcome after a boring sermon from the priest. Made the lunch tastier. BB chose a seat near Ram and Sita.

'What you say, Sita?' BB's eyes were mischievous as she asked her directly. 'Britain too much freedom. All women do bad things. Even married, they want other man, badmash nai? Very, very bad, Kali yug.' She rolled her eyes heavenwards, then quickly returned to scrutinise Sita's face.

Sita just smiled, but the food almost choked her. She played with the food, frowned, held her tummy and made out that she was in pain.

'Men, women all just doing love, love, very bad.' BB continued. 'Husbands too soft. Often not know what is happening under their noses. Right Ram?' She gave him a challenging look. Ram who was enjoying the food was trying to make out if the cumin in the curry had been roasted first or put in to the sauce in raw state. He had not paid a blind bit of attention to the women's conversation, but had vaguely heard the last bit.

'Yes I suppose so,' he nodded not wanting to disagree or start an argument. He took another mouthful and decided that the cumin was roasted that was why the taste was different.

'Ram, what you think?' BB persisted.

'About what? Sorry I was not listening.'

'About love affairs, of course,' Reena butted in fascinated by BB's grilling of Sita. She had cottoned on that sparks would soon be flying.

'A lot on TV shows, I suppose,' he said not happy that his attention was drawn to inane conversation.

Sita got up from her seat.

'I've had enough, Ram. I've a tummy ache. I'll wait in the car if you don't mind.'

'Why you leaving in such hurry? Lunch not nice or something I say?' BB asked, her face all lit up, eyes pinning Sita's discomfiture.

'I'm not feeling too well,' mumbled Sita and hurried away. There was something wrong Ram realised slowly. He got up and made his excuses.

BB had a parting shot. 'The husband always last to know.'

Reena had watched the charade. She could wait no longer.

'You don't mean Sita…?' Her saucer like eyes widened more, her face puckered in a shocked smile. Ram heard the comment

'Oh my God can't be Sita! She and Ram have been together for ages.'

'Well, I not believe either, till I saw them myself.' BB smacked her lips, pausing to give effect. 'You know it's man she works with, a gora.'

'Oh no, at her age? Her daughter married herself!'

'Aree, aree, all bad, no? Kaliyug has come to earth as predicted. Bad, bad times, no?' BB rolled her eyes in disgust.

'I just can't understand. A colleague you say. Maybe they were discussing work. You must be mistaken BB.' Reena was still stunned at the news.

BB embellished the fact a bit more. A bit of masala always makes the story more interesting. She had only seen Neil and Sita walking towards the car in the surgery, but she added that she had seen them hugging and kissing. The rumours were obviously true. Sita would not have reacted the way she did. Almost ran out on them.

BB helped herself to another ladoo, gloating at the triumph.

'I blame Ram, too soft in every way. Who would run after chocolate gateau if there is ladoo in the house?' Reena commented as the news filtered around the table.

They spent a lot longer at the table, and BB stuffed her face with more sweets as she recounted the details.

The secretaries at the surgery had noticed the new relationship between Sita and Neil, but thought it was just banter. Saroj Sharma's young nephew, Raj who was doing his six-month GP training at the surgery, relayed their gossip, more as a joke. He was not aware how rumour spreads. Saroj had wasted no time telling BB, her close friend. BB had now confirmed her doubts by tackling Sita directly. It was a free for all now. BB could not have chosen a more public place. The mandir was the centre of the small Indian community. The whispers were all around the temple within a few minutes. Mission accomplished, BB heaved her bulk out of the narrow chair.

Prasad and Lata kept quiet. The gossip was hurting their close friend. They attempted to quell it. 'Let's not talk without knowing the facts,' said Prasad. People just turned away from him.

'I always thought she was strange. Too westernised,' said Maya, putting her tuppence worth in.

'I know she talks about books and plays, not very Indian,'

'She never cared about saris and jewellery, or even cooking.'

'Why, she allowed her daughter all freedom, discos, staying late, no control.'

'What control when you yourself are behaving in such a way?'

The comments came thick and fast.

'I really thought they were like Ram and Sita' said Prasad quietly, 'a perfect pair.'

BB was pleased with her work. The damage was done. This was her day. She had never forgiven Sita for not 'curing' her daughter Kulvinder. In her ignorance, she had felt deep inside that if Sita had 'treated' her Kulvinder, she would not have become a lesbian. Somewhere in her mind, she had harboured that feeling of revenge, someway of getting her own back. She would follow all the angst and misery of Sita's tattered future. She would have plenty to fill her days. She would follow the aftermath avidly. The scenarios already played in her mind. Would Ram leave her? Would Sita leave Glasgow or have the gumption to run away with her lover? How would Uma cope with this trauma?

BB felt triumphant as she cast her mind on to her next project. She thought about the newly widowed Vijay, her mind turning to find a suitable young lady for him. Before BB could move Lata rose up to her in full height. She could take it no longer. She moved up close to BB, looked her right in the eye, and said in a voice that was quiet, deep and shaking with feeling, she said,

'What about your lesbian daughter Kulvinder? Why don't you tell them about Liz and Kulvinder in London or do you want me to do it for you?'

The crowd stood still, the intake of breath almost audible. They looked at BB. She drew herself up but watched as Prasad came up beside Lata.

'Well do you want me to add to that?' he said loudly.

The whispers about BB started, Reena's open-mouthed face changed. She was the first to recover and challenge BB.

'What are they saying Balvinder? That's terrible?' BB's face crumpled. She pulled her duppatta over her head and covered her face. She sat down heavily in a chair, looked down, shaking her head, drops of tears fell on the carpet. She had never expected that her secret would ever be revealed. She had no reserves of strength when confronted with the truth.

'Yes, she has kept that very quiet from all of you, but without knowing anything at all she is spreading rumours about Sita, in the temple of all places. I'm disgusted,' Prasad's jowls shook and eyes glared at the crowd. Lata drew him away from the crowd. They left, ashamed and angry at the same time. They could not take such awful snipes at their friend.

All those who had been at the receiving end of BB's tongue-lashing, were now able to see her for what she was, an old woman putting up a brave façade, attacking others to deflect anything that might come her way. They turned away from her, disappointed.

'Even Lord Ram had to put Sita through all that suffering once she came back from Ravan. Our Sita will have to go through hell.' The gossip about Sita now turned into one of sympathy and understanding.

Some started to discuss the Ramayana and argued that all Hindu religious scripts were just a reflection of human life and a guide or a code on how to live. Some marvelled at how a book written five thousand years ago could still resonate and give succour to life in the present day. Others related their own problems.

'Life is complicated enough without all this gossip,' said some.

'Nobody knows what happens behind closed doors. Poor Ram.'

The hurtful barbs now were aimed at BB. 'Lesbian! What is happening? She talked about Kaliyug. Look at what has happened in her own house!'

The crowd grappled with the news then moved on, some rushing to get some shopping done. Some others had the Diwali function to organise. The crowd melted away as duty called.

*

The icy silence in the car reflected the chill in Sita's whole being. Ram drove without saying a single word.

'Ram, listen to me. I'm not having an affair. You must believe me.'

She babbled on.

'Ram, you know that I'd never ever be unfaithful to you. I'd never ever hurt you or Uma. Please believe me… ' She cried, sobbed.

He drove even faster, wildly. Sita was worried they might have an accident. Ram so out of control was something she had not seen before.

At the house, he walked in and slammed the door. She thought that the door would fall off its hinges. He took a pile of her books that was on the table and ripped them, threw the pages all over. He kicked the brass plant pot and then gave her a look of sheer hatred. He ran up the stairs and came down in a minute with a small bag.

'Ram please wait. I need to talk to you. Please…hear what I have to say…'

He was out the door, slammed it so hard that the whole house shook.

He was a man of few words. What did she expect? She had done the worst thing to Ram. The guilt was overwhelming. Would anyone understand her feelings? Where would he go? She opened the window to get some air. The breeze fluttered in.

A page of a book that Ram had ripped fell at her feet. It was 'Madame Bovary.' The words of Emma 'Oh, why, dear God, did I marry him?' pierced her eyes and heart. She picked up all the pages and the torn books, and stood with them, unable to move or think any more.

Chapter 30

The weeks of crying and trying to reach Ram had made Sita pale with exhaustion. Uma had tried pleading with her dad. Lata and Prasad had tried their best. Ram was stubborn. He would not listen to any of them. He was not prepared to talk to Sita. She wondered about going to India for a while, work in her dad's foundling home 'First Step.' She could not leave her job in haste. They had to get a locum. There were too many hurdles to cross. Running to India would have given her a break, but she would have had to face reality on her return. She wanted to get back with Ram, wanted him to listen to her side of things. Sita was convinced that if she could talk to him and explain he would realise that it was an infatuation, that she had not committed adultery.

She clutched the pint of milk and was heading towards the car when she saw Mrs. Patel getting out of her car parked next to Sita's blue Toyota. Mrs. Patel was the type who would accost her unfailingly with a list of ailments whenever or wherever they met. She would question her endlessly on the medication, give her opinion on alternative therapies and chat for an interminable time. Sita gave a hesitant smile as she neared her. She was stunned to see that Mrs. Patel walked right in front of her, gave her a look of hatred, shook her head disapprovingly and then moved away without acknowledging her at all. Sita's hand shook as she opened the car door. She slid into the driving seat. The ignition switch immediately brought the tape that was in the car to life again. The Supremes singing 'When will we meet again?' and the line 'Are we in love or just friends' came on. She felt a silent tear wet her cheek. She switched the tape off and drove home.

It was eerie, the house without Ram. Mr. T the cat came over, brushed on her leg and meowed in a forlorn way that only cats could. She ruffled his neck distractedly, put the pint of milk in the fridge and switched the kettle on. She opened the cupboard for her mug then broke down in tears again. The sobs of confusion, sadness, guilt, loneliness wracked her body. The mug was in the sink. Ram would have washed it and put it away.

The water in the kettle boiled, the little bubbles visible in the see-through kettle, little globules jiggling around the glass jar of the kettle, like a crazy dance and then bits of steam escaped from the spout. She rinsed the mug, made a strong cup of coffee, sat on the red sofa. The scalding hot coffee hurt the tip of her tongue. She put down the mug hastily, tried to cool her burnt tongue. She picked up Mr. T and cuddled him close. His 'Whiskas' breath familiar, as his little whiskers brushed on her face. She was comforted as she nuzzled against his toasty warm fur. Mr. T. She remembered when Ram had brought the scrawny, little kitten nearly fifteen years ago, on her birthday. Uma was thrilled; Sita thought it was such a sweet gesture. It was not often he remembered her birthday. He would rush out later and buy a card, some flowers or chocolate from the petrol station, either when Lata had called to wish her or the early morning calls from her mum or dad from India reminded them it was her birthday. This had been a surprise. She had held the tawny ginger bundle close and cooed over it. Both she and Uma planned all the things to buy for the pet, what to call him and had looked up the vet.

'Did you go to the 'Cat Protection Society?' What a perfect gift for my birthday? Thanks Ram.' She gave him a big kiss. He shuffled a bit, held her at arms length,

'Yes…. Happy Birthday. I… it was Jim. His mum's cat had had the kittens. He asked me if I would take one. I thought both Uma and you would like it…'

'He's cool. He's mine,' said Uma, 'Mum, and I'll take care of him.'

'Of course. He's so cute. A lot of responsibility though.'

Sita and Uma were deciding on the cat's name when the programme with Mr. T came on the TV. They felt the ring around his neck made him look as if he had a huge gold chain like Mr.T. He also had a funny tuft of hair on the top of his head that never behaved and stood straight up. They giggled as they christened him. Mr.T grew up to an enormous size as befitted his name.

*

The mobile's ring tone was loud. It was Neil again. He had called and texted every day. He could not accept that Sita would stop loving him. He had not given up. She needed time to think. Getting away seemed the

223

right thing to do. She wanted a place that she could get away from it all, nothing that reminded her of Ram or Neil. She called Uma and told her of her decision. She was very sympathetic.

Chapter 31

He had left the house and never gone back. All Sita's pleadings to return, to listen to her version of events he had ignored completely. The rage that he felt, the humiliation was too strong. It was a shock, her supposed infidelity. Now he was not even sure if she had cheated on him, but the mere thought that she was infatuated with Neil, enraged him. He knew on reflection when he returned to calmer moments how BB had always spread vicious rumours, yet he had believed her and left his wife of so many years. It was that feeling of guilt, perhaps that he had never been able to show his love for her, his inability to articulate his feelings; his assumption that she would understand, that wrung his heart. Ram had lifted the phone so many times. He had torn heaps of paper as he tried to write to her but the words were never adequate. He thought of Lord Ram in Ramayana. Even God in the legend had taken his wife Sita back after a rigorous test of her fidelity, after her encounter with Ravan who had imprisoned her. But, not him. He had no strength to go through with it. His feelings of anger, shame, and guilt all rolled into a thick ball of hatred, then one of self-pity. The longer he dwelt on it the worse it got. He was unable to forgive her, forgive himself, or pick up where he had left off. His way of coping was to shut the event from his life, compartmentalise it, and throw it into a corner of his mind. His feelings of hatred for his dad, his inability to voice his love for his first love Vidya at Jipmer, his shyness, his quietness made him a vulnerable, emotional mess. He could recognise the deep self-loathing that he had. He coped the only way that he knew how. His work became his life. He cut himself off from the world that they had known as a couple. His one companion, Jim, from the SNP was his only contact with the past. He cocooned himself in his new state of loneliness. 'Rely on yourself,' came to his rescue again. The code that he had always lived by.

Uma never questioned him after the initial pleas. He had asked Uma to bring all his belongings from the house. He stayed at a hotel to begin with, and then moved to a small flat. Uma and Ewan supported him and saw him through his difficult time. Uma's tears and her sensible words came back to him. She played a mature role in the crisis. 'Dad, I love you both. Don't ask me chose between the two of you. I am always here for both of you.' She was torn between the two of them obviously, but she was sympathetic, just what he needed. She came to him when he needed her, made sure that there was no deliberate meeting of Sita, Neil and Ram. Both at Diwali and Christmas, she meticulously organised so that she saw both her parents but at different times. Ram found her love and support touching.

He had found Sita's hairclip, a brown tortoiseshell, the design of a webbed pattern with light reddish brown streaks on dark brown. The clip with stainless steel claws to hold the hair that strayed, hair that got blown away and not remain in a prim and proper fashion, restrained and neat. The shape of it tugged his heart. He picked it up, the smooth shell-like feel, evoked memories of a peaceful time, a time of being one with each other. This small article had brought back the whole person to life. A small inanimate object that had once graced her person was in hands. The clip, which had touched her curly hair, he wanted to stroke her hair now, hold her close to him, and smell the jasmine scented hair. He wanted her. He missed her.

His intense feeling of self-loathing about his inability to articulate his love for her took over. His father's loud voice would thunder out and say things to people without any semblance of shyness or hesitancy. Why had he inherited his mum's meekness, shying away from simple gestures, gauche, restricted by series of doubts? He hated himself. The glass of whisky numbed the edges of his despair. He got up and refilled his glass.

Two sayings came to his mind. Was it Virginia Woolf who had written 'You do not find peace by avoiding life?' He was avoiding facing the future. He preferred life moving on without any challenges. He found it hard to retract his action taken in haste. His pride made him feel he would be crawling back to her, accepting that he had made a mistake in leaving her in a rush, not waiting to listen to her. The longer he left it, the harder it became. He had spurned Uma's overtures to get him to talk about it. 'Let a man lift himself by his own Self-alone and let him lower himself for this Self alone is the friend of oneself and this Self is the enemy of oneself.' The words of the Bhagavad-Gita Gita, spoke the truth again. He knew what he must do but could not find the strength to go through with it.

Chapter 32

Sita had to get away, get her thoughts together. As soon as the plane touched the tarmac, she was overwhelmed with mixed feelings. Racially, genetically she was one with the environs in India but in her heart, mind and soul, she knew 'she belonged to Glasgow.' There were some advantages being in India which she had never noticed as a child, not being stared at, no name calling assuming her land of birth to be neighbouring Pakistan. She felt at home and yet felt that having spent more years in Glasgow had changed her perceptibly. The new India was so different in many ways. The IT industries, the affluence of the middle classes, had given a new confidence to the citizens. All the multinational companies were vying for a piece of the Indian economy. She found it strange to find that some British-born Indian youth were seeking their future in Bollywood, or starting their business ventures in India. It was a complete reversal to what it had been like when she had left India.

She had booked for a full fortnight at an ashram. She did not tell her family in India. Only Uma knew where to reach her. She wanted the trip to help her through this emotionally wrought period.

The ashram was in a tranquil, beautiful setting, close to the beach in the coastal town of Cochin in Kerala. The atmosphere was one of calm, and peace. She could hear the sounds of the ocean in her room, the waves crashing or rippling softly on to the golden sand that she could view from her window. She felt close to nature, the rooms simple but spotlessly clean.

The first week went in a whirlwind of emotion and activity. Sita followed the structure of the day at the ashram. She was amazed at how the rituals made sense in helping her cope with this awful feeling of helplessness that she could not get rid of. She was grateful to the guru, who patiently explained the reason for the various treatments and their benefits to her. Simple ones like making sure that she rose early every morning and greeted the dawn with a 'surya namaskar', the sun salute of yoga.' Practising some of the basic yoga asana, eating a healthy diet and

227

meditating were encouraged. It suited her to do things that were completely new. It took her mind away from the raging conflict within. The luxury of getting all her needs seen to was wonderful. One of the days she was sitting quietly by the small lake at the ashram, an American woman, Mandy spoke to her. She chatted to her for a brief time, to get a respite from thinking.

'Isn't it fantastic, to unwind and just soak in the atmosphere? You Indians are so friendly.' Mandy rattled on. Mandy Kukur was from Palo Alto in San Francisco. It was good to have some company. They both had something in common. Mandy was trying to get over her acrimonious divorce from her husband Mark. The stress of going through the harrowing months had left her in need of a holiday. Sita empathised with her. Ram walking away was still hurting. She needed this holiday to heal and move on. They formed a friendship. It was easier for Sita to be with Mandy. Most of the Indian women her age in the ashram had come with husbands.

The second week at the ashram, she felt the routine soothing and she relaxed a bit more. This was the place to find her inner peace and make her decision. The ashram lived up to all her expectations. The stay confirmed what she had always felt, that it was the simple life that allows one the time to deal with life's traumas. The week flew in, with the routines of the ashram, the Ayurvedic treatments, the time to meditate. This change was exactly what she needed. She had to make her mind up about herself, she needed to be alone and make a decision after proper thought. She was not going to do anything in a hurry and regret it later. She felt rested and renewed.

Looking at the golden sunrise early on the last morning at the ashram, she made her decision. The trip back was less painful. Having made the decision gave her an inner strength. She was composed. She could face the future. Uma picked her at the airport. Mr. T. was in the car, purring happily at seeing Sita. She got him out of his box and cuddled him. Glasgow's grey sky and the piffling rain were reassuring. She felt she was back home, ready to face her future. In the car the pleasantries over, Uma turned to her 'Mum, you're looking better. The ashram must have helped you.'

'Yes, I am better,' Sita nodded in agreement.

'Are you getting back with dad? Shall I try asking him to meet up with you? He must have cooled off by now.'

'I never left him, Uma. It's not for me to get back to him. I don't think he wants me. Did he ask you once when I was away or talk to you about me at all?'

'No, he didn't. I'm sorry. It's so awful to see you both like this.' Uma squeezed her hand gently.

'I don't think he cares for me at all. His pride is more important to him, obviously.'

'Mum, I don't know. Maybe he's still confused.'

'Confused! You mean Aunty BB's word is more important than mine? Should he not listen to me, his wife, rather than a gossipmonger?'

'Mum, I can't even broach the subject with him. He just walks away.'

'That's typical of him, bottles everything up. I can't understand him at all even after all these years with him.'

'Mum...what are you going to do?'

'I am quite clear now. I have my job. I'm not running away. I'm going to get on with my life. I've done nothing wrong. You may not like the decision that I have made but in time you'll understand. I don't care about BB or anyone else for that matter.'

The words 'are you going to live with Neil' were at the tip of Uma's tongue. She hesitated, Sita looked tired, exhausted. Instead she made her a simple tea and toast with the bag of shopping that she had brought with her. She waited till Sita had a shower.

'I'll see you later mum, take some rest.' Uma left with Mr. T.

After a jetlagged sleep, Sita got up to face her new life. She put her mobile on charge, unpacked and decided that she'd call the surgery next morning and inform them that she'd be back on the Monday. She sat on the red sofa, the old faithful that had seen each milestone in her life, pondering on her life of solitude. She heard a car draw up in the driveway and the headlights shone briefly in the room as the person parked. She opened the door. Maybe Uma was calling again to see that's she was okay.

It was Neil. She withdrew in shock. He walked in.

'I missed you so much Sita. Why didn't you tell me that you'd left for India?'

'How…how did you know…?' she blurted out still standing at the corner of the porch, unsure and dazed to see him.

'I had to call Uma to find out you were okay. I thought you'd fallen ill. She told me everything.'

He shut the door behind him, and turned. She ran into his arms, the tears fell warm on his shoulder.

'I was going to call you. Neil… I love you …need you more than ever.' Her muffled voice was interspersed with sobs.

'I know, I know…I need you too,' he said gently, and held her tight.

Chapter 33

Glasgow 2008

The cacophony of voices on TV discussed the news on the referendum on Scottish Independence. The eerie bluish light reflected on Ram's face. The clinking ice swirled in the glass of whisky in his hand in a tight grip. He watched with smug satisfaction. The SNP had won the last election in Holyrood. In power, they showed the swagger of the winning party. The routing of the Labour party in the country where it was born seemed to give this win a special poignancy. An Independent Scotland seemed a closer reality now. Ram felt all the years of his hard work as an activist in the party had at last borne fruit. Wendy Alexander looked jaded, like her counter part Gordon Brown in Downing Street. The Crewe and Nantwich By-election win by the Conservatives was touted as ringing the death knell of the Labour movement in Britain. After the effervescent high of Tony Blair's win in 1997, his disastrous 'invasion' of Iraq was bleeding the party to its slow death.

The mobile trilled beside him. He switched it on.

'Uma has had a lovely baby girl. You must come and see her.' He could hear the excitement in Ewan's voice.

'Congratulations. Is Uma okay?' Ram stood up. A rush of joy gripped him. He held the glass in his hand in a tight grip, and then put it down on the mantelpiece. The crystal reflected the prismatic colours of the rainbow, as he paced around.

'How is the baby?' Ram's usual reticence vanished. He rattled a few more questions. 'Was it a normal delivery? Did they look after Uma properly? Were you with her?'

'Hold on dad. Mum and daughter are fine. I'll tell you all about it when you're here.' said Ewan, the pride in his voice sweeping over the line.

'Great, of course I'll be there right away.' Ram switched the mobile off. He paused. The enormity of the moment made him dizzy with excitement. He recalled holding Uma as a baby all those years ago. A silent tear welled up. His baby was now a mother. He rushed out of the door, ran back in to get his wallet and drove over to the hospital, and parked in a careless way, not like his normal self. He remembered being with Sita at her difficult birth with Uma. The scenes of their closeness, the wonder as they had both gazed at baby Uma swaddled in a pink blanket, flashed in his mind.

He entered the maternity ward, stopped short at the room and hesitated. There was a group of people. Ewan saw him, 'Come on in granddad,' he ushered him in.

Sita and Neil were bending over the baby's cot. The awkward pause was broken by a loud wail from baby Mia, who was protesting loudly, her pink face, writhed in little wrinkles. Her tiny fist crunched in a tight ball flailed around. Sita picked her up gently and handed her to Uma. The wail slowed to a whimper, and then it was quiet again. Ram placed the teddy, the balloons and the flowers on the bedside table, the little purchases that he made in the hospital shop. He was amazed at the things available in the little shop, recent changes that he had never noticed. Ram was pleased when Neil moved away from the cot and walked over towards the door. 'I'll get some fresh air and leave your parents to fuss over you, Uma.' He gave her hand a squeeze and moved out of the room. Ewan and his uncle and aunt followed Neil.

The awkwardness when all were around the bed eased a bit. Sita, Ram and Uma looked at the tiny bundle, and a million thoughts ranged wildly in each of their minds. Uma was pleased that her parents were both at her bedside. Ram was still squirming, not quite sure what to do or say, yet happy to be there for Uma, a mixture of emotions that unsettled him.

Sita said, 'Was the breech birth terrible, Uma?

'Mum, you'll never believe. The baby must have a lot of you in her. Yes, just like you, as grandma used to say, arriving upside down. But I'm fine, everything went well. The staff here are great. '

Ram stood beside Uma, holding her hand, gazing at her and the baby in turn.

'Dad, look, look at her left cheek. She has your dimple.' Uma smiled at her dad. Sita looked up at him, and then averted her eyes. The dimple and his curl that she had found so endearing she thought to herself. Sita busied herself with the flowers that were on the table.

Ram touched the baby's little hand.The baby held on to her grandpa's finger. His heart gave a lurch of pleasure.

'I'll get a vase to put these in,' Sita said and hurried away to the nurse's station. Ram gave Uma and the baby a hug.

'I'll see you again. Don't want to tire you both,' he said and left. He passed both Ewan and Neil outside the maternity ward, gave a nod and hurried out to the car park. He drove slowly out of the hospital. His feelings swayed between the joy of the new baby and seeing Sita again. Even after all these years, it was painful seeing her and Neil together. She seemed happy, though she had hardly glanced at him. They were weaving a kind of unspoken dance around each other, evading, avoiding each other and keeping their lives as separate as possible. She had grey flecks in her hair, the hair in a shorter style. She wore glasses, though she had still maintained her slim shape. He realised he had noticed all these details, more than he ever did when he was with her. A deep sense of shame gripped him. He still loved her, but his pride had got in the way. It still rankled when he saw her with Neil. The jealous feeling reared its ugly head, try as he might to quell it. He wanted to turn back the clock, wish he had forgiven her, or at least listened to her. A poem, 'Distance' that he had read somewhere came back to him.

The closer we are the greater the distance

Unspoken now, misunderstood in silence

Words on tips of tongues, deftly stifled

Hurting inside, the heart muddled.

The closer we bond, the more we hurt

By words said too quickly, or terse

That tone, that voice, honeyed for friends

Changes so, when homeward bound.

Stepping on eggshells, crackling fear,

Tread soft or you'll hurt one so dear.

When words fail the actions seem bold

The distance grows and love turns cold.

He drove back to his empty flat. The whisky glass lay on the mantelpiece where he had left it as he had rushed out to see his new grand daughter. The neat flat, perfect in every way was in contrast to his life. He picked up the glass. The ice had melted. The whisky was diluted. He gulped it then moved over to the drinks' cabinet, poured himself a good strong dram and drank it neat. The fiery liquid slid down his throat smoothly. Alex Salmond's face wreathed in smiles, stared back at him from the newspaper.The headlines read: 'Referendum on Scottish Independence. 'Bring it on,' says Wendy.' The words on the page became a black burr as his eyes focussed on them but he took very little in. The words recognised by him did not quite seem to reach his brain. He persevered. The 'macchattering' classes and their opinions, he thought cynically. Nothing mattered now. The faces of Mia, Sita, Uma, Ewan, Neil flashed by in front of the words. Mia holding his finger, Sita glancing up at his dimple, the cot, and the flowers were like a jigsaw puzzle, pieces lay jumbled in his mind. He could make no shape, no sense of it at all. He folded the newspaper neatly, put it away in the recycling bag, changed and went to bed. He switched off the bedside lamp and lay in the dark.

The morning sun streamed through the curtains and hurt his eyes. The answering machine bleeped every few minutes. Ram turned over and put the pillow over his head. He did not want to get up. Not this morning, perhaps never again. The machine persisted. The bleeps annoyed him. He woke up shuffled his way to the hallway and thumped the machine hoping it would fall silent. It was the voice, the familiar soft tones that he would never forget. It made him stop, catch his breath and listen to the message.

'Ram, I'm coming to Glasgow for a Conference next week. Any chance of meeting you?'

It was Vidya.

Maybe it was good to get up and face the world thought Ram. He straightened the answering machine, made the bed, cleaned the whisky glass and made sure the flat was in order. He had a shower and planned for the day ahead and his future.

He called her.

Chapter 34

Eileen and Sita sipped their red wine.

'I like your new hairstyle. The streaks look good, takes years off you.' Sita admired the young looking Eileen. She was like her old self again.

'Hides my grey well. Can't get back my old colour again, dyed it too many times.' Eileen smiled and patted her hair.

'So is the course okay?' Sita asked Eileen. The red wine in the glass swirled as she held it to her lips.

'I felt scared at first but I am really enjoying getting back to work. Things have changed so much.'

'You'll make a good matron. They're talking about introducing the battle axes again.'

'Hey, less of the battle axe bit. I thought you said I look good!' Eileen threw a small piece of tissue at Sita, screwed up her face in mock anger.

'I'm glad that you're back on your feet. I was worried for you.'

'You've gone through the mill too. We've both had an awful time haven't we?' Eileen's concern was clear in her voice.

Sita nodded.

'How's Neil?' Eileen asked.

'Oh, keeping busy. We both enjoy life to the fullest.' As Sita saw her enquiring look, she added, 'No regrets at all. I am really happy.'

'So what else is new?' Eileen leaned forward to hear.

'Nothing great, Neil and I are involved in fundraising for the latest scanner that the hospital can't afford to buy. Not much changes in the NHS.' They both laughed.

They parted after making a firm date to meet again.

*

Sita drove over to see Mia and Uma.

'Mum, Ewan's Uncle Charlie and family from America are coming over for Mia's birthday.' Uma was excited.

'All the way from USA for her birthday?' Sita was surprised.

'Well, they heard about the homecoming year and planned it to coincide with her first birthday.'

'Homecoming! Of course.' Sita said.

'They left Glasgow seventy years ago and want to keep in touch with the family.' Uma continued.

'A big party to organise, then, I'll help you Uma. Don't worry.' Sita laughed.

Home, culture, roots, depths of our being, home is where one feels right, thought Sita. She lay in bed beside Neil. Her life was with him now. Her life with Ram flashed for a moment. She sighed. She could not erase twenty years of her life with him. The rain spattered on the window, as Neil cuddled her close. She thought of the happy little family of Uma, Ewan and baby Mia. The breech birth, the upside down life that had been predicted for Sita had become true but she had taken charge of it and changed it, made it her own. Her life with Neil was now filled with love and happiness.

She was truly 'twice born,' entwined in the two cultures enriched by the Indian womb that had nurtured her being and the Scottish cradle now that nurtured her soul, her heritage and future unique. She closed her eyes and fell asleep enveloped in love's warmth.

Printed in the United Kingdom by
Lightning Source UK Ltd., Milton Keynes
137065UK00001B/412-423/P